DRAGON BITES

STORMWALKER, BOOK 6

ALLYSON JAMES

JA / AG PUBLISHING

CHAPTER ONE

Janet

"Heels, check. Party dresses, check. Lipstick, check. Cash for g-strings, check." Maya Medina hefted her bright red overnight bag as she opened the door of her pickup waiting in the dirt lot in front of the Crossroads Hotel. "Ready to go."

My bag held a few more sensible things like jeans and T-shirts, but I'd thrown in my one sexy dress and high-heeled shoes. No makeup—I didn't wear it, and with Maya around, no one would be looking at me anyway.

I'd promised Maya a girl's weekend as soon as I got done with my three totally selfish weeks with Mick riding the back highways of the West and up into Canada. We'd camped when we felt like it, stayed in luxury hotels when we felt like it …

No battles, villains, dragons, goddesses, or demons to interrupt us. No bad storms stirring my Stormwalker magic. Waking up next to Mick every day in the morning sunshine was the best thing that had happened to me in a hell of a long time.

Now Maya herded me out of town again. I'd barely had time to make sure all was well with my hotel, wash my underwear, and repack. I'd said good-bye to Mick earlier this morning, wanting to do it alone before the hotel guests were up. Our good-byes could get steamy.

It was nine now—we'd make Vegas by mid-afternoon if we didn't stop too often. I tossed my shoulder bag onto the floor of the pickup's passenger seat and climbed up after it. "Ready."

"Hot damn." Maya slid behind the wheel and started up the truck. "Okay, some ground rules." She touched her fingers as she counted them off. "No magic. No demons. No destruction. No ruining my clothes, my sanity, or my weekend. Got it?"

"Got it. I need a vacation too."

"You just had one," she reminded me teasingly. "While I was here working."

Maya happened to be the best electrician in Magellan. When she wasn't fixing the wiring at my creaky old hotel, she was running around our small town keeping everyone else's in order.

"Vacations with Mick can be … intense," I said. "Not bad intense, but let's just say I'm ready to relax. I've already got my spa day booked."

"Too tame for me," Maya said. "I'm going to haunt the casinos, the night clubs, and the male strip shows. Nash can suck it."

Nash, the Sheriff of Hopi County, was Maya's boyfriend and definitely not a party guy. All work and more work was Nash's motto. He loved Maya, and she him, but they mixed like oil and fire.

Maya beamed me a huge smile as she gunned the engine. The truck's wheels spun and we headed for fun and freedom.

We hadn't made it to the end of the dusty parking lot before a thud sounded in the back of the pickup. I cranked my head around to see my half-sister, Gabrielle, launch herself into the truck's bed, following the duffel bag she'd thrown into it.

Maya slammed on her brakes, and the truck skidded us sideways. "No, Janet," she snapped. "Just no."

Gabrielle peered through the cab's open back window. "Come on—what am I going to do skulking around here by myself? You should be keeping an eye on me, Janet."

Maya answered before I could. "You can go home to Janet's grandmother. Aren't you supposed to be there anyway?"

Gabrielle rolled her eyes. "Ruby is doing nothing but fussing over Pete's wedding. If I go home, I'll have to run errands and clean the house—which is pristine already." She switched her dark gaze to me. "Your grandmother is truly out of control."

My father, Pete Begay, planned to marry Gina Tsotsie, the lady he'd fallen in love with, later this month. Grandmother, thrilled Dad was marrying a respectable, ordinary woman after all these years, was going overboard with preparations. They'd have a traditional wedding with all the trimmings, with a special hogan being built for the occasion. Grandmother called me often, not to ask my opinion, but to regale me with all the things she expected me to do. I couldn't blame Gabrielle for not wanting to be in the middle of the chaos of home.

I sighed to Maya. "If we don't let her come, she'll follow us, or make things go wrong with the truck until she catches up. Easier to bring her along."

Maya gripped the steering wheel. "You keep her under control then. If she gets herself into trouble, I'm ditching her. You too. I'm not wasting my weekend chasing her around."

She spoke from experience. Gabrielle and I shared a mother, a malevolent goddess of Beneath, who was as crazy as she was powerful. Gabrielle had inherited her magic and also some of her insanity.

"Yay!" Gabrielle punched the air then sank into the bed, resting her back on the cab. "We're going to have so much *fun!*"

Maya sent me a dark look but she stepped on the gas and we flowed out onto the desert highway, heading west, a stream of reddish dust rising in our wake.

THINGS WENT WELL AT FIRST. THE DRIVE, WHICH I ALWAYS liked, took us through Flagstaff with its high mountains and soaring pines, and then down a long hill back to the desert, the sheer cliffs and rocks calling to me. It was October, the air crisp and cool but still warm enough to enjoy. We turned north at Kingman and moved through ever more barren land along the Colorado River to the new bridge that soared nearly a thousand feet above the river from cliff to cliff.

We drove into the afternoon sun, to the glitter on the horizon that was Las Vegas.

The city had grown even since I'd been there a year or so ago. It spread farther across the valley floor every year, flowing out toward the eleven-thousand foot mountains on its edge. Businesses and houses sprawled in a tangle, but the draw for outsiders was the long road of towering hotels, now gleaming under powerful sunshine, that offered every enter-tainment imaginable.

Gabrielle had remained quiet during the ride, hunkering down in the back to sleep. As we pulled into the parking garage of the hotel, she popped up again, leaping out of the back as soon as Maya stopped.

Maya had reserved one room for two people. I thought we'd have to pay extra for Gabrielle, but by the time Maya and I reached the desk to check in, Gabrielle had completely vanished. I mean literally. One second there, the next second gone.

We didn't mention her, got our room keys, and headed up to the fifteenth floor.

Gabrielle waited for us near the door. She leaned against the wall, arms folded, a little smile on her face.

Maya stalked past her and stuck the key into the slot. "How did you know which room we'd get?"

Gabrielle shrugged. "I made the computer kick out the room number I wanted and scooted up here to wait for you."

"You can do that?" I asked as we entered the room.

"Sure. Can't you?"

I chose not to answer. Gabrielle can work quiet and subtle things with her magic I can't begin to comprehend. I could do tiny spells to unlock doors, or I could destroy small towns. Anything in between was difficult for me.

The computer had given us a suite. Two bedrooms surrounded a small living area with a sofa bed, and a huge bathroom connected the bedrooms. A giant window showcased the city and the mountains, which were already dusted with snow.

"Thanks, Gabrielle," Maya said grudgingly.

"Don't mention it." Gabrielle flung herself down on the sofa and dropped her bag next to it. "I'll sleep here."

I knew she wasn't being kind, taking the foldaway bed. It

was closer to the front door, so she could sneak in and out when Maya and I were fast asleep.

Not that either of us planned to sleep. This was Vegas, baby.

We showered, put on our party clothes, and headed out, me in black, Gabrielle in a glittering blue dress. Gabrielle was very pretty, I had to admit, with a roundish face, long straight hair, and eyes so dark brown they were almost black. Maya, in a bright red short thing, mile-high heels, and knockout beauty, outdid us both.

The first stop was the all-you-can-eat buffet where I discovered how much food Gabrielle could put away. As I watched her shovel in sirloin steak and a mountain of potatoes, followed by three different desserts, I wondered if her parents had starved her. Sadly, that could have been the case.

Maya's body didn't have an ounce of fat on it, but not from dieting. She took plenty of helpings from all the food stations, including a large hunk of prime rib. I ate more modestly, worried I'd fall asleep if I stuffed myself, and I didn't want to sleep until daylight.

Afterward we hit the casino, and I played slots. I heard my grandmother's voice in my head warning me of gambling addiction. She disapproved of casinos in general, and was angry that the Navajo Nation had finally decided to build casinos and resorts. She'd been of the school who thought the Diné should stay firmly out of the gaming business.

Gabrielle had no worries as she stalked to a blackjack table and charmed her way onto a seat. That particular table had a high minimum bet, and I had to wonder where she got all the chips suddenly stacked in front of her.

I watched her win a little, lose a little, win again. Sure enough, I saw a spark of light brush the cards right before she was dealt a hand that gave her twenty-one. I marched right over and took her out of there. The last thing we needed was for her to get arrested for cheating.

"Oh, come on, Janet, these places have tons of money," Gabrielle insisted. "They can afford to lose a little."

"Where did you get enough to buy all those chips in the first place?" I demanded.

Gabrielle shot me an innocent look. "Colby might have lent me some money. I told him I'd double it."

I growled as I continued to drag Gabrielle out, over her protests.

Maya had already grown bored with gambling and was ready to hit the male revues. We found one in a hotel a block off the Strip, and Gabrielle shoved most of Colby's money into the g-strings of the well-muscled, slick-bodied dancers.

We made it back to our hotel in the small hours, tired, but determined to stay up the whole night. What else was Vegas for?

"There's another restaurant down there," Gabrielle said, tugging me along a less-traveled corridor of our giant hotel. "And a chocolate fountain. Seriously, Janet, a fountain that pours *chocolate*. You should get one for the Crossroads."

Cassandra, my hotel manager, would look at me with cool eyes if I suggested that, and explain about costs, liability, return on investment, and other things I gladly left to her.

The halls we traversed led to the spa, the pool, the gift shop, the garage, and a bridge to a shopping mall—the maze of corridors met in one massive intersection under a domed ceiling.

Down one of the corridors, I saw Mick.

I paused, surprised, sure I'd been wrong. I had another fleeting glimpse of him walking away from me, and then he ducked into shadows and was gone.

I knew Mick wasn't here. He told me he'd be running

errands while I was gone and maybe going out into the
desert to meditate. Dragons did that, apparently. If he'd
changed his plans, he hadn't mentioned it—I'd had no
messages from him all night.

But I knew Mick. I recognized his stance, his walk, his
untamable black hair, his broad back, the dragon tatts on
his arms.

I started quickly down the corridor, craning for another
look.

Maya came after me. "Janet, what are you doing?"

"I saw Mick," I said. "I swear it was him."

"Oh, yeah, I forgot to tell you." Gabrielle fell into step
beside me. "I talked to Mick while you were packing. He said
he had to blow town for a few days. He didn't say where, but
he looked kind of grim. You know, resigned to something."

I halted and stared at her. Gabrielle gazed back at me, not
the least bit contrite. "Seriously, you're just now mentioning
this?" I demanded.

Gabrielle shrugged. "I forgot. Don't be mad. Mick's a big
dragon. He can take care of himself."

Except when he couldn't. I started down the hall. There
was the off chance the man I'd seen *hadn't* been Mick, but I
needed to know.

I called over my shoulder to Maya and Gabrielle. "You
don't have to wait for me. Go enjoy the chocolate fountain—
I'll catch up."

"No way." Gabrielle's light footsteps sounded behind me.
"If this gets exciting, I want in."

Maya said nothing, but I heard her heave one of her long
sighs and tramp after us, her stilt-heeled shoes clicking on
the bare floor.

The corridor bent out of sight into deep shadow, very few

lights burning. The fancy Italian tiles of the main hotel vanished, and soon we were walking on concrete slab.

"Maintenance," Maya said with the confidence of one who knew her way around the bowels of every building. "The boilers and electric panels will be down here."

"Cool," Gabrielle said. "We can mess with the lights."

I didn't bother to tell her no. My skin prickled with unease, as though it sensed the electricity Maya talked about, concentrated and crackling in one place.

I caught the faintest whiff of an acrid stench—brimstone, fire, and a heavy cluster of very dark magic.

Gabrielle sucked her breath. "Shit, what *is* that?"

"What?" Maya, without magic of her own, couldn't sense what we did. "I don't like this, Janet—let's go back."

I wholly agreed with her. I would have turned around and raced out, maybe back to the male strip show, which had been refreshingly mundane, except that I'd seen Mick come this way.

And if there was bad shit going on in this hotel, I couldn't let the man I was going to marry face it alone.

I continued, Gabrielle a step behind me, the rise of her deadly magic pressing my senses. Maya followed, muttering that it had been too much to hope we'd keep out of trouble.

We walked a long way. The corridor curved to the right and then to the left, then took us onward in a straight line.

The hall finally ended in a double steel door that at any other time I'd believe led to a maintenance room. But the miasma that came from beyond coated the doors in darkness, a sticky residue that warned us to stay the hell out.

I didn't want to reach for the door handle. I knew the thing would be locked, only the privileged admitted. I'd have to find a way to tamp down my magic to trickle it into the lock without blowing up the door and the walls and ceiling around it.

Gabrielle darted forward and snapped a spark into the keyhole. The door handle exploded.

Maya ducked and slammed into the wall, cursing as the handle sailed past her and clanked to the cement floor.

I tensed, waiting for who knew what to rush out of the dark opening.

No one appeared. Gabrielle and I exchanged a glance and then we started forward, Maya close behind us, still cursing.

We stepped into darkness. Gabrielle lifted her finger, a light springing from it to show us a hall painted black—floor, walls, ceilings. At the end of it was an opening, from which emanated a red glow.

The stench grew as we neared the arched doorway with a curtain hanging across it. The curtain was white, and I saw as we neared it that it was a bed sheet.

I caught its edge and carefully lifted it.

The roar beyond pushed at me like a wall, red light surging and flaring high. The room I looked down upon was vast, filled with people shouting, screaming, cheering. They were crammed together, standing, in a semicircular space like a sports arena but with no seats, shouting down at the floor far beneath.

A wave of sulfur and heat smacked my face, along with stinging smoke.

When the smoke cleared I saw a creature from hell on the black sands of the arena floor. It had a thick body twice his height, a long neck, two massive legs, tentacles, and a snout full of teeth. Not a dragon, which was a creature of beauty, but a demon from one of the many hells of Beneath.

Facing it, naked, his body covered with cuts, his hair caked with blood and sweat, was Mick.

CHAPTER TWO

I halted in shock, too dazed to make a sound. Mick circled the creature in the arena below me, his hands spread, watching it circle him.

The room was dark except for the red glow rising from the floor and the faint light of incongruous exit signs over the doorways.

Any moment now, Mick would turn dragon and launch himself into the creature, or he'd let fly from his hands the fire that would incinerate it.

Any moment.

Mick remained human and continued to circle, slipping once in the blood on the sandy floor. The creature had a gash across his belly but it didn't slow him.

Turn dragon, I silently willed Mick. *Take him down, and we'll go upstairs and celebrate. We'll check out that chocolate fountain.*

The creature struck. Its tentacle caught Mick on his side and flung him across the arena, Mick landing smack into the wall. He slid down but came to his feet, shaking himself, and went right back into the fight.

The crowd roared. They were human and non-human, a mix of demons, Nightwalkers, men, and other things I couldn't figure out in my panic. Most cheered on the demon, though some yelled for Mick as he faced the monster once more.

"Why isn't he going dragon?" Gabrielle demanded from beside me, Maya peering over both of our shoulders. "Why isn't he flaming the son of a bitch?"

I had no answer. I watched mutely as Mick ducked another blow from the tentacles, got under the creature's reach, and thrust his hand to the cut in its belly, tearing open the gash to let blood rain down.

The demon screamed in rage, kicking and flailing, a huge claw sending Mick tumbling again.

Now was the time for Mick to blast him with fire and end this game.

Game. I realized the fight was indeed a game, gladiatorial combat, with a dragon pitted against a demon, the spectators cheering on their favorite. This was Las Vegas, which meant they'd probably bet large amounts of money on the outcome. The demon was the favorite, I guessed from the amount of cheers it got.

But why wasn't Mick fighting as a dragon? Or using his magic to give him an edge?

I scanned the room for any sign of a magic dampening spell but sensed none. If Mick remained human and fought with his bare hands, it was by his own choice. It also meant he didn't have a chance.

The demon struck again, this time slamming Mick to the floor and leaping on top of him.

A scream left my mouth. It was drowned out by the cry of

the spectators, thrilled that the favorite was about to win, the loser to—what? Die?

Magic welled inside me, my Beneath magic building and swelling while I desperately tried to ground myself with Earth magic to keep it controlled.

I felt the buildup in Gabrielle as well, power that could annihilate the entire arena and everyone in it, including Mick, and us too if she lashed out.

Mick scrambled out from under the demon, his body covered with blood, and staggered to his feet. He looked up and straight at me, his eyes black and full of fire.

"No!" he shouted.

How I heard him over the noise, I don't know, but the word bore into my brain. Mick's eyes held desperation, even fear—not of the beast he fought, but of me and Gabrielle.

I grabbed Gabrielle's arm. "Wait! Stop!"

She flung a glare at me, her eyes gray-white with power. "Why? What the fuck?"

"Mick says no." I had to yell into her ear. "He must have a reason."

Gabrielle kept glaring at me, but she lowered her hand, sparks swimming in her fingers.

Below us, Mick danced out of the creature's reach, the demon enraged. The beast struck again, and Mick ran behind it, kicking and punching until the writhing creature swung around.

Mick grabbed the now furiously bleeding gash in the demon's belly and yanked it open. A hideous stench filled the arena, cutting through the brimstone smell. Mick kept pulling, his strength amazing, until blood, filth, and entrails poured out of the creature's stomach.

It screamed and flailed, trying to grab Mick with its claw-ended tentacles. Mick held on, his body bathed in gore as he emptied the creature's insides onto the arena floor. Maya swung away, hand to her mouth, but Gabrielle and I watched in fascinated horror.

Mick jumped aside, and the demon crashed to the ground, thrashing, moaning, dying. The spectators yelled and cursed as their favorite writhed in agony.

Mick lifted one of the stone blocks that lined the edge of the arena, returned to the creature, and rammed the rock through its cranium into its brain. The demon stopped flailing, went limp, and all light left its eyes. Mick was never one to let a creature suffer, not even a hell-bred demon.

The few spectators on Mick's side went crazy, punching the air, shouting and gleeful. If odds had been long on Mick, they'd just won a ton of cash.

Two men in cowled robes walked out to the arena. They studied the demon, obviously dead, and then moved to Mick, who waited, panting and bloody. The two men—probably the refs—conferred, and then one raised Mick's arm.

The crowd booed, the winners melting away to collect their money, leaving the unhappy spectators yelling abuse.

Mick raised his head and looked at me. He was covered from head to foot in red and black blood, and from behind the blood, his dragon-dark eyes blazed in rage.

At *me*. Mick was furious at me for being there. He was telling me to get out and stay out, to leave this to him, whatever *this* was.

Right. Like that ever stopped me.

More robed men came in to drag away the dead demon, now a pathetic corpse. Mick gave me a final admonishing look and disappeared through an arched opening below.

"We have to get down there," I said.

"How?" Maya, her face wan, her lips pale, scanned the arena. The rows where the watchers stood fed out into halls like the one we'd come through, giving no direct route to the arena floor.

"Fly," Gabrielle suggested.

"Oh sure," Maya said, but Gabrielle held up a hand, magic dancing on her palm.

"Not *fly* like flap our wings, silly, but glide down. I can do that—"

"No," I said firmly. "Bad idea to attract attention in a place like this. Mick obviously got down there. There has to be a way."

I started back out the direction we'd come, lifting the bed sheet and entering the black painted hall again.

Maya clicked after me. "There'll be stairs connecting the arena to these floors, or a tunnel to outside or another hotel. Fire codes." Her voice was shaky, breathless.

I'd seen Mick in the blank hall and then he'd vanished, suggesting he'd gone through a door or stepped into an elevator.

"How did he get down there so fast?" Gabrielle asked. "It took us a while to find the arena, but not that long. By the time we reached it, he was already fighting."

She had a point. Either we'd wandered around back here longer than we'd thought, or something in the air had made us lose track of time, or I hadn't actually seen Mick. No—it had been Mick, but maybe I hadn't seen him *here*.

"I might have seen a reflection," I said. "He has the magic mirror with him. He always does."

Gabrielle groaned, eyes rolling. "Gods, you're not going to talk to that thing, are you? You promised you'd leave it upstairs."

"I did. It's in my suitcase."

Mick and I each carried, at all times, a shard from a magic mirror that hung in the saloon of my hotel, plus Mick made sure a piece was ground into the side mirrors on our bikes. While annoying, the mirror was the most reliable means of communication we had, and several times, the mirror had meant our survival.

I also used the mirror to keep in touch with Cassandra, my extremely competent hotel manager, whenever I left the Crossroads, or to talk to Mick when we were apart. The mirror had been disappointed that I'd left it in the hotel room tonight for our girls' night out, but it was probably consoling itself by looking through whatever mirrors in the hotel it could. It might be an inanimate object, but it was a total perv.

I didn't want to go all the way back upstairs for it, but I realized I didn't have to. I hurried out of the back halls and to the main part of the hotel, Maya and Gabrielle behind me.

The decor of the casino contained mirrors on every wall, pieces of mirror glittering on the columns that rose to the dusky ceiling. Security sat above that dark ceiling, watching the gamblers on the floor from the nest of their observing offices, and other guards patrolled the floor, watching, watching.

I walked up to a column and chose a piece of mirror at random. "Mirror, mirror, on the wall..."

"What are you doing?" Maya demanded, while Gabrielle let out a breath of resignation.

"Come on," I growled at the diamond-shaped mirror.

No one else in the casino could possibly hear me over the electronic whir of the slot machines, bells announcing a winner, the *clink, clink, clink ... clink, clink, clink* of coin payouts, shrieks of joy or curses of dismay.

A security guard noticed my interest in the column and started to stroll over.

"Answer," I commanded the mirror.

"You didn't finish," the mirror's petulant voice came to me. Only a magical person could hear it, which, for the moment, meant me and Gabrielle. "You have to finish the incantation, or I'm not saying a word."

I ground my teeth, shifting on my stupidly high heels in impatience. "All right, all right," I growled. "Mirror, mirror, on the wall, who's the fairest of them all?"

"I am, of course, honey," the mirror drawled in its drag-queen tones. "What do you want?"

"Mick. Did he have you project his image where I'd see it?"

"No, I did that all by myself. Mick didn't want you anywhere near, but I knew he'd need you. He's in trouble, honeybunch. *Bad* trouble."

The security guard was almost upon us. They didn't like loiterers in Vegas hotels. Either spend money or get out.

"I saw. How do I find him?"

"I'll show you," the mirror said excitedly. "Follow me!"

The tiny mirror flared with light, then the one next to it, then one on the next column. I followed the flashes, Maya and Gabrielle on my heels. The security guard halted and watched us go.

"There." Gabrielle pointed as a mirror flickered down the hall that led toward the shops.

We scurried after it, three young women in tight party clothes running like crazy across the casino. We went by the hall where I'd first seen Mick, the mirror guiding us on past the chocolate fountain toward another hall and the entrance to the parking garage.

I spun to follow a flash into another maintenance corridor, this one full of gray walls with pipes running everywhere.

A narrow elevator door waited halfway down this hall-

way. Its bell dinged as we approached, and the door slid
open. We peered inside, but saw nothing more sinister than a
small, plain elevator that smelled a bit of diesel.

Maya and I hesitated, but Gabrielle charged inside. "You
coming?" she demanded.

I darted in after her. Maya paused one more moment,
then rolled her eyes and plunged inside.

Gabrielle reached for the bottom button, *4B*, but the
button for the third subbasement lit before she could touch
anything. The doors shut, and the elevator eased downward.

None of us spoke as we descended. The elevator halted
on 3B with a gentle bump, shuddered once, and the doors
slid open.

We peered out in trepidation, but found nothing more
than a gray-painted, silent hall, similar to the one upstairs.

Light flashed to my left, and I trotted from the elevator to
follow it.

I felt Gabrielle tense behind me as we went, the rise of
her magic like static in the air. Maya brought up the rear in
silence.

The hell grew darker as we walked, and soon we heard
the noise of the arena, the crowd surging to a roar as another
match commenced. The sound was more muffled, however,
farther away.

The stench hit us a moment later—not from the arena,
but from doors we came upon that lined the corridor. Each
door was made of thick steel, some with small grates, some
completely solid, but all locked from the outside, secured
with chains and giant bolts.

There was death down here, and fear and rage. The creatures inside the cells waited to fight until they died and they
knew it. I felt their resignation, terror, anger, determination.

Something large threw itself against one of the doors as

we passed, but the door barely rattled. Magic kept these cells sealed, I sensed, not just the locks and chains.

The tiniest flicker sparked on the dull gray steel of one of the doors, the magic mirror leading me where I needed to go. I knew Mick was behind the door—the bond that stretched between us pulled at me.

Before I could do a thing, Gabrielle exploded the chains with a strike of Beneath magic. She never had debates with herself about whether or not she should use her magic—she just let fly. Maya and I danced back as pieces of metal flew past us and pinged into the cement walls.

Gabrielle grabbed the door and flung it open, her magic negating whatever had held it shut. "Mick!" she yelled. "We're here to rescue you."

Mick, naked and blood-streaked, his hair matted with filth, lifted his head from where he sat on a stone slab against the far wall of a dark and tiny cell. Manacles circled his wrists and ankles, chains leading from these to rings in the wall.

Mick glared at us for a heavy moment before he sent a snake of fire magic to slam the door in our faces.

CHAPTER THREE

I stared at the blank steel door, the panel over its grate tightly shut. Mick, captured and enslaved, was inside, but the glower in his eyes had told me that the three of us were the last people he wanted to see.

"Gabrielle," I said, holding down my worry as best I could, "open the grate. *Gently*," I added hastily as she lifted her hand to blow it apart.

Gabrielle sighed and gestured with her forefinger. The panel over the grate popped open, letting out the acrid scent of dragon and blood.

I stood on tiptoes to peer through the grille. Maya, tall enough, especially in her high heels, looked in next to me.

"*Dios*," she said. "You stink, Mick. What are you doing in there?"

I couldn't have put it better myself. Mick rose and crossed the four feet of his cell to face us, his chains rattling.

"I'm here by choice," he said. "It won't be forever, I'm paying off a debt, and you need to stay out of it, Janet."

He delivered this speech then scowled at me with

dragon-dark eyes as though I should turn around and toddle home like a good Stormwalker.

Believe it or not, the answer was a mountain of information for my usually cryptic boyfriend. A few years ago, he wouldn't have even told me this much.

"What kind of debt makes you have to fight demons without using magic?" I demanded. "You could have destroyed it *and* the refs in five minutes and blown this place. Come out of there—you can clean up, and we'll go home. I'd love it if you were in one piece when I marry you."

"Valid points," Gabrielle said from my other side, on her tiptoes. "Scrag whoever stuck you in here, Mick, and let's party. Or I can scrag them for you, if you want."

Mick took on a look of ancient patience. "I'm not using magic, because I promised. Rules of the game. I will pay my price and finish it. If I'd known the games would be in Las Vegas, in this hotel, *this* weekend, I would have made sure you didn't come here. I'm pretty sure this is someone's idea of poetic justice."

Gabrielle spoke before I could. "You mean you're being forced to fight to the death like a gladiator?"

"Something like that." Mick nodded as though this were the most reasonable thing in the world. "No magic allowed, at least in my case. A physical fight only."

My mouth went dry. "No magic means you can die. Who the hell would make you do that? And what is this debt? I don't remember you involved in anything this big —this *weird*—"

"It happened a long time ago," Mick interrupted. "Before you were born, in fact. I arranged to pay off the debt now so I can marry you with a clean slate. I didn't know exactly when the payment would be arranged, didn't know until late yesterday, and as I said, I didn't know until I arrived that it would be *here*. I went to a pickup point out in the desert, was blindfolded, and brought here. I didn't have time to warn you."

"Yesterday." I knew that now was not the time to berate him for not telling me, but I couldn't stop myself. Mick and I had agreed to make sure we both knew about any danger that befell us, so we could back each other up. Typical Mick to think fighting to the death was a trivial thing he could take care of when I wasn't looking.

"I planned to be done with it and home before your vacation was over," Mick said. "You deserve some time off."

"So do I," Maya put in hotly. "But for once, I agree with Gabrielle. We can't leave you in there to be killed. The door's unlocked—let's go."

"I bet it won't be that easy," I said. "There will be some kind of contract, maybe a compulsion, that requires Mick to fulfill the debt. That's how these things work. Right?"

Mick gave me a nod. "I have to finish what I've started." He softened into the smile that could make me melt at ten paces. "And then I'm free. We'll celebrate when I get back to the Crossroads."

If he survived the games. The demon he'd faced had been huge and powerful, and Mick had barely bested it. I had the feeling each opponent would be harder to beat than the last, until Mick either died or won his final match.

"What exactly did you do?" I asked. "And to whom?"

"Lost a fight," Mick said without embarrassment. "When I was younger, against a being vastly more powerful than I was. He was killing another and I decided to intervene, cocksure enough to believe I could best him. To save my life, and that of the one I was trying to help, I agreed to fight in his games, signed a contract in blood."

"Shit," I said softly. I shivered, the chill clammy on my

bare arms. "I can't leave you here. I'm not going to lose you again."

Mick shook his head. "I can't go, not yet. If you stay to wait for me, Janet, you can't interfere. *I* have to finish this, one way or another."

"And if you don't finish it? If you refuse to play the game?" I knew the forfeit would be dire, but I wanted to hear it.

"Then not only will I forfeit my life, but everyone I know and love will be hunted down and killed. No exceptions."

I figured it would be something like that. Mick didn't respond to threats to his own physical well being—if the cost had been only his life, he wouldn't care. He was a dragon, and dragons didn't have much use for fear. Very little on this Earth was more terrifying than themselves.

Gabrielle cocked her head. "Do you have to *love* the person who gets destroyed, or just know them? 'Cause that lets me out. You barely like me."

Mick shook his head. "It means you, Janet, Maya, Colby, Janet's grandmother and father, Gina, Cassandra, Pamela, Fremont, Nash, Jamison, his daughter and wife, everyone in Magellan, Drake, and pretty much any friend I've made in my long life."

"Oh." Gabrielle blinked. "Even Drake? Wow."

Drake was a dragon, former toady to the Dragon Council. He and Mick were uneasy allies at the best of times, and I imagined the uptight Drake would not be happy to be lumped in as one of Mick's friends.

"All right, Janet, you heard him," Gabrielle said. "We have to leave him to it."

I didn't budge. Mick gazed back at me, unmoving, but I read a world in his eyes.

"Who would do this to you?" I asked.

Behind me, Maya said, "Um, Janet. Maybe *him*."

Him was a man walking slowly toward us. He was tall and wore a dark suit brushed by the few lights in the hall, his silk tie a hue that changed from dark green, to black, to dark red as he neared us.

His face was attractive, well shaped but with an edge to it, one that said he didn't give a crap whether people thought him good-looking or not. His hair was dark red, the light above him burning it redder, and a trim beard of darker shade of red framed his face.

His eyes ... I had no idea what color they were. I thought brown, but when he turned to the light, they were black, and then a brilliant green, then gold, then back to brown again. Iridescent, like his tie.

The man didn't look any more threatening than any well-to-do man walking around the casino upstairs. His aura, on the other hand, told me a different story. It was ever-changing like his eyes and tie, flashing, flickering, dissolving to nothing to reform again. He smelled of fire and ash, like most dragons, but the bite of the fire was so ancient it was mellow.

The mellowness did not mean he wasn't dangerous. The older a dragon became, the more powerful he grew. The three on the Dragon Council were ancient and bad-tempered, but the energy I sensed from this guy was ten times what I got from Bancroft, one of the strongest dragons on the planet.

Which gave rise to the question—if *this* dragon were so old and powerful, why had I never heard of him?

"Oh, my." Gabrielle folded her arms, leaning against me as she assessed him. "*He's* nice."

The dragon-man halted about six feet away from us. "So this is the Stormwalker." His voice was deep and rich, the syllables carefully pronounced, as though English wasn't his first language. He didn't have a marked accent, but his speech was careful, almost musical.

Gabrielle answered him. "Yeah, she's the Stormwalker, and can kick your ass, so don't get any ideas. My sister is wicked powerful. I'll tell her to go easy on you, though, because I have a thing for dragons."

The man had been gazing into my face with the rudeness common to dragons, but now he flicked his attention to Gabrielle, his eyes changing to deep black.

"And this is the goddess-child?"

"The what?" Gabrielle drew herself up, the crackle of her power rising.

"Gabrielle," I said calmly. "Shut up a minute." I fixed the unknown dragon-man with a steely glare worthy of my grandmother. "Who are you, and why did you force Mick here?"

His gaze moved back to me, the eyes now dark blue. "Does my well-being depend on my answer?"

"I can't hurt you, and you know it." While I might be a Stormwalker with a good dose of magic from my Beneath-goddess mother, I had a hard time against dragons. Whenever I bombarded Mick with my magic, he absorbed it, deflected it, or threw it back at me. "You're a dragon. Which dragon? Why haven't I ever met you before? Or heard of you?"

"I keep to myself," the man said, sounding amused. "I'm not surprised Mick never mentioned me—it is an alliance best forgotten. The other dragons don't speak of me either." His lips twitched. "For fear I might hear them."

I wasn't sure what that meant, but it couldn't be good. This dragon didn't radiate menace exactly—not like the remaining members of the tripartite Dragon Council. *The*

Mighty Three, Colby called them. He didn't radiate the good-natured energy of Colby either, nor the quiet strength of Drake.

He didn't exude anything at all, but he probably didn't need to. He simply *was.*

"You can call me Titus," the dragon said in his rich voice. "Janet Begay."

Titus would be short for the multisyllabic names dragons had. Mick's was Micalerianicum, which he thankfully never expected me to say.

I didn't wonder too much how Titus knew about me, because while Mick was a very private person and rarely spilled the details of his life, everyone in the magical world knew I was his mate and soon to be his wife. Titus probably already knew about my Beneath magic, my hotel, my friends, my relationship with Mick—everything.

What bugged me was that I'd never heard anything about him. Not from Mick, not from the other dragons. Why not?

"Pleased to meet you," I said in a flat voice. "Are you the reason Mick is in a cell, and fighting for his life?"

"No," Titus said smoothly. "Mick is."

"I know Mick is here because he's too damned honorable for his own good," I said angrily. "I meant—are you the one he made the bargain with? And why?"

"To answer your questions in order: No, and it's none of your business."

"It's dragon business, you mean."

"Only because Mick and I are dragons," Titus said. "This has nothing to do with the dragons in Santa Fe who think they run the world. This involves Mick and me, and Mick's life. He owes a debt. He's paying it, and I'm assisting him." Titus looked us over, his gaze taking in Maya, assessing her and the threat she might pose. I saw his dismissal of her as human and harmless. "Why don't you three ladies go enjoy yourselves? Mick will join you when he's done."

I stepped up to Titus. He was a foot and a half taller than I was, and his eyes held the coldness of a vast, forgotten cavern. "Let me understand. You're compelling Mick to fight demons and who knows what else with his strength alone, and you expect me to go off and play until he's finished or dead? How can he possibly win without his magic? That demon nearly killed him."

"But it did not," Titus said. "Dragons are strong, even in our human forms, Ms. Begay, amazingly strong. You know that."

"Don't humor me. You'll pit him against deadlier and deadlier creatures until he can't win, won't you?"

"Would I?" The glint in his dark eyes was unnerving. "And if you stay to watch, you'll be tempted to reach out and help, and then Mick would forfeit the match. That means with his life."

"Who would kill him?" I demanded. "*You?* If you're hot to see Mick go down, why don't you fight him yourself?"

Titus gave me an unruffled look. "That was not the agreement."

"He means he's afraid," Gabrielle said. "He knows if he and Mick go one-on-one, he'll be nothing but a dragony smear on the floor. *This* way he can get Mick killed without having to mess up his suit." She edged closer to Titus and brushed a finger over his pristine sleeve.

Titus's gaze flicked to her before returning his focus to me, and his lips quirked into the ghost of a smile. "Your friends are protective, Ms. Begay. Interesting. That one doesn't even have any magic."

He gestured to Maya, who lifted her chin and stared right back at him. "Because I have a boyfriend who won't give a shit who you are if you do anything to me." Nash Jones was a magical null—a man who could absorb magic, even the most deadly, and negate it without it harming him. But he could be killed physically—a dragon could easily crush the life out of him.

"Janet." Mick's voice rolled from the cell. "I'll be all right. Let me finish this, and we'll go out on the town."

He meant to be reassuring—*Relax, baby, I got this*—but I was anything but reassured. Dragons were complicated beings. There was more going on here than a simple payment of a debt, I was sure of it.

Dragons are also enigmatic to the point of madness. There's nothing they enjoy more than *not* explaining a situation.

I shot Mick a frown and turned back to Titus. "Tell you what. You let Mick go, waive this debt, and I'll let you live."

Titus studied me without alarm. "You have just stated you can't hurt me."

"Not with my Earth magic, it's true. But I wield more than that, and I have Gabrielle as my backup. How about you release Mick, and I'll make sure Gabrielle doesn't turn you into a pile of ash?"

"Aw." Gabrielle rubbed Titus's sleeve again. "I wouldn't do that. He's cute. I could enslave him a little, though, if you want, make him be a good dragon."

Titus gazed at Gabrielle's finger brushing the fabric of his coat, his expression unchanging. He wasn't worried about her, which worried *me*.

Dragons are very much Earth magic—grounded in power as old as the bones of the world. Beneath magic, on the other hand, came from the time before this Earth was created, older and white-hot. Dragons were nearly indestructible, but only nearly.

"Janet." Mick's rich voice wove the syllables of my name. "Trust me." He gave me the words he'd been telling me since he first met me. "Be patient, and all will be well."

I searched for any hint that he didn't mean it, was trying to pass me a message, but I found none. He really believed he could survive.

"Seriously?" I demanded, glaring at him through the grating. "You want me to walk away and let this asshole let loose any kind of monster on you just to see how you defeat it? *If* you can. While I do—what? Sit in the audience and chew my nails? Try to stop myself saving you? Or go dancing with Maya and Gabrielle and leave you to it? Screw you, Mick."

Mick returned my gaze, unblinking, but I noted that his eyes were still black, his dragon eyes. When he was relaxed, his eyes were a deep blue, beautiful like a deep lake in the sun.

I had to choose. Let Mick keep his honor and fulfill his bargain—and maybe die—or fight Titus on the spot to get him free?

I opened my mouth to give him my decision—Gabrielle and I would dust this guy, and I'd grab Mick, and we'd run—when a couple of things happened.

First, I noticed Maya had wandered down the hall and was talking to someone in a soft but adamant voice on her cell phone.

The incongruous surprise that she'd found a signal down here and my curiosity as to who she'd be calling was drowned out by the second thing—the noise of a wall exploding behind me, and the roar of a giant, crazed being as it broke out of its cell and hurled itself toward us.

CHAPTER FOUR

A nightmare filled the corridor, all eyes and sinuous body. It couldn't rise to its full height, so it stretched its bulk lengthwise, like an enormous snake.

"Woo!" Gabrielle yelled. "Everyone get behind me!"

She ran at the monster, her hands full of white magic, her feet moving with a dancer's grace. She wanted to fight it single-handedly, I realized, and expected the rest of us to take cover.

Forget that. But I had no storm to help me, Mick was in chains, Titus only stared mildly down the hall, and Maya, though she'd sensibly fled the other way, was still on her phone.

Gabrielle sent a ball of crackling white Beneath magic to the dark, sinuous body of the demon. It had a dragon-like head, though thinner and narrower, and pointed teeth sticking out around its snout like an alligator's.

Gabrielle's magic struck. The creature whipped itself out of the way at the last minute, and the magic bounced off the ceiling and plummeted downward. The demon whacked the ball of brilliant light with its talon, then screamed when the talon burned.

The creature dropped, fixing its red eyes—all eight of them—on Gabrielle.

She laughed. "You wanna play, do you?" She gathered a more intense ball of magic, one that would bring down the ceiling and probably most of the hotel above us, and drew back her arm like a major-league baseball pitcher.

"No!" I yelled at her.

Chains exploded in Mick's cell. He charged out, flinging away the manacles as he strode past Titus, who did nothing to stop him.

Mick wore not a stitch, his torso caked with dried blood and covered with abrasions. The demon caught a whiff of the blood, snarled, and started for him.

Gabrielle leapt out of the demon's way, her feet connecting with the wall. I scrambled past Mick and Titus as the demon whipped past Gabrielle, heading for Mick.

Mick waited, his eyes black in the gloom, arms outstretched, as though ready to embrace the demon as it came on. He snarled a very dragon snarl that was nothing but noise to me, but the demon abruptly halted, blinking its eight eyes at Mick.

Gabrielle, the crazy woman, launched herself from the wall and landed on the demon's back. The demon roared, whipping its head this way and that, trying to find the flea clinging to it. Gabrielle loaded her hands with magic, ready to plunge her power into the demon.

Mick snarled again. The demon swung around once more, fixing on Mick as though it understood him.

Gabrielle raised her hands high, Beneath magic glowing around them. "Stop!" I shouted. If she struck, she'd get hit

with the magic too, like a person tasing herself by holding on
to her tased victim.

My sister crashed her hands to the demon's hide,
plunging magic into its body.

The creature howled, and Gabrielle screamed, shud-
dering as though she'd been struck by a thousand volts. She
slumped forward, the magic dying, but she didn't fall. She lay
flat on the demon's back, and I heard her faint laughter.
"Wow, what a trip."

Mick growled more sounds at the beast. The demon
raised its head, eyes filled with pain, and met Mick's gaze in
understanding.

It turned itself around, somehow managing to squeeze
itself down like the snake it resembled, to navigate the
narrow hall. Gabrielle remained limp on its back as it slunk
toward the cell it had broken from.

I turned to Mick, my eyes wide. "What the hell did you
say to it?"

Titus answered for him. "He explained the consequences."
Titus hadn't moved during the entire encounter, and now he
brushed off his coat sleeve as though annoyed by a speck of
dust. "Every being here has come of his or her own accord, to
fulfill a contract. She knows what will happen to her children if she breaks out and flees."

"Her?" I asked, staring at the retreating creature.
"Children?"

Titus gave a brief nod, and Mick's expression told me he
knew this too. "She signed the contract," Titus said.

"Aw." Gabrielle's voice drifted down the hall. "Poor
snaky." She patted its hide. "How about we kill Titus and
blow this joint?"

She was talking to the demon, I realized. I heard the creature growl, a sound like Mick had made. Gabrielle cocked her head to listen, then she nodded.

"Yeah, I like that idea," she said to it. "Close your eyes."

"Gabrielle!" I yelled, but too late.

She let loose. Magic left her fingers in streaks of lightning, streaming along the walls in a blast of white fire that had me hitting the floor. When I climbed to my feet, I saw that Gabrielle's magic had burst open every cell door. I heard chains shatter, creatures bellowing in surprise and pain.

Mick sprinted after the demon with Gabrielle still clinging to it. Another deluge of Beneath magic burst from Gabrielle, the air so bright I had to duck away and fling up my arms to shield my face. Even Titus flinched and closed his eyes.

I lost all track of Maya. Hopefully she'd headed upstairs and the hell away from the hotel.

When I could see again, it was to watch Mick leap to the demon's back and reach for Gabrielle. I dashed after them. Mick was resistant to Beneath magic, but *resistant* wasn't the same as *immune*.

I didn't make it two steps. The creatures Gabrielle had freed flowed from their cells, bellowing and shrieking. They filled the corridor with not only a crush of bodies but also a stench of excrement mixed with brimstone.

Many of the demons crashed their way to the far end of the corridor, seeking a way out, breaking down walls as they went. Others slithered around the creature filling the hall, Gabrielle riding it like a bronco buster, and headed for me.

No, not me. Their rage was focused on Titus, who turned to face them, his eyes still screwed shut from the bright flare of Gabrielle's magic.

Well, shit.

If Titus died, would Mick and the rest of the arena's combatants be released from their contracts? Would they hurry quietly home, or would the demons burst out into the hotel upstairs and wreak havoc, with Gabrielle spurring them on?

Mick turned and shouted at me. He put magic into that yell, so I could hear and understand: "Save Titus!"

No time to ask him why. The adamance in Mick's command jolted me—he'd never ask without good reason.

In the second after Mick's shout, I was throwing myself between the surging demons and Titus. I dug deep inside me for the Beneath magic Gabrielle tossed around so easily, and slammed up a wall of it in front of me.

The demon leading the charge smacked into the energy and screamed as its hide sizzled. It bounced away, whimpering, and the others halted uncertainly.

I faced a motley crew of beings from every hell ever opened. Some were human shaped, some flickering from man to animal and back again—skinwalkers. I saw giant beasts and small ones, the smallest of them raising its claws to shoot streams of liquid at the magic shield. The liquid slid ineffectually down my barrier but burned into the concrete floor like the strongest acid. Smelled like acid too.

Titus regarded me in surprise and with a little more respect. "Hmm. I should put *you* into the arena."

"Not if I can't fight without magic." I clenched my teeth so they wouldn't chatter with the energy surging through my body. "I couldn't arm wrestle one of these guys."

Titus put his head on one side, studying me with very dragon-like assessment. "Individual restrictions are set for individual combatants, according to their abilities. Each fight is different."

His lack of panic irritated me. "Well, right now, these

combatants want to take out their hostility on you, so you might want to make a run for it."

Titus shook his head, to my surprise. "I'm as bound here as they are. I can't run."

What? "Great. So what do we do?"

"We see what you and your sister can accomplish."

He spoke as though he had no stake in the outcome of this fight. I tamped down my anger and concentrated on keeping the barrier steady against the demons trying to figure out how to break it.

Mick was busy attempting to tame Gabrielle. He had his arm around her, but she ignored him, enjoying herself blasting holes in the walls. If she burned her way up through the hotel, a whole lot of people would die.

But she was on the other side of my barrier, out of my reach. I had to leave it to Mick to talk her down.

Most of the creatures released simply tried to escape, but the ones just beyond my barrier had murder in their eyes, the need for vengeance.

Some of these creatures came from the hells of Beneath— which was the remnant of the world before this one, from which the first humans had emerged. Those beings might be able to best me. Already power crackled as they prepared to raise their magic against mine.

Then there were hells that contained Earth-magic crea- tures, like the dragons—the demons that emerged from those were different, but just as dangerous.

At the moment, the Beneath demons and the Earth-magic demons had a common cause—breaking through the barrier and killing me and Titus.

The ceiling imploded in a cloud of dust. Instead of falling in and crushing us to death, it peeled slowly open, Gabrielle holding it up with her power. She did it easily, Mick's efforts not stopping her at all. Her laughter drifted among the chaos.

I was sweating, my legs shaking with the effort of keeping my shield up and the demons away from us. The acid-flinging one tried again, and this time, my barrier wavered the slightest bit. My heart sped in panic. Not the way I wanted to die.

A demon escaped through the hole in the ceiling. And another, and another. The creatures facing me caught on, and they began to turn away and fling themselves upward, slithering, climbing, flying out through the upward tunnel Gabrielle had created.

Gabrielle shouted in unholy joy, Mick growling at her. The beast they rode lunged for the hole, Gabrielle clinging to its back, Mick hanging on to Gabrielle.

After a few turbulent moments, Titus and I stood alone in the corridor, dust filling the air and making me cough.

I closed my hand to disperse my barrier and sagged heavily, catching myself on the wall. My nerves buzzed, and I felt sick, as I always did after I wielded too much magic. I needed Mick to ground me, but at the moment, Mick was busy trying to keep my little sister from destroying Las Vegas.

My legs buckled, and I started to slide downward. A pair of strong hands caught me. I felt a bite of fire, smelled a whiff of ash, and found myself landing against the soft cashmere of Titus's suit.

"What are you?" he asked me, his eyes changing from blue to silver to black as he stared down at me in dragon curiosity.

"I'm a Stormwalker." One weak as a kitten at the moment. "Usually," I amended.

"Interesting. Mick didn't catalog all your abilities."

I wanted to stand up and give Titus an indignant look,

telling him my abilities were none of his business, but my body wouldn't obey. I had to lean on Mick's enemy and soak up the Earth magic within him, drawing on it to stabilize me.

"Probably because he was too busy trying to stay alive," I croaked.

Titus put his hand under my elbow. "You all right? You're taking magic from me."

I nodded, my long hair falling into my face. "Sorry. Can't help it. Your Earth magic is bolstering mine so I can calm down the other side of me. Mick usually takes the edge off."

"Hmm," Titus said again, studying me with eyes that remained dragon-black.

I drew a ragged breath. "You and I need to have a long talk. But right now, we need to go upstairs and stop demons from every imaginable hell from killing all the people in the casino."

Titus raised his brows. "Yes, I think you're right. On both counts. Shall we?"

He turned me around, his grip on my elbow inflexible, and led me down the corridor in the opposite direction of the hole, where the ceiling was still intact, and to the elevator, which amazingly still functioned. The arena was quiet now, the audience having fled.

I heard the screaming as soon as the elevator doors opened on the ground floor. Titus had helped me regain some of my equilibrium, and I ran, if shakily, down the maintenance halls to the main part of the hotel. Titus moved ahead of me in a graceful sprint, running lightly even in his elegant suit.

The casino was like a scene from a creature feature. Demons swooped and swirled or slithered across the floor— three were busily ripping down chandeliers, while others knocked over slot machines, nearly crushing people beneath them. Still others plowed through the card tables, scattering chips, cards, chairs, and people.

Fleeing humans streamed out the doors, meeting with a crush of those outside struggling to see what was going on. The sun was hours away, but in the heart of Las Vegas, the lights were bright as day.

Gabrielle rode the demon, who flung its body every which way, its giant tail causing havoc. Mick hung on grimly behind her.

I caught up to Titus and grabbed on to him for strength as I gathered my power once again to stop the demons. Titus's eyes widened as he felt me drag his magic out of him, but he caught on quickly and let me take it, at the same time building dragon fire in his hands.

I'd have to strike at all the demons at once, and I'd have to kill them. I knew most of them didn't want to be here, were as trapped as Mick, but if I didn't stop them, this hotel and likely most of the city would become a bloodbath.

I shakily gathered my force, Titus flinching as I pulled hard on him. At the same moment, Maya pushed her way in from the street through one of the casino's revolving doors.

Behind her strode a man with buzzed black hair and gray eyes, a Taser in his hands. This man halted in front of the demon Gabrielle rode, aimed the Taser at her, and shouted, "Stop!"

CHAPTER FIVE

The man was Nash Jones, Sheriff of Hopi County. What he was doing in Las Vegas, a long way out of his jurisdiction, and what he thought he could do with a single stun gun against a horde of demons, I had no idea.

Gabrielle's face lit up in welcome. "Nashie!" She waved. "Come and join my party!"

The demon under her eyed Nash in trepidation. It didn't care about the Taser, or the puny human holding it, but it sensed about Nash what I knew—that he ate demon magic for breakfast.

While the demon halted in worry, one of the acid flinging creatures ceased knocking over slot machines and leapt at Nash's back, black fluid spewing. Where the liquid hit the carpet, the carpet dissolved into a hissing, stinking mess.

Where the liquid hit Nash, it did ... nothing. I held my breath. The acid was a physical manifestation and so should burn him without hindrance, but the liquid disappeared as soon as it touched him. Nash turned his head and fixed the demon with a gray-eyed stare.

The beast squealed in terror. The others caught its fear, turned to find the source of danger, and recoiled.

Now they only wanted to get away, demons flying or running like animals in terror, but they didn't know where to go, and the destruction increased as they panicked.

"Janet!" Mick shouted at me. "Open a way!"

I knew what he meant, but what he was asking was onerous. Easy for him to throw out the command, but such a thing would take all my strength, and might be beyond my ability.

I grabbed Titus, dragging him after me as I stumbled toward the hole Gabrielle had blasted up from the basement.

"Help me," I said, jerking at his finely tailored sleeve. "We have to give them a way to escape."

"We do that, I die," Titus said, far too calm for my liking.

"If you don't, they'll attack you, and I don't know if I can hold them off. And you die."

Titus took his time answering, as though he had to weigh my argument. "All right," he said finally. "What do we do?"

"You hold on to me so I don't implode." I turned my back on him and positioned his hands on my waist. "That would be messy. Ruin your suit."

Titus rumbled a dragony noise that sounded almost amused. He threaded his fingers through my belt loops, holding me steady while I leaned over the hole in the floor.

I looked straight down several floors, through pipes, wiring, and broken cement, to the basement where the cells were.

Had anyone else working in the hotel known what kind of arena was down there? Or that cell blocks had held creatures from every hell imaginable? Or had Titus managed to keep it a secret except to those in the know? Humans would have to believe in demons, or simply not care, to watch and bet on combat like that.

I drew a long breath and gathered my magic.

I felt a second wave of Beneath magic forming with mine and jerked around to see Gabrielle slide from the demon's back and approach me.

She joined me at the precipice. "Let's send these poor guys home, Janet," she said, her voice serious.

"Thank you," I answered cautiously. "You know how to open a way?" I didn't think she could—opening a vortex to Beneath took a combined power of Earth magic and Beneath magic, and Gabrielle had been unsuccessful at attempts to open one before, which had upset her very much.

She gave me a look of confidence. "Not really, but you can show me."

I shuddered at the implications of teaching Gabrielle how to open a gate to Beneath, but at the moment, I didn't have time to be choosy. I gathered my will, focused on the crack in the floors below and sent my magic there.

Gabrielle's power joined mine a second later, flowing down to encourage the Earth to part and open. Not simply to make a hole, but to open a way to another dimension, to Beneath.

Beneath wasn't all one place—nothing so simple. There were pockets of different hells, each populated with its own brand of demons. The space my mother dominated wasn't the same as the one under Area 51 or those reached via other vortexes throughout the world.

At the moment, we couldn't worry about who went where. We just needed these demons out of here before people died.

The trouble with opening a gate to Beneath was that we couldn't be certain what would come *out* of it—demons of all shapes and forms, skinwalkers, and things no one had a name for.

I'd just have to hope that me and Gabrielle, with an assist from Mick, Titus, and Nash, could keep them at bay. I grabbed Gabrielle's hand.

The jolt of joining with her lifted me a few inches off the floor. My magic was a blend of the frightening mindlessness of Beneath mixed with the solid, dark, almost homey Earth magic, but Gabrielle was pure power.

I'd had no idea how much spun through her, but it was incredible. How she held all that inside her and still lived amazed me. I'd be out of my mind, blithering in a straight-jacket, with people having to feed me through a grate in the wall with a very long spoon. My respect for my little sister rose.

Gabrielle was giving me a wide-eyed stare, as though what was inside *me* astonished her as much.

Then she clenched my hand, grabbed my energy, mixed it with hers, and sent the combined might into the basement.

Concrete and stone exploded in a fiery wash. Wiring sparked, and then came a flash so bright it obliterated all other light. It died into darkness the same time all the electricity went out.

To hear a casino silent was a strange thing. The machines ceased whirring, bells no longer rang, and the flashing, glittering lights sputtered out. Even the artificial Las Vegas noon outside the windows went dark. A few moments later, a backup generator clicked on, and dim light tried to leak through the lobby.

Another white-hot light flashed upward, one so fierce Gabrielle and I scrambled a few steps backward. Then the Earth parted with a groan.

Underneath Las Vegas is high desert floor, and under that

is water—aquifers that feed the city. The entire downtown area is sinking, apparently, from the constant drain on these aquifers.

We hit one. Water geysered through the hole, drenching all those in a circle of a dozen feet, but Gabrielle and I didn't stop, our magic continuing to drill through heavy water to the bedrock far, far below. After a minute or two, the precious water ceased flowing and began to drain into the realms of Beneath.

A vortex opened. It rotated, slowly at first, then spun faster. Most of the demons dove for it in glee. Others tried to hang back but were pulled toward it whether they liked it or not.

The beast Gabrielle had ridden slithered past us, making for the hole. "Bye-bye," Gabrielle called after it. "You take care of your kids, now."

The creature turned its great head, its gleaming eyes resting on Gabrielle. I saw gratitude in its expression before the creature turned away and slid into the depths.

Others quickly followed, the vortex sucking them down into the Earth.

Gabrielle whooped. The beasts flowed past us, faster and faster, until the last of them vanished in a rush, like grains of sand draining down an hourglass.

I glanced at Gabrielle, and she nodded. Our magic in sync, we reached down and began to pull the vortex closed.

The Earth resisted, rocks and dirt digging in stubbornly. The magic that came from Earth—the magic that enabled dragons and Changers, witches and Stormwalkers to exist—didn't get along with Beneath magic, as I was made aware every day of my life.

The Earth magic we'd touched to open the way to Beneath was old and strong, and I had the sense that it wanted to dive into the Beneath world after the demons and destroy all there.

A strange thread wound up into my mind, a whisper to become one with the Earth, to let that magical part of myself take over. To dive into the hole and surround myself with dirt and rock and the solid magic they contained. To burrow in and stay, to release my Beneath magic forever.

It was enticing, that whisper. The thought of giving up the madness that lurked inside me was tempting. I could curl up in a cocoon while my Stormwalker magic kept me alive, and melded me with the Earth, my father.

I started to fall forward, anticipating the coolness and calm of being surrounded by soothing soil, while the Earth lured me into sleep without dreams.

Something hot flashed through my arm and a terrible strength jerked me backward.

I blinked open my eyes and realized I'd been leaning far, far over the edge of the hole. Gabrielle, her fingers wound tightly through mine, hauled me back, her Beneath magic like hot, stinging needles.

I saw her worried face, her mouth shaping the word, "Janet?" but I couldn't hear her.

The Earth was crying out to me, begging for me to come to it. To heal it or release it—I wasn't sure which.

I wanted to. Everything in me wanted to throw off Gabrielle's hold, jump down into the warm depths, and release all my sorrows.

My hand seared as Gabrielle's Beneath magic tore into me. I screamed, or thought I did, but I couldn't hear that either.

Then Mick was beside me, at the edge, and the Earth reached up to embrace *him*. I yelled at him to get back—or tried to. I couldn't speak, couldn't move, couldn't make a sound.

The Earth is awakening, I heard distinctly in my brain, and sensed a joy on top of that.

I wanted to laugh, to welcome the voice, to open my arms for it.

Gabrielle's mouth was moving again, and so was Mick's. The ground sucked at Mick's feet—it would take him. We'd join hands and fall into the vortex, be swallowed by it, together forever. The thought elated me as much as it terrified me.

Mick called out over the crowd, though his voice was silent to me, and I sensed someone rush up behind me.

Gabrielle's shriek bore into my brain, and then her touch was gone. A pair of strong arms closed on me from behind, and sound abruptly returned.

I heard shouting, screaming, the babbling of the patrons in the casino, and the crack and roar of rocks and concrete slamming together at my feet.

The enticing whisper of the Earth cut off, as did the flow of Gabrielle's magic. My own magic streamed backward out of me into the man who'd grabbed me—Nash, the magic null.

I yelled as the magic left me, Nash and I outlined in an eerie glow. Then, with a low *whump,* my power hit the spell that made Nash a magical drain, and the light flickered out.

He didn't have to squeeze my ribs so hard, I thought irritably. I struggled to breathe, but I couldn't break his hold. My friends—Mick, Gabrielle, and Maya, with Titus behind them—stood still and watched Nash calm down crazy Janet.

Nash finally eased away from me, his gaze on me sharp. But I'd be all right now. No more whispers from the Earth, no more double dose of power from myself and Gabrielle, no more demons, no more vortex. All gone.

I turned to tell Nash that a simple touch would have done, but my leg bent, the floor rushed at me, and I never remembered hitting it.

I WOKE IN A SOFT BED IN A SUMPTUOUS HOTEL ROOM WITH TOO many people in it.

Mick, dressed in a pair of jeans and nothing else, sat on the bed next to me, his back against the headboard. His arms and chest were deeply scratched from his battle in the arena, though he'd washed off most of the blood.

My head rested against his hip, a comfortable place to be. The warmth of Mick cut through my fatigue, the tingle of his healing magic stealing through my body.

Nash stood in the middle of the room, arms folded over his gray polo shirt. Maya slumped on a sofa behind him, her legs dangling elegantly over its arm. Titus the dragon sat in a chair near the window, silhouetted by the bright lights outside, one pristine trousered leg crossed over the other. Gabrielle …

I struggled to sit up, alarmed. "Where's Gabrielle?"

I tried to remember what happened. We'd watched the demons dive for the worlds below, and Gabrielle had been right next to me. A voice had told me to jump with the demons, not to Beneath, but into the Earth itself. It had started to grab at Mick too, as though it sensed the incredible Earth magic within him and wanted to embrace it. Then Nash had pushed Gabrielle aside and seized me.

Had the vortex called out to Gabrielle? In my mind's eye, I saw her spread her arms and laugh in delight as she leapt from the edge.

"She took off," Maya said in a groggy voice. "Titus tried to stop her, but she fought him and went."

"You should have kept hold of her," Nash growled at Titus. "She's too dangerous to be out there on her own."

"That is obvious." Titus brought his fingertips together. His clothes were as impeccable as ever, as though a shield had kept them clean from the dust and chaos of an exploding hotel full of demons. "I thought the Stormwalker more important to save."

Mick put a hand on my shoulder, more magic snaking in to find my hurts and ease them. "Don't worry too much, Janet. I have friends out looking for her, with strict instructions to report to me."

My eyes widened. "Friends? What friends?"

"Men and ... non-humans I call on when I need a little assist," Mick said, at his most reassuring. "They arrived swiftly to my summons."

I fixed my wavering gaze on Nash. "What are *you* doing here? I'm guessing you were who Maya was talking to on the phone, but there's no way you could have made it here so fast from Flat Mesa."

"That's because I wasn't in Flat Mesa." Nash's cool eyes held no judgment. "I was already in Las Vegas, on business."

"He means he was keeping tabs on us," Maya said. She didn't sound surprised or annoyed, only resigned. "He knows how much trouble I'm sucked into whenever I'm with you and decided to make sure he was on hand to get us out of it."

I couldn't argue with Nash's logic. He'd pulled Maya and me out of wreckage in Las Vegas before.

"Thanks," I said with sincerity.

Nash gave me an acknowledging nod. "Titus and Mick were explaining to me how there was an illegal fighting ring set up in the basement of this hotel."

I let out a short laugh. Leave it to Nash to hang a label like *illegal fighting ring* on supernatural gladiatorial games involving demon-kind.

I turned to study Titus, the details of the fight returning to my brain. "When we were in the basement, you said you were as bound as the demons, and if you let them go, you'd die."

"I did." Titus didn't change expression—all dragons have a tendency toward understatement and ambiguous answers.

"Why? I thought you were running the games."

"He is," Mick said. "But at the behest of another. He was as compelled to obey as I."

When Mick becomes dragon serious, his speech grows archaic. The bad boys in the novels I read talk all kinds of grunge, but Mick, the baddest bad boy I've ever met, says things like *at the behest of*, or *arrived swiftly to my summons*.

"I hope you're going to explain that," I said.

"I'd be interested myself," Nash added.

Titus rose. He was a large man in his human form, like Mick, and looked comfortable in the well-tailored suit I suspected had cost thousands. Mick was more at home in biker clothes, but dragons chose their looks and stuck to them. Colby had opted for Yakuza style tattoos, and Drake, like Titus, dressed in designer suits, usually black cashmere with black silk shirts.

Titus straightened his iridescent tie with careful fingers. "Mick and I are bound by a promise made centuries ago," he said. "Exacted from us by a dragon slayer."

Nash's derisive huff rang through the room. "A dragon slayer? Are they anything like those Nightwalker slayers that came through Hopi County this summer? You and Mick couldn't fight off a few obnoxious humans with crossbows?"

Titus didn't laugh, and neither did Mick.

I remembered Mick mentioning a dragon slayer when we'd been protecting Ansel, our Nightwalker friend, from being killed by vampire hunters. I'd thought Mick joking at first, but he'd given me a dead serious look and said dragon slayers were real, and very dangerous. He hadn't elaborated after that, and I'd forgotten about it amid more pressing business.

"Dragon slayers are nothing like Nightwalker slayers," Titus said in his dragon-deep voice. "They're the most dangerous things in the universe—they have to be, in order to defeat dragons. There are no unsuccessful dragon slayers."

"No live ones, he means," Mick said. "The unsuccessful ones became dragon fodder."

"If there is anything left of them to eat." Titus spoke matter-of-factly.

"Ew," Maya said, her face wrinkling. "You *eat* people?"

"Dragon slayers aren't people," Titus said.

"He means that literally," Mick broke in as Maya drew a breath to object. "They are powerful mages, or demons, or some combination of the two. The dragon slayer who made the contract with us began as a human then became a mage and segued into demon as the power consumed him over the years. I told you I fought him, to save another. He was determined to bring me down and he nearly did. I had to beg for my life. He offered it to me, for a price."

"Yes," Titus said. "I was there. The one Mick fought so hard to save was *me*. But I was near to death, and Mick could not prevail against him. The slayer made us both promise to fight in these games, with me to host them, choosing the combatants that would be hardest for Mick to beat. He enjoys such irony. The slayer wishes to rid the world of dragons and demons, and this way he gets entertainment from it. And money. *Much* money from those who will pay to watch and wager."

"Really?" Maya said. "But you both must have grown stronger since then. Mick, you said you were only a young dragon at the time. Why didn't you find him and confront him again?"

Titus looked at her as though she'd lost her mind. "We signed an agreement," he said, sounding almost shocked.

Of course. Dragons and their damned honor. They'd abide by the contract if it killed them—which this one had a good chance to.

"Was he there at the fight?" I asked. "Why didn't he try to stop you? And Gabrielle?"

Mick shook his head. "He doesn't always attend. He enjoys watching from afar. But he is deadly, and he is determined," he continued grimly. "And now that we've released all the demons and broken free of the games, he won't stop until he finds us and makes us pay."

Gabrielle

WHILE BIG-SISTER JANET WAS SNUGGLING WITH HER BOYFRIEND and confabbing with Nash and Titus, I went out looking for the dragon slayer.

How did I know about the dragon slayer? The demon told me. Not so much *told* me as conveyed it through flashes of thought, anger, and fear. This dragon slayer hadn't confined himself to dragons, according to her, but turned his attention to all large monsters who might be a threat to humankind.

Since Janet was pretty beat up after that show of magic, I

considered it my duty to go find the slayer and put him down.

Janet had been amazing, I admitted. She doesn't give herself credit for all she can do—she's been brainwashed into thinking she can't use her power to kick serious ass. The people holding her back are all afraid of her and want to control her. Afraid she'll kick *their* asses, so they put these weird restrictions on her, and now even she believes those restrictions are right. I sympathize—same thing happens to me.

Whenever she does tell everyone to fuck off and lets loose, she is one powerful magic chick, and I love her for that.

The patrons of the casino had applauded after we'd sent the demons back to their hells and the lights had come on—I guess they thought it was a performance, maybe a taste of what they'd see in the hotel's theatre. Humans can be so oblivious.

I figured this dragon slayer must be somewhere nearby—he'd keep tabs on how his gladiatorial games were going, right? Someone like that wasn't going to trust that everything would go well without him.

Ergo, as Mick would say, he must be around here somewhere.

I started with the hotel. I'm good at sensing auras, like Janet is, so I opened myself up to them as I wandered through the casino.

That was a mistake, because all those auras came crushing down on me. None were anything but human, but humans can be complicated. They ran the gamut of emotions—excited, depressed, scared, worried, elated, angry, frustrated, or bright with sexual satisfaction. I almost fell to my knees under it all, and had to stumble outside and lean against a marble pillar by the door to catch my breath.

Nowhere had I sensed a being gloating because he'd captured all those demons plus a dragon or two, or fury because Janet and I had set them free.

"Get you a cab, ma'am?" The doorman, decked out in a tailcoat and top hat, gestured at a queue of taxis.

I was surprised to see taxis, because these days so many people use those services where you summon ordinary citizens and they drive you around in their family car. I think that's weird, but I didn't want to get into the back of a dirty cab either. The one that had brought us back from the male strip show had smelled like vomit.

"How about a limo?" I asked on impulse.

"Sure thing." The man held up his hand and whistled, the sound cutting the night. In a few moments, a sleek black car pulled up to the curb.

It wasn't a stretch limo, or one of those Hummer ones with a bar and dance space, but it was a lovely car. I slid onto soft cushions in the back seat, and told the driver to charge the fare to Janet Begay in room 1589.

"I don't work for the hotel," the driver said. He was good looking, in his twenties, dark hair, blue eyes. *He* could have danced at the strip club.

I sat forward, resting my arms on the back of his seat. His picture ID on the dashboard said his name was Amos. "It's all right. Janet's good for it. She's my big sister, and will do anything for me."

I sent a trickle of magic down the seat and into his shoulder, not enough to hurt him, but enough to make him see things my way. Amos shot me a smile, which made him even more pretty.

"Where does your sister want me to take you?" he asked.

I thought a moment, pretending I wasn't winging this. "What's the most luxurious hotel in Vegas?"

"That would be the *C*," he answered without hesitation.

"Is that like the one in Los Angeles?" Cassandra, Janet's hotel manager, had worked for the *C*, the ultimate in decadence and personal attention. Too personal, she'd decided.

"Same guy owns both. This one just opened up a few months ago."

"Sounds interesting." I flopped back onto my seat, figuring a heavy hitter like the dragon slayer would pick the most opulent place in Vegas in which to hang out. "Take me there."

"You got it."

Amos put the car in gear and rolled out of the driveway.

CHAPTER SIX

Gabrielle

I loved this, I thought, as the car slid smoothly into traffic. I expressed my wish, and it was granted.

No one scolding me, telling me to calm down and be quiet—*Do what everyone says, Gabrielle, because you're too crazy to be trusted.* Ha. Being out on my own was already so much better.

The night was warm beyond the darkened windows of the limo and full of light, the power outage caused when Janet and I had opened the vortex already forgotten. I gazed at the tall buildings we passed, all flashing and waving and trying to grab my attention. *Come inside,* they said. *Delights await. Food, drink, money, sex. Whatever you want.*

I didn't believe the promises of the signs, dancing lights, and jetting fountains—people will say anything to take your money. I'd lived in Las Vegas right after I'd left home, though I'd worked at a grocery store in Henderson, trying to be "normal." I'd given that up pretty fast. I'd rarely come down to the Strip to sample its enticements, but in those days I'd only had vengeance on my mind. No time for enjoyment.

Amos chatted to me as we went. He was from California, and had been driving here a couple of years. He told me he had a girlfriend he was trying to save up to marry, an ex-girlfriend who was kind of stalkery, and brothers he partied with whenever he went back to California.

I listened with interest, enjoying Amos going on about his ordinary life, which sounded so much more peaceful than mine.

Traffic was dense and it took a while to move down the Strip, but finally, Amos pulled into a long circular driveway that rose steeply to the front door of the C.

Unlike most of the other hotels, this one didn't have a skyscraper attached. A gigantic fountain display in front of the entrance spewed light instead of water. A massive garden identical to the one at Versailles—so said Amos—lay behind it.

The hotel was in the style of a French chateau, like Versailles itself or maybe the Louvre—I'd never been to either place, but I'd seen pictures. Janet and Mick really needed to take me to Paris.

A doorman, even more smartly dressed than the one at the hotel I'd left, opened the car's door for me.

"Here you go," Amos said, sounding regretful. "Have a good time."

I considered. "Why don't you wait for me? I'll hire you for the whole night. I might need to check out some other places."

Amos brightened. "That would be cool."

"Wait then. Janet's good for it."

Amos gave me his most handsome smile. "Your big sis must love you a lot."

I leaned forward and patted his arm. "Oh, she does."

At least, I hoped so. She'd be bitching at me for running out on her, but she'd be plenty happy if I caught the dragon slayer for her.

I blew Amos a kiss and slid out the back door, thanking the doorman. Two bellmen leapt to open the hotel's front door for me and I smiled at them as I sailed inside. Everyone was so courteous.

I stepped into unbelievable opulence. Yep, if I were an all-powerful dragon slayer, I'd stay here.

The casino took up most of the floor, but this one had fewer slot machines and more card tables than the other hotels we'd visited tonight. People around these tables weren't the comfortably dressed tourists and retirees I'd seen elsewhere but wore high-fashion clothes—slinky dresses for the ladies and suits or at least coats and natty shirts for the men.

The casino's lofty ceiling was soft white, resembling a Mediterranean building decorated for the very rich of the past. A cool breeze blew through it, as though suggesting that the ocean was right outside.

I noticed most of the women had men with them, the kind who touched his lady's back when escorting her across the room. The women put slender hands on their men's arms, wrists dripping with diamonds.

These beautiful people sat at baccarat tables that were partitioned off from the other card games, each table with its own crystal chandelier and tuxedoed dealer.

"May I help you, ma'am?"

A suited man with a Bluetooth in his ear had approached

me and now gave me a look of stern scrutiny. I noted there were others like him stationed about the casino, making sure the wrong element didn't enter their fancy hotel.

I was still in my glittery blue party dress, but I was a mess from rescuing all those demons. Riding the female snake demon had scared the shit out of me and also been the most fun I'd had in a long time.

I'd *connected* with it. I'd felt the demon's terror and fury, the kind that had raged through me whenever my so-called dad had gone on a drunken rampage against me and my stepmom.

Thinking about my parents led to some very bad memories, which I shoved swiftly away. I couldn't focus on my mission if I wallowed in the past.

"Where's the ladies' room, sweetie?" I asked the well-dressed security guard. "I need to freshen up."

He pointed the way. I saw him discreetly motion to another guard, telling him to keep an eye on me.

I waved at the second guard as I sashayed into the bathroom. A look into the mirror told me things weren't as bad as I'd feared, but I needed to rinse my face, comb my hair, and fix a rip in one side of my dress.

The tear I repaired with magic, my hair with a little water and my fingers. I didn't have a purse—that was smashed somewhere under our hotel—so I'd have to live without a comb until I could hit a store.

I ducked into a stall to do my business, and heard two women come in and linger in the lounge portion of the bathroom.

"Honey, are you sure?" one asked in concern.

The second's answer had tears in it. "He's on the phone all the time, and never talks to me anymore. I saw his texts to her one day, and he ..." The young woman drifted into sobs. "And tonight he's acting like everything's fine."

"Oh, honey." True sympathy oozed from the first woman. "Do you want me to have Ron talk to him?"

"No." Panicked. "I don't want him to know."

I flushed and burst out of the stall, heading to wash my hands at the sink. The two women jerked around to stare at me, but the poor thing in tears couldn't stop crying.

Both ladies wore satiny, expensive dresses, and jewels that could feed a small family for a year. Their skin was far too pale for the hot Nevada sunshine, and their hair had been cut, highlighted, and styled in an upscale salon, probably the same one for both.

The woman comforting her friend gave me a look of embarrassment tinged with hostility—but hey, they should have checked whether they were alone before they went off about their problems.

I dried my hands and faced them. "So your idiot husband not only wants a trophy wife, but a trophy girlfriend too?" I asked the teary-eyed woman.

"This really is none of your business," her friend began, but my heart went out to the poor crying rich girl who was learning that money couldn't buy her everything. I'd grown up in a trailer with a drunk, and even I knew that.

I tossed my terrycloth towel into a hamper—no paper towels for this bathroom. "Here's what you do," I said. "You find the hottest guy in this place and flirt like hell with him. Take him dancing, buy him drinks. Make the dickhead you're married to realize you aren't going to roll over and let him cheat on you. Then you hire a limo for yourself, the hot guy, and your girlfriends, and you go out on the town. Steal your husband's phone before you go, drop it on the ground in front of the limo and tell the driver to run over it. I have a car waiting out front—driver's name is Amos. He'll help you out. Tell him Gabrielle sent you."

The sad woman listened, her eyes swimming with tears. "I'm not sure I could do that."

"Why not?" I put my hands on my hips. "Sounds like your perfect husband doesn't appreciate you. Sell those rocks he gave you, buy your own place, and find yourself a boy toy."

She shook her head while her friend listened, open-mouthed. "I don't want that," the cheated-on woman said. "I just want things the way they used to be."

"Take it from me, sweetie, no, you don't. You want what you *think* you had—I bet your husband was a philandering asshole from day one, just good at hiding it. Take your own life into your hands, and tell him to suck on it. If you don't let him have a hold on you—then you win." If only my stepmom had listened to me when I'd tried to tell her that.

"I think I agree with her," her friend said, sounding surprised at herself. "Allan is a shit. I always thought you were too good for him."

"There you go." I spread my hands. "Don't forget—steal cell phone, smash it. First, though, maybe send some texts to the girlfriend—you know, like they're from him. 'I decided I hated you, bitch.' Or 'You're so ugly, looking at you gives me a migraine.'"

The friend laughed quietly, and even crying girl smiled through her tears. Maybe they weren't so bad for privileged, rich, flawless women. I guess not everyone's life is ideal.

I tipped them a wink and moved out the bathroom door. Look at me doing all kinds of good deeds tonight.

Waving again at the security guard, I went to the cashier's counter to pick up some chips.

I can't do mind magic—like put people in trances or anything—only the simple suggestion like with Amos—but I

made the computer on the other side of the cage think I'd
handed the lady a good credit card, and it told her to give me
about ten grand in chips. I'd done a similar thing to get the
hotel suite for Janet.

I distracted the cashier with patter, and she shoved chips
at me, looking faintly puzzled. There were so many chips,
she gave me a little wooden carrier for them. I thought I
looked elegant gliding through the casino, my neatly stacked
chip carrier at my side.

The two ladies came out of the bathroom. They pasted
bright smiles on their faces as they approached a group of
sleek-suited men who took no notice of them.

What was with these guys? Were they so convinced that
their women would drop their panties whenever they
snapped their fingers that they no longer had to be decent
to them?

Bought and paid for, I heard Grandmother Begay's voice in
my head.

I paused a step. When did I start thinking of Ruby Begay
as *Grandmother*? She wasn't *my* grandmother.

Pushing the troubling thought aside I changed my direction to make for the guys. The two ladies, still a few yards
from their husbands, caught sight of me. *Which one?* I mimed
at them.

The friend gestured to the tallest one, with blond hair,
cool blue eyes, and a superior smile. He was trying to domi-
nate the conversation, making his friends acknowledge that
he was leader.

I headed for him. A couple of the men in the small group
saw me coming. They showed interest—of course they did. I
was cute, young, wearing a tight blue dress with shimmering
sequins, and I wasn't married to them.

One said, "Hey, darling, what's your rush?"

I ignored him. I pretended to trip and banged right into Allan the Dickhead.

He looked down at me with scorn that quickly turned to lechery as he steadied me on my feet. "Careful, honey." He looked me up and down and said, "Out of curiosity, are you Asian?"

A lot of people mistook Indians for Asians. Thank that land bridge in Alaska so many eons ago. "Chinese," I lied.

"I like Chinese," another of them quipped. "Got any fortune cookies, honey?"

Could they disparage any more races at the same time? They were *all* dickheads.

Janet would be proud of me, because I did *not* toast the whole group and dust their ashes off my hands. I kept to my objective and turned away, tossing a little smile over my shoulder as I went.

"Sorry, dudes. See ya."

As I passed the two ladies on my way to the card tables I slipped Allan's phone, which I'd lifted from his coat pocket, to the friend—she'd make sure crying girl followed my advice.

"You can do so much better than those assholes," I said. "Hey, come partying with me—we'll find us some sweet guys and go dancing."

Both shook their heads, as I knew they would. They were too afraid to break free at the moment, but I'd planted the idea in their heads. They had a spark of defiance in their eyes as they regarded the cluster of men, who were busy looking at *me*, not their wives, the shitheads.

Those guys were so screwed, and they didn't even know it yet. I laughed as I sauntered away. Mission accomplished.

And then I saw him. Not so much *him* as the aura of black, white, and brilliant red that wrapped him like a cloak.

The power washing off him—a blast of Earth magic like I've never felt before—brushed against my Beneath magic and sent every nerve buzzing.

I'd found him.

The dragon slayer. Right in front of me.

CHAPTER SEVEN

Gabrielle

I came to a dead halt, my hand tightening on my chip holder as I prepared to draw on my power for the kill. Teach him to mess with my dragons.

The dragon slayer looked right through me. He glanced around, as though checking out the casino, but never noticed me frozen in place, gaping at him. My jaw had to be on my chest.

I snapped my mouth closed, relieved but at the same time offended. Couldn't he sense that the bad-assest mage in the Southwest was right in front of him?

Apparently not. Maybe because I wasn't a dragon? Or a snake-bodied demon? Or did he just not think me a threat?

He turned away and moseyed through the casino, scanning the tables before he chose one. Passing the time before he hunted another dragon?

I followed, doing my best to look innocent. Men tried to stop me as I slid past them—asking if I were alone, if I wanted company, if they could buy me a drink. Because of course, a young woman walking around by herself could only be dying to hook up with a guy, any guy.

I brushed past these eager gentlemen—or gave them a shove out of my way if they were too insistent. I didn't want to use magic to push them aside, because that might alert the dragon slayer. He hadn't noticed me as a girl in a slinky dress, but guys flying across the room on a jolt of power might give him a clue.

The dragon slayer bulked out his elegant suit, like a wrestler who'd stuffed himself into formalwear to glad-hand the right people. His hair was a cross between brown and blond, as if he couldn't decide, and his eyes were dark in a squarish, flat face, nose a little beaky. Not bad looking—in a brutish way—but Amos, my driver, was much more handsome.

The dragon slayer sat down at a baccarat table. I slid onto the empty seat at the other end of the horseshoe-shaped table, setting my rack of chips on the green felt.

I'd never played baccarat before, but I figured it couldn't be all that hard. Casino games are fairly easy—it's knowing how much to bet and when to stop that's difficult.

The baccarat tables I'd glimpsed in other casinos had been tan with bright markings, but this one had an old-fashioned feel to it, like the rest of the hotel, as though we'd been transported back a hundred years ago to a posh place on the Riviera.

I studied the numbers and words painted on the felt but had no idea what to do.

"You can bet on the bank or your own hand," a well-dressed, silver-haired gentleman next to me said. "Is it your first time?"

He could have put innuendo into the question, and I'd

have punched him, but he seemed genuinely nice, so I let it slide.

"It looks fun, so thought I'd try it," I said, making myself sound ingenuous.

"The minimum bet at this table is a thousand dollars," the man said gently. "That's this one." He touched a yellow-bordered chip. "You sure you want to do this?"

"Of course." I plucked two chips from the carrier and stacked them in front of me.

The man raised his silver brows and then copied me, putting down a bet of two thousand.

The dragon slayer laid down a stack that made five thousand. I only smiled and waited for the dealer to take cards from the shoe and slide them to me on a wooden paddle. So much more elegant than having the dealer's fingerprints all over the cards, and probably more sanitary too.

My cards were a two and a three.

"That's good," my new friend said. "In baccarat, you need to stay below or at nine. Tens and face cards are worth zero." The dealer slid cards to him, a king and a three. "You can ask for another card, but you have to be careful. The tens place isn't counted, so if your cards add up to, say thirteen, that only counts as three."

I wrinkled my nose. "Really? Who made up that math?"

The gentleman smiled. "Bored card players in the eighteenth century."

"Couldn't they count back then?"

"I think they wanted to make things more difficult."

Of course. Where was the fun if you won too easily?

The dragon slayer received his cards. The dealer drew a five and a seven for the bank, which by this bizarre way of counting, equaled only two points.

"I'll take another," I told the dealer, then grinned when he turned over a four. Nine points—hot damn.

"Very good," my new friend said. "I see I won't be so lucky." He had another face card, which meant he topped out at three points.

The dealer gave the other players cards as they wished, then the game was over. A stack of chips came at me by way of a small plastic rake, and the same rake scraped away my new friend's chips. The dragon slayer received a payout too.

I narrowed my eyes as I watched the slayer. He sat casually, a slight slump to his broad shoulders as he stacked his chips with big fingers and placed another bet.

The gentleman leaned to me. "You need to move your chips or they'll be your bet on your next hand."

I considered, then shrugged. "Let it ride."

He looked worried. "Are you certain? You could lose it all."

"Doesn't matter. I'm here to have fun." I nodded at the dealer to let him know my bet stood.

"Good for you." My friend put down two thousand, which he lost at the end of the hand. He let the chips go, unperturbed.

I lost as well. I didn't have to—I could have slid some magic into the card shoe to give me nine points again, but I chose to stay cool. The first hand I'd won by luck alone, which was an exciting feeling. Plus, I didn't want to dribble out too much magic in a place like this.

Cassandra had told me about the man who owned the C hotels. He was called Christianson, and he knew all about magic. He had once employed Emmett Smith, the Ununculous—top mage in the world—to make his guests' dark, kinky wishes come true.

I'd think a man like Christianson would know when

someone used magic to cheat in his casinos. Janet had handed Emmett Smith's ass to him a few months ago, but another dark mage could have taken over his position.

More cards, more bets. I shoved six thousand dollars in chips onto the felt. The dragon slayer bet five thousand.

Cards turned over. My friend next to me relaxed a little when his points totaled eight. "Staying right here," he told the dealer with a warm smile.

The dragon slayer asked for another card. I forgot to, because I was too busy watching him, and lost my chips on a hand of only two points. The dragon slayer won a big stack.

I'd felt a tingle as soon as the dealer plucked the card from the shoe and slid it to the dragon slayer.

I didn't have any Earth magic in me, and in my youth had never been good at detecting it, but that had been before I'd hung around with Janet and Mick. I'd become much better at sensing it now, especially since I'd moved in with Janet's grandmother.

Ruby Begay was a strong Earth-magic shaman, and Janet's dad, the sweetheart Pete, had Earth magic in him as well, though more modestly. Gina Tsotsie, Pete's fiancée, had some too, which she worked into her pretty jewelry.

You can't be around that much Earth magic, twenty-four seven, and not get used to its buzz. Grandmother Begay pretended she never used hers, but I knew she zapped a little into the food she cooked—I'd seen her do it. I'll never tell, though, because her meals are wonderful.

Now, as I sat at the elegant, old-fashioned baccarat table, I sensed the little spark and smelled the whiff of warm dust that meant Earth magic was in the air.

Was the dragon slayer nuts? He'd be caught by the magic-savvy hotel owner and either flayed alive or taken out into the desert to be shot and left as a lesson to others. Did goons still do that in Vegas?

The dragon slayer didn't appear to care—he just kept on cheating, his flick of magic barely discernible.

As the game went on, my new friend beside me won and lost, taking his money or letting it go with equal grace. No magic there. I tried to emulate him, pretending that victory or defeat meant nothing to me.

I had my fingers on the table during one hand when the dragon slayer was dealt his third card, and I definitely felt the bite of magic snaking toward the dealer. I sent a subtle trickle of my own magic over his, and the slayer ended up with a face card, which brought his points to the grand total of four.

He blinked and frowned, while I hid my smile of triumph.

Another deal, and then my silver-haired friend, who was down to his final chips and a hand of two points, made a resigned gesture. "One last card, and then I retire. Do be careful, all right?"

"Don't go," I said on impulse. I liked him—so few people were nice to me, and I was enjoying the novelty. "You'll win, I'm sure."

He shook his head. "The cards aren't with me tonight."

"Oh, I don't know," I said. "I have a feeling your luck is about to change."

I sent my tendril of magic to the dealer, and the next card brought my friend's point total to nine. The dragon slayer lost completely, and I resisted crowing with laughter.

"See?" I said. "Your luck is changing."

My friend didn't scream in joy or jump up and down like people in ads for Las Vegas do. He looked mildly pleased, gave me a smile as he pulled in his winnings, then laid down another thousand-dollar chip.

The slayer looked up and over at us. I gave him a five-fingered wave, but his gaze didn't settle on me—it rested on my distinguished gentleman friend.

The man beside me exuded no magic at all, so why did the slayer stare at him so sharply? Did he assume the wicked flash of magic from my end of the table couldn't possibly have come from the Apache woman in party clothes?

I kept grinning at the slayer until finally he flicked his gaze to me.

The ice in his stare froze me to the bone. There was power in this one, no mistake. I don't know why that worried me—I didn't have to be afraid of Earth-magic beings. Did I?

Smile in place, I showed him a spark in my fingers. *It's on, honey.* I saw a glitter of magic in his hand, his response. *Oh, yeah. It's on.*

My view of the slayer was cut off when my new friend blocked it by bending to me.

"A word of advice, my dear," he said in his smooth voice. "Have nothing to do with that one. I know young women find men such as he exciting, and I'm guessing my warning will only make him more attractive, but please believe me. I've heard things about him, bad things. And no, you can't reform men like that, no matter how hard you try."

Aw, what a sweetie. Distress showed in his brown eyes, concern that I'd throw myself away on an asshole and end up beaten, barefoot, and pregnant in a rundown shack some-where. I'd never in a million years let that happen to me, but my friend was so kind to worry.

I patted his arm, noting that the sleeve of his jacket was ultra-soft. "Trust me, I'm not interested in the guy, except to take vengeance on him for a friend."

I'm not sure he believed me. "Just be careful—he is not a

good man. I have a daughter about your age, and I'd say the same to her."

I blinked back tears as I tightened my grip on his arm. "Can I pretend you're *my* dad? Mine was a total dick. He's dead now."

"I'm sorry." He looked bewildered but sounded genuinely sympathetic, which was a new one for me. I released him and held out my hand.

"I'm Gabrielle. I'm not usually so awful—well, okay, maybe I am. At least, my sister thinks so."

"I'm Cornelius." He had a warm handshake, a firm clasp. "A strange name these days, but my family hoped it would lead to great things. Tell your sister you are not awful."

"Thanks." I flushed as I let go and turned to accept more cards. I wasn't used to pouring out my feelings, not my true ones, and now I was a bit embarrassed. Not sorry though. Cornelius, on the other hand, was unruffled, with an easiness about him.

The hand dealt me wasn't good, but I was learning in this game that points could change radically with the flip of a card.

I placed my bet, asked for another card, and sent an invisible frisson of magic into the deck so the slayer's six thousand dollar bet went bust.

Winnings were pushed to Cornelius and to me. "Betting on the bank, that's the way to go," I decided, laying my chips in the "bank" space.

"The hotel will take a percentage," Cornelius warned.

I shrugged. "That's all right. It's their table."

The dealer's points in the next hand totaled nine, letting me win, while the slayer lost again.

"You have a cool head for games," Cornelius said with a

touch of admiration as I calmly stacked my winnings. "I think you'd enjoy Monte Carlo."

Monte Carlo, the exotic name of another place I'd never been. I hadn't been most places. I'd grown up pretty much a prisoner in my own house, and now Grandmother Begay didn't want me out of her sight, unless I was with Janet and her watchful dragon boyfriend. Mick didn't let me get away with shit, like the big brother I'd never had.

"I'd love to go," I said wistfully. "But big sis—you know. She's protective."

"Well, I'll just have to speak to her," Cornelius said warmly.

This was turning into the best night of my life. I was making new friends, winning a bunch of money, and tweaking the nose of an all-powerful dragon slayer.

Who turned to the dealer, stuck out his arm to point to me, and said clearly, "She's cheating."

I lifted my hands and stood up, wide-eyed. "What? What are you talking about?"

I'd risen to show that I couldn't possibly hide any kind of cheating device on my person and that I didn't have a purse or a phone. And anyway, the cards the casino used were plain cardboard, and the shoe was a simple wooden device. No electronics or magnets could manipulate it, and since the dealer laid the cards out, face up, six inches in front of each of us, I wouldn't have any opportunity to switch them for different ones.

Didn't matter. At one push of a button from the dealer, security guards, five of them, materialized and headed over.

Cornelius rose to stand beside me. He held up his hand as the guards neared. "It's all right," he said. "I'll vouch for her."

The guards, to my surprise, stopped.

The slayer, now on his feet, growled at Cornelius. "What

are you doing? I *saw* her."

Cornelius gave the security guards a mild look. "I'm not sure about *him*, though."

The guards instantly turned and moved to the slayer. "Sir," one of them said. "Please come this way."

I wanted to dance around and do a fist pump but decided to remain dignified. The slayer's eyes glittered in a dangerous way, but I watched him make a decision to not argue. With another glare at me, he took up his chips and quietly left the table.

"Payback's a bitch," I told him, as the guards led the slayer past us.

Yes, it is.

I don't know if I heard his words projected into my head, or if I simply knew that's what he was saying. Either way, it chilled me.

I abruptly wondered what he'd do to the security guards once they were out of sight, and started to follow, leaving my chips behind.

Cornelius caught my hand. "No, my dear. Let it go."

Would the dragon slayer kill the guards? Or simply talk his way out of this to keep his low profile?

Whatever he would have done next became a moot point, because at that moment Colby came in through the casino's front door, followed by a tall, darkly attractive and very irritated Drake.

The dragon slayer whipped his head around like a lion catching a scent. Power built up in him like a tidal wave, and the guards slid away from him, looking confused.

The slayer turned for Colby and Drake, who had both frozen in shock.

I shook off Cornelius's hold and started running for the dragons, but too late ... far too late.

CHAPTER EIGHT

Gabrielle

"Out!" I yelled at Colby as I rushed at the two dragon-men, putting myself between them and the slayer. What the hell were they doing here anyway? "Go, go, go!"

The dragon slayer came swiftly up behind me. I swung to face him as Colby and Drake fanned out in fighting formation.

The slayer had shucked his suit coat to reveal a plain black T-shirt under it—not a great fashion statement, but one that wouldn't hinder him when he wanted to fight.

I saw that before darkness swallowed him. I didn't know what kind of weird magic he was working, but it had a suffocating bite that pressed at me.

"You stay away from my dragons!" I shouted. Real mature, but the slayer's rising power was immense, terrifying. I'd never felt anything like it.

I conjured hot Beneath magic in my hands, squashed it into a ball, and threw it at the slayer.

The white magic hit the black and swirled like yin and yang, before all the magic coalesced into fragments and hurtled back at me.

I dove for the mosaic tiled floor, but not quickly enough —shards stung me as I went down, and I heard a rip as my dress tore. Sequins littered the tiles and smeared blue sparklies on my skin.

I climbed unsteadily to my feet, blood trickling down my face.

"What is wrong with you?" I yelled. "Janet bought me this dress!" I'd fallen in love with it when we'd seen it on a sister-bonding shopping trip, and I'd hounded her to get it for me. She'd done it to be sweet, not because I demanded it. I knew that.

The slayer blinked at my reaction, but fuck him. I loved this dress.

My hands shook as I fashioned the furious power within me into tiny knives and sent them directly at the slayer. "See how *you* like it!"

I'd meant to cut his clothes to shreds, make him stand there embarrassed and half-naked in the middle of this elegant casino, but my magic never reached him. It ran up against the translucent black miasma around him, once more mixed with his magic, and streamed back to me.

"Now that's just rude," I shouted as I headed for the floor again.

Colby and Drake put themselves in front of me, barriers between me and the slayer. So sweet of them. They were trying to defend me, but they'd just die.

I scrambled up and attempted to push past them, but they stood side-by-side, a hard-muscled, dragon-man wall. Any other time, I'd find this sexy, but at the moment my heart pounded in fear.

"Get out of here!" I screamed at them, beating my fists on their shoulders. "He's a dragon slayer. He'll eat you for breakfast. I have a limo waiting outside. Go, and I'll cover you."

If I expected them to say, "She's right," and run like sensible dragons, they disappointed me.

Drake glared at me over his shoulder with sloe-dark eyes. "We know who he is. Take yourself away, and we will deal with him."

"We heard about your shindig at the other hotel," Colby put in. "We've been looking all over town for you."

"Why?" I scowled. "I was handling it."

Colby looked me up and down. "What part of handling it includes getting covered in blood?"

"Colby, this guy's deadly," I said desperately. "Would you *go?*"

The dragon slayer assessed the dragon-men with narrowed eyes. I expected him to gather his powers and enslave them with a gesture, but he only watched them, sizing them up.

Colby's muscle shirt and low-slung jeans showed off the artwork all over his body. Drake wore a black suit with a silk tie, the ends of dragon wing tatts rising from the coat up his neck to his jaw. He'd caught his long black hair into a ponytail to stay neat and out of his way, and it flowed down his back in a straight, satin fall.

Both men could morph into big-ass, terrifying dragons, but I was scared to death for them. This slayer had *Mick* cowed and obeying his commands, and while I loved Colby and Drake I knew Mick was the more powerful dragon. Titus seemed like he was plenty deadly, and he was going along with the dragon slayer too, the demon had told me.

The slayer continued to gaze at Drake and Colby, who remained stoically in front of me. The others in the casino were watching in curiosity—or busily ignoring us. Most humans can't see magic when it happens, so they'd probably only watched me hit the floor, snarling while the three men stood around staring at one another.

My friend Cornelius was heading our way. I didn't want him to become collateral damage, so I spun away from Colby and Drake and ran to intercept him.

The slayer caught me in the side with some kind of magic torpedo. The blow spun me then lifted me high, higher, and slammed me against the stone wall far above the casino floor. I was pinned like a bug against the plaster, and now everybody could see up my dress.

I struggled to loosen myself, but the dark magic held me fast.

"How did you do that?" I yelled down at the slayer. "This is some really cool shit. Drake, Colby—now's your chance to *run!*"

Did they? No. The stubborn pains in the ass held their ground and shot dragon magic at the slayer. Fire arced through the air—hot, deadly dragon magic that would incinerate the slayer where he stood.

The slayer glanced at the two dragons and flicked his finger. The fire hit a wall. The flames became one flat mass, fixed in place, burning nothing.

The dragons snapped off their flames, Colby's lips parting in shock. "Well, fuck," he said.

Drake remained silent, but I had the amazing sight of seeing him actually show some consternation.

And then there was Cornelius. He spoke animatedly to the security guards, giving orders like a battle commander.

The security goons swiveled as one and headed for the slayer. Another was on the phone—talking to whom? Paramedics? The fire department? Would the firemen have a tall enough ladder to get me down?

To hell with this. I called up some of my baddest magic, the kind Janet and her grandmother were teaching me to keep hidden and under control so I wouldn't go around leaving huge craters in the world, ones littered with dead bodies.

But this had gone far enough. The terror that had consumed me when I'd battled Emmett Smith not long ago, and *lost*, was threatening to engulf me again, and I couldn't let that happen. I couldn't let this shithead dragon slayer destroy people I'd come to care about. He had to go down.

I opened my arms, sucked in a breath, and called to the magic in the deepest part of me.

What I used everyday—the little balls of power to sting people or make them leave me alone, even what I'd combined with Janet to open up the Earth and send all those creatures away—that was on the surface.

I hadn't told anyone, least of all Janet, or gods forbid, Grandmother Begay, what kind of power, connected to Beneath itself, I could channel through my body. That was the reason Emmett, the Ununculous, before Janet destroyed him, had wanted what was inside me.

Emmett had succeeded in sucking away much of my power. He'd separated *me* from *it*, leaving me a broken shell at the bottom of a wash. Drake had found me, and Colby had carried me home, taking care of me all the way.

But Emmett hadn't been able to steal everything. I'd managed to keep one tiny piece of me from him, the one that had a direct link to Beneath. I'd been crazy afraid he'd find it, because if he'd opened that link and used it, the world would have been finished.

I'd realized as I fought Emmett that night that I didn't hate the world as much as I thought I did. It had fun people in it, like Colby, and good people like Janet's father and his girlfriend, and Fremont, Janet's plumber. I'd done everything I could to make sure Emmett didn't destroy what little happiness I'd found.

After Janet had battled Emmett, she'd returned my magic to me, but I'd had to lie low for a while at the house in Many Farms to recover.

Even Grandmother Begay had been kind to me—at least at first. Her idea of helping someone get well was badgering them so much they'd haul themselves out of bed and run away in self-defense.

But now I was back, and more bad-ass than ever.

I touched the chink that led to places Beneath and let its amazing light fill me.

"Hey, dragon slayer," I called down to him. "Slay *this*."

I shot my power straight into him.

The dragon slayer wasn't human. I felt that as my magic touched his. He had once been human, long, long ago and still held that shape, but he was demon inside, a pure Earth-magic demon, an ancient one.

There was a darkness in him, and a heaviness, like the ground trying to close in on me. I smelled muddy dirt and tree roots, as though I'd burrowed into the Earth to get at him.

The slayer stiffened as I opened him up and let Beneath magic fill the cracks I made inside him. The power he used to hold me at the top of the wall snapped off, and I started to fall, but I caught myself with a shaft of magic and slowed my descent.

As soon as my feet touched the floor, Colby tackled me.

I shrieked and tried to roll out from under him. I'd tasked

my Beneath magic to seek and destroy Earth magic, and Colby was full of that.

"Let go of me!" I pummeled him, but Colby's solid flesh didn't budge. "I don't want to hurt you."

"Stay down," Colby admonished. "Let Drake deal with the dickhead."

"The dickhead will kill him. And I might kill *you*. Get up, you big lump."

Colby's face hovered over mine, his light blue eyes glittering with a mixture of warmth, anger, fear, and relief. He was one good-looking dragon, and in any other circumstance I'd love having him on top of me.

But I pushed and heaved to get away from him. For the moment, my magic had dampened—which I think was me instinctively trying to keep from toasting him to a cinder.

I wasn't sure, though, how well I could control this most dangerous part of me. Grandmother was trying to teach me self-control, but I wasn't a very good student.

A wailing scream came to us, a bellow of a dragon in pain. Colby was off me in a second, hauling me up and putting me behind him.

The screaming came from Drake. His beautiful suit was in shreds, and blood ran down his face and through his hair, as though something had raked huge talons over him from head to foot. The dragon slayer held his fingers like claws, laughing as Drake bellowed.

Drake's neat ponytail came undone, his hair sticking to his face as dark blood dripped from the top of his skull. His skin was cracking, heaving, letting out flashes of red-hot light.

He was trying to go dragon, but the dragon slayer's magic prevented him.

I broke from Colby and ran straight at the dragon slayer,

letting my power come. I couldn't reestablish the link to Beneath again—that needed concentration—but I didn't have time to worry about that.

I launched myself into the dragon slayer and took him down.

Weird—the scent that came from him was like the deep woods where I'd grown up, after the summer rains. It brought back memories—me running wild as a kid, losing myself in the trees, and then the hell I got when I finally went back home.

The slayer smelled like the bite of winter snow and wood smoke, again scents that held both comfort and fear for me. Winter meant I had to stay inside with my awful dad, but on the other hand, I liked the cold. The White Mountains were a beautiful place.

The memories flashed through me as I looked into the slayer's eyes, but I fought off my confusion and let my power surge through him. "You leave my friends alone!"

"They're not your friends." The slayer spoke in a calm voice, his tone resonant, thick and dark like his aura. "They're Earth-magic beings who will defeat you. Your Beneath magic will not prevail. The Earth is rising. You woke it, and now you will pay."

"What?" I shook him. "What the hell does that mean?"

The slayer's magic bit deep, stirring pain at the center of my being. I understood what Drake had felt, that core wanting to expand and explode, tearing my body apart on its way out.

I squashed the compulsion, but my distraction was enough to let the dragon slayer throw me off, climb to his feet, and run.

Drake roared in pain. He scrubbed at his face, trying to hold himself together, his clothes in bloody tatters.

"Colby, get him out of here!" I shouted, and raced after the dragon slayer, who was heading for the line of French doors at the back of the casino. "*You*, stand still so I can kill you."

Colby wasn't listening. He started after me, leaving Drake to be surrounded by security guards, who looked like they weren't sure whether to draw their weapons or call an ambulance.

Out of the corner of my eye, I saw dark mists close around Drake, the kind dragons drew about themselves when they were preparing to shift. If Drake went dragon in here, he'd bring down the building.

I couldn't stop to make Colby do what I wanted. The slayer was getting away.

The slayer ran out of the casino and into the beautiful gardens. I chased him down avenues lined with lemon trees and hedges and around fountains and flower beds.

The slayer ran like a human being, but one who'd trained for marathons. I kicked off my high-heeled shoes and sprinted after him. The gardens were deserted in this hour of dawn, although I startled a couple in passing who'd come out to enjoy a moment of passion.

A gate on the other side of the garden led to a swimming pool. The dragon slayer leapt over the gate, the kind opened by a hotel key card.

I heaved a sigh, grabbed the top, and vaulted over. The iron grill reached up and tore the seam down the side of my dress, the one I'd already stitched back together with magic. *Damn* this guy.

The pool area was empty, the pool not yet open for the morning. I leapt across deck chairs, gaining ground, and with a furious snarl, launched myself into the slayer's thick body.

He lost his balance and tumbled straight into the pool, me on top of him. Our clothes were quickly soaked, his dragging him down. I smiled hotly, my ruined dress no more burden than a bathing suit.

Instead of fighting his way to the surface, the dragon slayer wrapped his hands around my neck and started to choke me. I floundered, struggling to get free of him, but he was terrifyingly strong.

We sank, he strangling me. I stabbed him with my magic, but my jabs met the spongy feeling of mud, and he didn't let go of me.

Water went up my nose and down my throat, I couldn't cough, couldn't breathe.

Blackness consumed me. I was dying—strangled and drowned at the same time, by an Earth-magic mage I didn't even know. Not really the way I wanted to go.

A ton of regret rose up in me, and I wanted to cry, but I was too busy dying.

Tingling darkness, terror, and grief swallowed me whole, and I barely felt the new set of hands dragging at me before I was gone.

Colby

I REACHED THROUGH THE DARKNESS SURROUNDING DRAKEY, grabbed him by the back of his now ruined coat, and dragged him outside to a huge spread of garden with pruned trees that didn't grow naturally in this climate.

"Hold it together," I growled while I swatted at the tendrils of his magic that swirled around me.

Getting covered in another dragon's magic is unsettling. I flinched and said "fuck" a lot.

Finally, I threw Drake behind a high hedge that would screen him from the rest of the hotel. He could either go dragon and get the hell out of here or hunker down until he healed himself.

I deserted Drake and sprinted back toward where I'd seen the slayer run out, chased by Gabrielle. I couldn't leave her to fight a man who knew how to reach into the heart of a dragon and use the dragon's own magic to tear him apart.

The back of my mind told me Gabrielle wasn't a dragon and didn't have anything to worry about, but the thought of the slayer anywhere near her made my scales itch.

Janet's magic mirror had gleefully showed me earlier tonight how Gabrielle had broken a ton of demons out of bondage and sent them back to Beneath, which was why I was here. I'd winged up to see if she was all right. Drake, who'd been with me at the time, insisted on joining me.

So we run into the hotel, and there she was, trying to chase off a dragon slayer.

She'd fought valiantly to protect me and Drake when she could have scuttled off and left us to it—there was more honor in Gabrielle than anyone gave her credit for.

I saw the dragon slayer running like hell across the garden, Gabrielle right behind him. For a second, I admired her long, sexy legs as she sprinted after the guy, her beautiful face set in determination.

But she didn't understand her danger. I ran after them.

They went so fast that they disappeared into the pool area long before I got there. Fucking pool gate got in my way, so I ripped it from its hinges and threw it aside.

I heard the frantic splashing of water in the dark. My

dragon sight showed me roiling, bubbling foam in the pool, pale in the dawn light, and my heart squeezed in fear.

Before I could leap in to rescue Gabrielle, the churning ceased. The dragon slayer pulled himself heavily out of the pool to flop on his stomach on the tiles around it and lie in a limp heap, his breathing ragged.

The pool settled down, showing me scraps of blue dress and smoky tendrils of blood.

Gabrielle? Nowhere in sight.

CHAPTER NINE

Colby

The dragon slayer was down, his magic deflating—I could feel it back off like pressure easing in a descending plane.

I bolted to the other side of the pool and stepped on him with my thick-soled motorcycle boot.

"Where is she?"

I should just break the guy's neck. But not when the slayer knew what had happened to Gabrielle and I didn't. Her dead body wasn't in evidence, but there was a lot of blood and the remains of a blue dress floating in the water.

The slayer mumbled something. Weak, dazed, vulnerable. The dragon fire in me burned, itching to come out of my fingers and fry him whole.

I satisfied the itch by grabbing him by his hair and knocking his head against the tile. "Where. Is. Gabrielle." Each word was accompanied by a thump of skull.

"Took ..." the man rasped.

"Who took her? Where? Why?" Smack, smack, smack.

"Don't … know …"

I felt the man's power trying to resurge. I couldn't be here when he restored himself, or I'd be dragon meat.

I hadn't met this dragon slayer before, but they were mostly the same. *See dragon, kill it now*—dragon either escapes and has nightmares the rest of his life or ends up as a lifetime supply of dragon burgers.

If he didn't know what had happened to Gabrielle, he was no use to me anymore, and too dangerous to be allowed to live. I needed to kill him now and go find her.

As I tightened my hand on his neck, a shadow fell, one too vast to be anything human. A huge black dragon, so close I could see the individual silken black scales, hung over the pool house, its bulk covering the pool, the attached bar, and part of the garden beyond.

Drake, obviously back together again, hovered like a hummingbird, except he didn't buzz his wings—he went for slow, ponderous flaps.

Black threads of magic came out of his talons to crawl over the dragon slayer and wrap him tightly, a few brushing me in passing.

I knew what *those* were, and no way was I letting Drakey catch me in his binding spell. Not again.

I dove away from dragon and slayer, but unfortunately, the only place to go was into the pool. I found myself in nine feet of water, sinking rapidly to the bottom.

Swimming and me didn't mix—land dragons don't float too well. I crawled along the bottom until I reached the shallow end and rose to my feet, gasping for breath. I climbed ponderously up the steps, my jeans and shirt sodden, water in my boots.

Drake already had the slayer smothered in threads of the

binding spell. They were magical strands, not tangible ones, but I knew from experience they'd shackle him more solidly than chains.

Drake was one powerful dragon—something I'd never admit out loud—and when he exerted his will on those he bound, it was a terrible thing. I remembered my body obeying everything he said, even half my mind obeying it, while the other half of my brain was screaming at me to get away.

No matter how hard I'd struggled, I'd been trapped. Gabrielle, the sweetheart, had reached through those bonds and freed me.

It hadn't been Drake's choice to enslave me—he'd been following orders and had no choice—and I didn't hold it against him. But damn me if I'd ever let him do it again.

By the time Drake finished his spell, the dragon slayer was a cocoon of black cords. Drake had used far more magical ropes on him than he'd ever wrapped around me, but then, I wasn't a deadly slayer.

Drake flapped away while I squished around the pool to the slayer and stood looking down at him.

"Okay, we'll start again," I said. "Where's Gabrielle? You know, the lovely lady who was kicking your ass."

The man glared at me. He was an ordinary-looking human, with brown hair, brown eyes, skin darker than white but lighter than that of anyone of color. Bland, that's what he was. Mr. Bland.

"You should get some tatts," I said, holding out my well-inked arms. "Human bodies are kind of dull to me—at least the male ones are—but they take decoration well. Got these done in a little shop in Tokyo, in Shibuya, tucked next to the best onkatsu stand in the world—three stools and a guy cooking like crazy behind the counter. You'd never know that stand was there if you didn't know it was there."

Mr. Bland only stared up at me, so I nudged him again. "One more time. Where's Gabrielle?"

"I told you," he said through his teeth. "I don't know."

If he answered like that, smothered in a binding spell, it meant he really didn't know. My fears deepened. She couldn't have just vanished, could she? Not that I knew a hell of a lot about Gabrielle's magic. But all the blood scared me.

Drake strode in through the gate as a human, one as naked as a newborn. His skin was dark, his hair black, but he didn't resemble any one specific race of humans. He probably didn't think he had to, didn't think about it at all.

He had tatts, black lines depicting dragon's wings that covered his back and rose up his neck. I don't know where he had those done, but probably not my tattoo place in Shibuya. The guys there would be too cheerful for him.

Drake was one of the most obstinate, single-minded dragons I'd ever met. He'd been perfect working for the Dragon Council, because honoring his word was more important than breathing, but he'd quit them when he realized they didn't live up to his standards.

He eyed me. "I will need clothes."

I wrung out my sodden T-shirt. "You can't have mine." I'd need new ones too—these wet jeans were going to chafe like a some-bitch.

Drake moved to stand over the slayer. Tall and ice-cold, he gazed down at the man, a gleam of satisfaction in his black eyes. "You are bound to my will," he announced. "If I demand a thing of you, you will do it, even if it is to throw yourself over a cliff to your death."

"He's not kidding," I said. "Trust me."

The slayer glared up at both of us. "It doesn't matter. The Earth is rising. I am but a taste of what's coming."

Normally I ignore crazy statements like this one, but for some reason the words sent a tingle of warning through my body.

"See, I hate cryptic shit," I said, nudging him with my wet boot. Okay, so maybe it was more of a kick than a nudge. "*What* is coming?"

"She woke the Earth. She angered it. And now, it rises."

I kicked him again, harder this time. "See what I mean? Really hate it."

"I am but one vessel," the slayer said.

"Yeah, yeah." I was tired of kicking him, and besides, my socks were all squishy with water which was hurting my toes. "Aren't we all?"

"We must take him to the dragon compound," Drake said.

I gave him a wide-eyed stare. "Take a dragon slayer to a dragon compound? Now there's a great idea. He'll last, what, two minutes? Then die before telling us anything. Anyway, I thought you quit them."

"I did. But there are cells there that can hold him. His magic is strong, and he might eventually work his way free of the binding spell."

"Don't give him ideas. I understand your logic, but I have a better idea. Two actually. One, kill him and put him out of our misery. Two, since I want him to live a little longer, take him to Janet."

Drake paused a long moment, face impassive, while he weighed my suggestions. Then he gave me a nod. "I believe you are right."

"I am? Wow, would you look at that?" I said to the slayer. "Drakey agrees with me. Write it down. Date and time stamp it."

The slayer's lip curled. "It matters not what you do with me. You are obsolete."

I put up with squishy socks to kick him one more time. "Now you're hurting my feelings. And who the hell says 'it matters not?'"

"Take him," Drake said impatiently. "I need to clothe myself."

"Huh." I leaned down and hauled the slayer up and over my shoulder. Now that the binding spell was complete and specific to the slayer, it wouldn't grab on to me, at least in theory. "I'm surrounded by guys who talk in medieval poetry. Where am I taking him?"

"To Janet." Drake was already walking away toward the gardens, possibly to mug someone for their suit. I imagined him waiting a while until he found a man his exact size with his exact taste before he struck.

"Great." I adjusted the slayer's weight, and he hung limply without fighting me. "I always get stuck with the dirty work. So I'm supposed to drag you out, me soaking wet, through a posh hotel casino and lug you back down the Strip to find my friends. I'd much rather stay here and find out what happened to Gabrielle. If she's hurt, you, my friend, will pay with your life. Understand?"

Janet

MICK LED US AT A RUN THROUGH THE C HOTEL AND OUT INTO their gardens. Security tried to stop us, but Nash flashed his badge and we charged through. I don't think it was so much the badge that did the trick as our determination and Nash's air of authority. The whole world backed down from Nash when he was after a culprit.

I was right behind him and Mick, with Titus following me. I didn't like Titus behind me, but I didn't have much choice at the moment.

One of Mick's friends had called us while I was struggling out of bed, saying he'd spotted Gabrielle at the C, fighting for her life. I'd thrown on clothes, and we'd charged over here.

I stopped in the middle of a vast swath of greenery bordered by hedges and trees pruned into careful cone shapes. Dawn light streaked the sky pink and touched fleur-de-lis shaped flower beds that pumped blue, scarlet, and gold notes into all the green.

Through this beauty came a dripping man covered in tattoos that rivaled the flowers' colors. He carried another man over his shoulder, that man half-conscious and helpless.

I darted forward. "Gabrielle? Where is she?"

The glare Colby turned on me could have started fires. "She was fighting *this* dickhead, but by the time we caught up to them, she'd disappeared."

Colby upended his burden and dumped a man I'd never seen before onto the grass. He was thick-bodied but not fat, the thickness due to muscles and sheer bulk. He, like Colby, was wet, clothes soaked.

Titus and Mick pulled back involuntarily, and I felt the deep bite of Earth magic in him.

"*You're* the dragon slayer?" I asked in surprise. He didn't look that dangerous, but then, neither had Emmett, the most powerful mage in the world. Nor had Pericles McKinnon, the second-most powerful.

"Dragon slayer under a binding spell," Colby said. "Drake's specialty."

Both Titus and Mick stepped closer to the slayer again,

and I sensed their dragon-ness awakening—dragons were
very, very good at taking revenge.

Studying the slayer with the eye of magic, I saw the dark
threads that wound him in a tight, unbreakable swath. If
those had been tangible ropes, he wouldn't have been able to
move or breathe.

"Don't kill him yet," I said quickly to Mick. "Not until he
tells us where Gabrielle is."

"I *don't know*," the dragon slayer said groggily, with the
impatience of a man who'd been asked the same question a
dozen times already. "Something hit me, and when I pulled
myself out of the pool, the girl was gone. What is she? She
crackles with demon magic. And why is a demon defending
dragons?"

Not demon—goddess, I could have told him, but he didn't
need to know my family history.

"You really don't know where she is," I stated.

"I keep saying..."

"Good." Mick went for him, dragon fire dancing in
his hands.

Titus's expression was stone cold instead of eager, and his
suit wasn't even wrinkled, but the ball of dragon magic he
brought to his hand was deadly. The dragon slayer, in the
next second, would be toast.

"You can't kill someone in your custody," Nash said. He
was ever a stickler for the rules of law and order.

"Dragons can," Mick said.

The dragon slayer held up his hands, his fear unfeigned.
"Wait! You need me. You need me against what's coming."

"What?" I bent forward, carefully avoiding Mick's line of
fire. "What do you mean *what's coming?*"

"He's been spouting that crap since Drake bound him,"
Colby said in disgust. "A ploy to save himself, I'm thinking."

"No." The dragon slayer shook his head, sending droplets of water flying. "I'm bound to the Earth, so closely that I know every move it makes—every tiny shift in its crust. That woman woke it when she opened the way to send my demons home, angered it by letting the wrong magic beings penetrate its heart. The Earth is rising. I guarantee it. It will bury every demon, dragon, and creature of darkness in its wrath. That is why you should not have tried to break your contracts with me, dragon creatures—your mistake will cost you everything you have."

I did not like the sound of this. Colby might be right that the slayer was trying to keep himself alive by feeding us a load of bullshit, but his words held a ring of truth.

He was talking about Gabrielle and me creating the vortex in the hotel to get rid of the attacking demons. But why should the slayer focus on her alone, when our magics had combined to create the hole? And what did he mean, *letting the wrong magic beings penetrate its heart?*

"He keeps saying that," Colby said. "*The Earth is rising.* Sounds like a bowel movement. Can we dust him now and find Gabrielle?"

"No," Titus said. The flame in his hands died, and Mick had dampened his as well. "We need to interrogate him. Find out exactly what he means." He gave Colby a nod. "*Then,* we dust him."

Colby grinned and jerked his thumb at Titus. "I don't know who this guy is, but I like him."

"You can't interrogate him here," Nash broke in. "The line of security guards behind us are going to stop believing I'm here to make an arrest and come for us."

I glanced around and saw the formation of about fifteen men in dark suits with earpieces and sunglasses in the morning light, all focused on us. These security guards weren't cheerful retired men in uniform; they looked like Secret Service agents ready to take down anyone who even remotely looked like a terrorist.

"I'll get him out," Mick said. "Best place, the Crossroads Hotel. We can bind him doubly there."

The Crossroads would be a good place to take the slayer, I agreed, but I definitely didn't want to leave Las Vegas before I found Gabrielle. Not only was I worried about her safety, but it would be foolish to leave her in this town alone. Grandmother would kill me.

So much for vacation.

Gabrielle

WHEN I FINALLY WOKE, I WAS IN A BED. A SOFT, COMFORTABLE bed, nothing like Janet's lumpy mattress in her bedroom in Many Farms. The room was much larger too, and beautiful, with a high ceiling painted like the sky, soft furniture, and tall windows letting in streaming sunlight.

I had no idea where I was. Not in the hotel suite Janet, Maya, and I had been sharing, not Janet's hotel at the Crossroads, nowhere I'd ever been.

And I was in bed. Unclothed. I took a peek beneath the sheet. My underwear, blue to match my dress, clasped my hips, but the rest of me was bare.

I dropped the sheet as the door opened and my friend from the baccarat table—Cornelius—walked in. He tiptoed in, as though thinking me still asleep, and I slammed the sheet and blanket to my chest.

He stopped halfway across the floor. "Good. You're awake." He sounded relieved.

"Are you a pervert?" I asked him.

He blinked. "I beg your pardon?"

"A pervert. Are you one? Did you take my clothes?"

Cornelius's expression cleared. "Ah, I see your concern. Your clothes were in shreds and had to be removed. But no, I didn't touch you. The nurse did."

"Male or female?"

"Chandra. Female. She's very professional. Worried about you, but she says you will be all right. We found you in time."

My heart beat quickly, and magic prickled in my fingers, as it always did when I was scared.

"In time for what?" I demanded.

"To save you from drowning." Cornelius didn't move from his spot in the middle of the carpet, which was thick and covered with roses. "The man fighting you was arrested, don't worry."

"Arrested." My mind was cloudy. I'd been battling the dragon slayer, who'd done his best to strangle me and drown me at the same time. Colby and Drake hadn't been there at the pool—I'd saved them from him at least.

That made me feel a little better, though I hoped Drake had been able to go dragon and heal himself. But Colby would have made sure he was all right, wouldn't he? The two acted as though they didn't like each other, but now that Drake had quit the Council, they watched each other's backs.

"Who arrested him?" I asked.

"My men didn't say—probably they don't know. A police officer and some formidable looking assistants came in and took him away."

"Your men." I looked Cornelius up and down. "You have men? Who are you? A mob boss?"

Cornelius shook his head, his smile faint. "I say *my* men, but they work for the hotel."

"The *C*. Wait, the *C* is owned by a guy called Christian-son. Is that you?"

"No. John Christianson is my brother. He owns the chain."

My heart beat faster. "And you were playing at the tables, because ..."

He shrugged, his cheekbones staining red. "I like to play. It relaxes me."

I remembered Cornelius losing hands and pushing away chips like it was no big deal.

"Now I understand why you were being so nice to me," I said, disappointed. "I was a big spender, and you were trying to keep me happy."

Why this hurt me so much, I don't know. I felt tears sting my eyes, like I was a big sappy baby.

Cornelius raised a hand. "Not at all. I saw a young woman a bit out of her depth, and as I said, you are the same age as my daughter, which made me protective. You put up quite a fight against that man. He was a magic user?"

I started and pulled the sheet higher. Cassandra had told Janet that John Christianson knew all about magic, had wanted her to help him fulfill some of his customers' darkest desires with it. Cassandra had quit the hotel and disap-peared, terrified of what would happen if Christianson found her.

Apparently Christianson couldn't work magic himself, which was why he'd hired Emmett and Cassandra. It stood to reason Christianson's brother would know all about magic too.

"Yeah," I said warily. "Pretty strong Earth magic in him."

"I'm not certain what that means. He was using his magic to cheat?"

"Sure was. Made the right cards come out of the deck for

him." I'd done the same thing, but I felt it prudent not to mention it.

"Hmm." Cornelius didn't look fall-over amazed that a mage had waltzed into his brother's casino and used magic to cheat, or that I'd figured it out and challenged him. "What do you mean by Earth magic?"

I shrugged, wishing I didn't have to lie flat, but I wasn't about to let Cornelius, no matter how kindhearted he was, get an accidental glimpse of my tits.

"Means magic rooted in this Earth," I said. "Like witches who focus on crystals or water to work spells—stones and water come from the Earth. Or Changers—they get the power to shift from the Earth. Dragons, too. Dragons were made from volcanoes, by volcano gods, which is why they can wield fire." I closed my mouth before I could mention dragon slayers who went after the dragons. I didn't know whose side Cornelius was on.

He wore a quizzical look, as though debating whether to believe me. "You know a lot about this."

"I'm kind of an expert. This guy was definitely using Earth magic. Smelled like dirt."

"And all Earth magic, er, *smells* that way?"

"Not always." Janet's Earth magic didn't—she smelled like a rainstorm when she used her Stormwalker powers—a good rainstorm that settled the dust and made the world fresh. Grandmother Begay's reminded me of rosemary. Mick smelled like fire, and Colby smelled like incense. I liked that. Drake smelled of incense too, but a different kind. Drake was cinnamon, while Colby was more like sandalwood.

"You describe it as though you don't have Earth magic," Cornelius observed. "But you fought like a mage. What kind of power do you have?"

Oops. Speaking of secrets …

"Oh, nothing special." I managed a shrug. "Can I get some clothes? I feel weird talking to you like this. Or are you holding me hostage? Keeping me naked so I can't run away?" Not that it would stop me. I'd be out the window and down the street in a heartbeat, wrapped in the sheet if that's all I could find.

Cornelius raised his hands in surrender and stepped back. "Nothing so dramatic. I will have Chandra check you over and bring you something to wear. Then you can choose any clothes you want from the gift shop, as much as you like. It's on me. As a thank-you for catching a swindler at our tables."

"And then I can leave?"

Cornelius hesitated a fraction of a second, and that small fraction made my wariness return.

"Of course, leave if you'd like. I'll have a car drive you anywhere you wish. Though I'd appreciate it if you stayed for a little while at least, and talked to me about how this man used magic to cheat. So we can be on our guard. I can have your luggage transferred from whatever hotel you are staying in, if that will make you more comfortable."

I sensed a trap, and I hated traps. They made me crazy and want to kill everyone in my path to get out.

But I was also curious. Why did he want to pick my brain? Cornelius seemed personable and polite—kind, even —but something was up.

Grandmother Begay said curiosity was Janet's downfall— she couldn't keep her nose out of other people's business, no matter how much trouble it led her into. Well, I was Janet's sister, so I guess the curiosity was genetic.

I flashed Cornelius a smile. "That would be great. Let me clean up, you give me dinner, or breakfast, or whatever meal we're on, and we'll talk."

"Excellent. Thank you—er, would you be so kind as to tell me your full name, my dear? For Chandra's records."

I wasn't sure why that was important, but what the hell? My human name was harmless. "Gabrielle Massey," I said. "I'm Apache."

"Are you? How intriguing. Well, I'll leave you to it."

Cornelius pressed his hands together, looked as though he might bow, thought better of it, and left the room with dignity.

I waited a few heartbeats until I was sure he wasn't coming back, and then threw off my sheets as I tore to the bathroom. I truly had to pee.

CHAPTER TEN

Janet

M ick arranged everything from the lobby of the C. I would stay in Las Vegas with Colby while Mick, Drake, and Titus took the dragon slayer back to our hotel. Once I found Gabrielle, Colby and I would return with her to the Crossroads.

Maya and Nash opted to stay in Las Vegas—that is, Maya refused to leave. She declared she wasn't missing her trip because of me and my crazy family, an arena full of demons, and a weird man who called himself a dragon slayer. She said this in a hard voice, but I could see she was concerned about Gabrielle as well, and didn't want to go until she was found.

Nash, to my surprise, chose to stay with Maya. He'd already taken leave to come to Las Vegas and keep an eye on her, he said, so he might as well enjoy his time off.

They left us to return to our original hotel down the Strip, Maya looking not quite sure what to make of Nash's decision.

Mick hired a car to take dragons and slayer to Arizona, and when it pulled up, he and Titus bundled the dragon slayer into it. Drake, dressed in jeans and a T-shirt, probably the only things he could find on short notice, climbed quickly in after him, the binding spell Drake had woven shimmering like silver between him and the slayer.

Mick gave me a hard kiss on my lips, first, to say good-bye, second, to tell me to be careful. I rose into the kiss, tasting his fierce determination and also his frustration.

I waved at him as the car rolled down the hotel's circular drive, the slayer wedged between Titus and Drake in back, Mick in the front. Colby and I stood on the walkway near the door to watch them go, a warm desert wind wafting up the slope.

I worried as much about Mick as I did about Gabrielle, my heart squeezing as the car pulled into traffic at the bottom of the drive. Drake's binding spells could be broken, and if this one gave way, Mick would be in a lot of danger. The magic coming from the dragon slayer was terrifying.

"Okay," Colby said as the car moved out of sight. "Now we seriously have to look for Gabrielle."

"Did you say you were trying to find Gabrielle?" A young man, a driver from one of the many limos parked in front of the hotel came to us, wide-eyed. "She asked me to wait for her, but then there was the big fight inside, and now she's gone. She all right?"

Before I could answer, Colby caught the young man's shirt in his big fist, lifting him off his feet. "Who are you?" he growled. "What do you know?"

"Colby, put him down," I said quickly. I resisted the urge to add, "Bad dragon."

The man's gaze slid to me. "You must be big sister Janet." His words were strangled. "I'm really worried about her."

"Colby," I admonished. "He can't talk if he can't breathe. Put him down."

Colby set the man on his feet with exaggerated gentleness and brushed off the front of his shirt. "So, talk."

"I already said. I drove Gabrielle here, and she asked me to wait. Then she chased that guy out of the hotel, and then you showed up."

"*Why* did you drive her here?" Colby rested hard fingers on the man's chest.

"She told me to take her to the best hotel in Vegas. Which is this one. Said you'd be good for the fare." He glanced nervously at me.

I sighed. "Of course she did. Don't worry, I'll cover it. What's your name?—I'll make sure you get the fee."

"Amos. But I'm not leaving until I know she's okay." He lowered his voice, conscious of the other drivers, the valet parkers, and the security guards hovering near. "There's rumors that weird things go on in this hotel. Bad things."

"And you brought her here anyway?" Colby demanded.

"It's all right if you stay in the casino and public areas. It's different when you check in. I didn't think she'd be staying, but she's the kind they like. Lots of money, lots of courage."

"Courage, yes," I said. "Money—not so much."

"She had enough to sit at the thousand dollar baccarat table," Amos said. "I saw her." He flushed. "I went in to check on her."

Gods, how the hell had Gabrielle convinced the casino to let her play a thousand-dollar minimum game?

Simple. She'd used magic, which had alerted the weird people who owned the *C*.

"I'm glad you were concerned about her," I told Amos. "Do you know people who work here? Can they help me find her?"

He looked eager. "Sure. I'll ask around, and meet you—where? They'll talk to me more if I'm by myself," he finished apologetically.

"Middle of the garden," Colby said. "Fewer people to overhear us."

"Got it." Amos looked us up and down, Colby in his very wet clothes, and me in the simple jeans and cropped top I'd put on so we could race out. "Not sure they'll allow you into the hotel like that. They have a dress code."

"I can change as soon as I can get my luggage here," I said. "I'll just go check in."

Colby's grin beamed out. "I like how you think, sweetheart."

What the hell? I moved to the etched glass revolving door. The best way to know what goes on in the evil lair is to walk right in.

Gabrielle

I SHOWERED, DRESSED IN THE BATHROBE CHANDRA, A CALM-voiced woman who told me she was from Nigeria, brought me, and I shopped.

I didn't even have to leave my hotel suite, a lavish apartment that seriously beat anything the Crossroads Hotel had to offer. The TV had a channel for the shop downstairs, not a static online thing where you clicked on something and added it to your cart, but a feed of the wares, with slim young women modeling the clothes and jewelry. It didn't look homemade either, but like a professional advertising company had put it together with sleek backgrounds and sulky, shoulder-tossing models.

The coolest thing was, you picked up the phone, told the shop which dresses and jewelry you were interested in, and they brought everything to your room.

I indulged myself asking for about twenty outfits and trying them all on before I settled on three. I picked all three because I couldn't decide between them.

Chandra stayed with me throughout, giving me her opinion without reticence. Between the two of us, we chose a shimmering knee-length silver dress with spaghetti straps. The dress hung on me like a wave of water, but at the same time was modest, no cleavage. Grandmother Begay was always on me about modesty, which drove me crazy, not that I had any intention of showing total strangers all I had.

We picked out a quieter blue dress with short sleeves for more casual occasions, and a red top and minute black skirt in case I wanted to go dancing.

I talked about getting jeans and a black shirt, like Janet wears, because she looks kick-butt in them, but Chandra wrinkled her nose.

"You need your own style," she said in her rich voice. "You have beautiful black hair and can wear bold colors. Don't settle for drab."

Chandra's blouse was a swirl of blue, gold, red, and green that made her dark eyes sparkle, and she'd wound a bright scarf through her hair. She smelled a bit of lavender, but clean, not cloying.

"Why do you work here?" I asked as I put on the silver dress to have lunch with Cornelius. "Are you a nurse for the whole hotel?"

"I'm not a nurse—I'm a doctor," Chandra said. "Or I was."

Her tone was sad, and I looked at her with more interest. "They won't hire you in the United States as a doctor? Why not?"

"Oh, they would if I went through the steps for the license, but that is not the path chosen for me." She gave me a cryptic look. "It is a long story, but one for another day."

Since I'd started hanging with Janet and her friends, I'd cultivated an interest in other people. I very much wanted to know Chandra's story, but she gave a firm shake of her head, and I knew she wouldn't tell me, at least not at the moment.

I'd also developed worry. Had Drake truly been able to go dragon and get away? I kept wondering. Since I hadn't seen pieces of dragon on the grass outside, I assumed he'd made it. What about Colby? And Janet? Was she safe in our hotel room with Mick looking after her?

It was new to me, this concern about people. I wanted to call Janet, talk to her, make sure everyone was all right, but I didn't know how. I didn't have a cell phone—Grandmother Begay didn't like them and she wouldn't let me have one. Pete, who absolutely hated technology, was trying to talk her into getting one for me so I could at least check in, but Grandmother was stubborn. I didn't have any money or credit to buy a phone on my own.

There was a landline phone in the room, but I'd have to ask the front desk for the number to Janet's hotel, and I couldn't trust that no one would be listening to my call. I didn't want Cornelius or his staff to hear exactly what I said to my sister. None of their business.

I would figure out a way to contact her, but for now, Chandra was hurrying me, saying Cornelius would be waiting.

She steadied me as I slid into a new pair of silver, strappy high-heeled sandals, and then she looked into my eyes, as though assessing my state of health. "You are strong and resilient. Just be careful."

Chandra stayed behind as I went out—why, I didn't know, but I had the feeling she wouldn't tell me that either.

I discovered a guard outside my door, one of the security guys with an earpiece. He only gave me a minuscule nod as I said hi to him, and he pointed the way to the elevator when I asked.

I met Cornelius in a restaurant tucked away on the second floor. This restaurant didn't flaunt itself like the grandiose ones I'd seen on the ground floor or have gimmicks like a chocolate fountain. The restaurant was hidden in a discreet corner behind a thick glass door, as though it let in only those in the know.

A man in a tux opened the door and admitted me into a darkened room with red walls and hidden lights that cast dramatic shadows over the black tiled floor. The foyer contained a hostess desk in front of a wall that hid the rest of the restaurant.

The maître d', also in a tux, greeted me in a quiet voice and told me that Mr. Christianson was waiting. He led me around the partition to a room that carried on the black and red theme, with discreetly spaced tables and chairs. *Simple,* the decor said, *and very expensive.* Chefs in pristine white coats and tall hats cooked behind a half glass wall.

Only a few people dined here in mid-afternoon—a couple who couldn't get enough of each other and a few businessmen and -women trying to impress one another.

Cornelius rose as the maître d' led me to his table in an alcove by a window. The smoked glass gave me a view of the gardens and the distant pool where I'd battled for my life. Cornelius held out my chair for me and pushed it in when I sat.

He seated himself again and said nothing while a waiter

laid my napkin in my lap for me. I almost punched him before I realized what he was doing.

Cornelius smiled as though he understood my awkwardness. I consoled myself that even though I didn't know how to act in a swanky restaurant, I looked kick-ass in this dress.

"The chef is preparing a meal to my order, but if you don't care for any of the dishes and want something else, you have but to ask." Cornelius gave me his kind look. "Do you drink wine?"

Another waiter hovered with a bottle. I didn't drink much, but I enjoyed a glass of wine every once in a while. Cassandra had taught me what good wine should be like, and Janet's saloon, when it was whole, stocked a decent selection. "Sure," I said.

The sommelier poured a dribble of red into Cornelius's glass. Cornelius smelled it, sipped it, closed his eyes to really taste it, and nodded. The sommelier, with a look of gladness, filled my glass then Cornelius's, and discreetly backed away.

I took a dainty sip, savored the wine's rich flavor, and set the glass down. "Very good." I knew better than to talk about how fruity or spicy or woody or whatever it was, because I had no idea. It tasted like wine to me.

Cornelius dipped his head as though pleased with my assessment. "I am certain you are wondering why I wanted to speak to you."

"Crossed my mind." I glanced around. "This is all very posh, and you're ordering food and wine for me like you're my sugar daddy. Is that what you want? To be my sugar daddy? I probably wouldn't mind for a while, because I like you, but I warn you, I'm a free spirit. I'd get bored, and that would be it. I'd be gone." I waved my hand at the outside world.

And if anyone tried to keep me from leaving, walls would fall down, and people might get hurt, including Cornelius.

Mirth danced in his eyes. "No, my dear. I have a wife I adore and a daughter, as I told you."

"One my age, yeah. She anything like me?"

"She finished her doctorate in engineering at MIT last spring. She's already started a job at a company in Germany —she's very excited. She loves Europe." Pride radiated from him.

"So," I said. "Nothing like me."

"You have the same determination," Cornelius said. "She decided her course and let nothing stop her. Her mother and I hoped she'd do her schooling in California and find a job closer to home, but she fought to get into MIT and worked hard to get her doctorate, no matter what. I see the same strength in you. If you set your mind on something, you will achieve it."

"I suppose that's true."

I sipped wine while I thought about his observation. I complained a lot about how much Grandmother Begay restricted me, but I also knew that if I didn't *really* want to stay in Many Farms and listen to her admonishing me to not destroy everything in sight, I wouldn't.

Grandmother Begay, Mick, and even Janet were convinced that they dragged me back to Many Farms every time I got restless and ran off, but I knew I would never return to the little house in the desert if I didn't want to.

And whenever I did get restless and run, where did I go? To visit Janet at the Crossroads or elbow my way into her girls' weekend with Maya. They hadn't wanted me to come, but they'd realized they might as well give in, knowing I wouldn't go away, because I was a brat like that.

Was I really? I took another gulp of wine.

"What I am talking my way around to is offering you a job," Cornelius was saying. "Are you interested?"

I choked on my wine. I quickly brought up my napkin so I wouldn't stain the beautiful dress, and wiped my mouth and streaming eyes.

Cornelius watched me in concern, but before he could signal the waiter to help, I shook my head, waving the attentive man off with my napkin.

"A job?" I gasped out. "Why would you give *me* a job? Doing what? Cleaning rooms? I'm bad at that. Ask my sister."

Cornelius's wide smile told me I amused him. "A job as a mage, my dear. You are quite powerful. I could use you here."

My heart thumped and a frisson of fear spread its way through me. "I thought your brother owns the hotels."

"He does, but I run this one."

I regarded him in suspicion. "What do you need a mage for? So guests can live out their icky fantasies?—I don't even want to know what any of them are. I can guess."

Not long ago, three men in a gas station in Winslow thought it would be great fun to put a shotgun to my face and demand I do whatever they wanted. They'd thought wrong.

My rage and fear had built into a killing fury, and I'd let them know my displeasure as I'd thrown them around the convenience store. If Janet hadn't stopped me, I'd have toasted them, and I knew it.

Of course, watching the guy's faces as shafts of magic had banged them against the ceiling had been very funny. The memory brought a smile through my trepidation.

The smile made Cornelius relax. "I do know what goes on at my brother's Los Angeles hotel, my dear, and I don't approve. Because of him, the C has gained an unsavory reputation, which I would like to negate. I want people to stay *here* without fear, and I will turn away those whose needs are distasteful."

I turned my wineglass by its stem. "And you want me to help you do that?"

"I want you for protection," he said. "To make sure that no people with dark needs or the means to fulfill those dark needs are allowed to stay at this hotel, and if they manage to slip in, to banish them."

"Like warding, you mean? I'm not sure you need *me* for that. I can do wards, but I'm more a fighting magic kind of girl. I have friends who are good at warding, though."

Mick, for one, who kept Janet's hotel safe. Cassandra for another, but I wasn't about to tell the brother of John Christianson that I knew Cassandra Bryson. She was still hiding out. She'd changed her name, but I had the feeling Christianson could find her if he wanted to.

"I'm not sure what wards are," Cornelius said. "I did mean I need you for fighting magic. My brother called me this morning saying his clairvoyants woke up with dire forebodings—told him *something* was coming. Something to do with magic. I don't understand everything John talks about, but he's usually not wrong. If the mages he's hired say something dire might happen, and might happen in the C, I'm going to listen."

I flashed back to the dragon slayer when I'd tackled him in the casino, after he'd tried to tear Drake apart. *Your Beneath magic will not prevail,* he'd said, staring at me with his intense eyes. *The Earth is rising. You woke it from sleep.*

I still didn't know what he meant, but the chill inside me when he'd voiced the words had been real.

"And your brother suggested that you hang out at the tables until you found yourself a mage?" I asked.

I didn't like the pain that suffused me as I spoke. I'd

thought Cornelius was being kind to me for myself, not so he could assess my destructive powers.

But wait, he'd been nice when I first sat down, and he couldn't have known about my Beneath magic then, could he?

Cornelius shook his head. "My brother told me nothing. I didn't realize you had … potential … until you began to fight the man who was cheating. I hope I haven't offended you, my dear."

He had, but I admit I was quick to take offense. All my life no one had wanted to be near me because I was crazy, had a drunk for a father and a hell-goddess for a mother, and pretty much endangered everyone I encountered.

So when someone showed interest in me, I immediately figured they wanted something, and it was painful when I discovered I was right.

"No," I said, smiling sweetly. "I'll get over it. Hey, you bought me this amazing dress."

"Which looks well on you. My compliments." Cornelius raised his glass to me.

"Chandra helped me pick it out. She has good taste."

"She does. A very talented woman, is Chandra. I'm trying to convince her to return to practicing medicine."

"What's her deal?" I asked in curiosity. Wondering about someone besides myself was more interesting and less unnerving. "She said it wasn't the path chosen for her. What happened?"

"That I do not know. I imagine Chandra will impart her tale when she is ready."

I deflated. I enjoy a good gossip. Grandmother Begay says she disapproves of it, and in the next breath tells me the dirt on every single person she knows.

"I'll let you think about my offer," Cornelius said. "Don't let talk of business spoil your meal. Ah, here we are."

The waiter brought over steaming bowls of orange-red soup with a dab of sour cream floating in the middle. "Tomato bisque," the waiter announced.

The steam rising from the soup smelled fantastic, and the crackling wafers of bread with cheese baked onto them looked good too.

Cornelius waved at me to start, and I lost myself in the soup. Grandmother Begay was a good cook, but she stuck with fairly ordinary dishes like stew and corn. This soup was heaven, with the bright taste of tomatoes soothed by the velvet texture of cream, contrasted by the savory saltiness of the bread.

The next course was a spice-rubbed chicken breast on top of a warm salad with pumpkin coulis, this being October. I had to ask what coulis meant, but apparently it's a sauce, this one spicy, warm, and pumpkiny.

I ate everything the waiter slid in front of me and still had room for the blackberry sorbet for dessert.

I learned more about Cornelius as we ate—how he'd convinced his brother to open a hotel in Las Vegas, and how John had agreed if Cornelius would run it. It was a lot of work, Cornelius said, but he'd been lucky to put together a good team. He wanted it to be the perfect home away from home for his guests.

He told me more about his daughter, and also his wife, who lived in Los Angeles, from where he commuted when he needed to be at this hotel.

Thankfully, he didn't ask much about me, or talk about the fact that I was Apache, only inquired with mild interest where I was from. I told him Arizona, and that was all. It's a big state with one massive city, a few less massive ones, and a bunch of towns. Let him guess.

Janet and Grandmother Begay would never approve of me working for Cornelius, or staying in Las Vegas, or having any kind of life of my own. I was the evil Gabrielle, who needed to be contained. Mick would try to talk me out of it, and if I argued too much, he'd simply carry me off where everyone wanted me to go.

Cornelius signaled for our empty sorbet bowls to be taken away and coffee to be poured. I didn't like coffee, but I sipped it to be polite. As far as coffee went, it wasn't bad.

I smiled at him over the rim of my cup, as the angry voices of Grandmother Begay, Janet, and Mick danced through my head.

"I've decided," I said. "I'll take the job. When do I start?"

Cornelius beamed in relief. He opened his mouth to answer, but was interrupted by a shout from the maître d'.

"I said you *can't come in here*, sir." The "sir" was obviously a placeholder for "asshole."

A big man in sweat pants and a T-shirt threatening to rip at the seams shoved the maître d' aside and strode across the restaurant, his blue eyes flashing all kinds of dangerous.

A wave of joy lifted me to my feet. "Colby!" I rushed at him and threw my arms around his large, hard body.

Colby lifted me, cupping his hand around my face. "You're all right," he said, his voice hoarse. "Thank all the gods."

CHAPTER ELEVEN

Gabrielle

Colby's hug crushed my ribs, and then he planted a fierce kiss on my mouth.

Fire filled my body, stirring up magic, which wanted to embrace him back—Beneath magic and Earth magic intertwining. I knew that was a bad idea and suppressed the urge, but I liked the heat flashing through me all the way to my fingertips.

Colby's lips were strong, hot, smooth, and he could *kiss*. Caressing, coaxing, heating, stroking. He didn't try to shove his tongue inside my mouth, but it didn't matter—his lips were plenty talented on their own.

I heard Cornelius, in his quiet voice, tell the maître d' and waiters to leave us. He didn't say a word to me, but I felt him standing nearby, watching in disapproval.

I eased back from the kiss. Colby cradled me against him, his hold so strong I knew I'd never fall. Sparks swam in his eyes, and I could barely breathe.

Colby set me down, but with reluctance, and with even more reluctance, slid his arms from around me. I wanted to cling to him, something I never do, but since we stood in the middle of a flash restaurant with my new boss right next to us, I suppressed that urge as well.

I didn't know what to do when Colby let me go. Wipe off my lips? I didn't want to—the kiss tingled there. Pretend nothing happened? I didn't want to do that either.

In spite of my wicked talk, I didn't have much experience with kissing, no matter what I'd once told people I'd done with Drake. Drake had let me run on without contradicting me—either he'd been too embarrassed to speak, or maybe he'd wanted Colby to believe more had gone on than had.

I'd never slept with a man either. In high school, guys were afraid to ask me out—when one had tried to get handy with me, I'd broken all his fingers. After that, I was persona non grata, the girl no one wanted anything to do with. Once I'd grown up and left home, I'd never found any man I trusted enough to want to kiss. Then I'd met Colby.

Colby eyed Cornelius in suspicion. "Who is this guy, Gabrielle? Why are you having lunch with him?"

"He owns the hotel," I said quickly. "I work for him now. Sorry," I told Cornelius. "This is Colby. My friends are a little … protective."

Colby's scowl deepened, and he spoke to me as though Cornelius didn't stand two feet from us. "What do you mean, you work for him? Janet is going crazy looking for you. I'm taking you to her before she zaps me with lightning or turns me into a toad or whatever."

I did want to talk to Janet, but not like this—not me being dragged off to stand before her like the bad sister in trouble again.

I didn't want Janet taking this away from me. Our own

mother had tossed me aside and chosen her over me, because Janet has two kinds of magic running around inside her while I have only one.

Now that my insane magic had actually done something useful for me, I wasn't about to let go of what I'd found and run back home. Many Farms wasn't even *my* home—it was hers.

I calmed my roiling emotions and spoke with haughty dignity. "Tell Janet she can come see me in my office, *if* she makes an appointment." I turned to Cornelius. "Do I have an office?"

Cornelius kept a wary eye on Colby, who I had to admit looked a bit like a gangster. "You will. But of course, if you need to speak to your family, do so."

Panic stirred inside me. "No," I said, trying to remain calm. "Colby, tell her I'm fine but that she needs to leave me alone for a while. Like I said, she can make an appointment."

Colby was not happy with this. On the one hand, I knew he sympathized with me and the fact that no one trusted me —he had a similar problem.

On the other hand, he was scared of Janet. He'd never admit it, but he knew Janet could fry the flesh off his body or at least make his life hell. And even if *she* didn't—she liked Colby—Mick would.

"Tell her I threatened you," I said, shooting him a grin. "She'll believe that. I bet *I* could turn you into a toad—want to find out?"

Colby backed a step, raising his hands. "I'll take your word for it. Are you sure you want to work for this guy? What exactly does he expect you to do?"

"Help him with magical problems. It's fine, really. I can take care of myself, Colby. Tell Janet to back off." I gave him a melting look. *"Please?"*

Colby shook his head. "I am so not getting between you two. I don't want to end up as dragon dust. I'll tell her, sweetheart, don't worry." He at last focused on Cornelius, taking in Cornelius's charcoal gray suit, elegant shoes, and well-groomed gray hair. "If you do *anything* to hurt her, you will answer to me, and you will not like that. All the mages in all the world won't help you then. Got it?"

Cornelius didn't look offended. "Of course," he said smoothly. "I want nothing but the best for Gabrielle. She is a very talented young woman."

Colby nodded. "Yeah, I agree with you." He gave Cornelius another narrow look. "I'll tell her, Gabrielle, but I can't be responsible for how she reacts."

"I wouldn't expect you to," I said, giving his arm a pat. "Thank you, Colby."

"Yeah, well." Colby looked uncertain—he obviously didn't trust Cornelius and wanted to grab me and run. But here I was, asking him sweetly to do this for me.

He heaved a resigned sigh. "If you need me, you call me, all right? I'll be here in seconds." He leaned toward me as though intending to kiss me again but straightened instead, brushed a finger across my cheek, turned around, and walked out. Colby's fine back view beckoned my gaze, which I gave it until he disappeared around the red wall that separated us from the door.

Cornelius looked pleased I'd sent him away, but my heart banged and ached, uncertainty filling me as I watched Colby disappear. He was someone from my real life—if my life could be said to be real. I wasn't sure I was ready to let that life go yet.

Cornelius offered his arm. "I'll take you to your office," he said. "Then you can make arrangements with your sister. I will have one of the larger suites with a kitchen reserved for you if you want, but I won't require you to live in the hotel. You are an adult; you make your own decisions, live where you like. It is your choice."

"Of course, I'd love to stay here," I said at once. Where else was I going to go in Vegas, with no money? The winnings from the baccarat table had been scattered who knew where while I'd fought the dragon slayer, and it had been pretend money anyway. Not really mine, like the cash Colby had lent me before I left home, which I'd thrown away on blackjack and male strippers. I'd pay every penny back, now that I had a job.

Colby was nowhere in sight by the time we emerged from the restaurant into the quiet hall. Another guard had the elevator waiting for us. Cornelius stepped inside it with me, the doors quietly slid shut, and I rose up, up, and up, toward my new life.

Janet

"She's *what*?"

I stared at Colby, openmouthed, while he returned his stubborn look.

"Staying here and working for the hotel," he repeated with a growl. "I didn't get all the deets." He was angry at her decision, I could tell, but he'd also decided to walk away and leave Gabrielle with the brother of a man who frightened *Cassandra*, one of the most powerful witches I'd ever met.

Then again, I didn't know who to worry for more, Gabrielle or this Cornelius Christianson.

We stood in the casino, the card games in full swing at three in the afternoon, the buzz of the roulette tables sounding over conversations and laughter. Everyone was well dressed and well groomed, quietly flaunting their jewels, overpriced watches, and the fact that they were here at all.

"Where is she?" I demanded of Colby

His cheekbones flushed, and he looked uncomfortable. "In her new office, I guess. She says you need to make an appointment."

My eyes widened, and I let out an exasperated breath. "Of course she did. All right. Where are these offices?"

"How the hell do I know? I didn't follow her—I came to find you."

I turned in a circle, seeing nothing but wealthy people gambling in the casino and bright sunshine outside in the gardens. Offices in a place like this would be well hidden.

Colby cleared his throat. "I think maybe you should leave her alone, Janet."

Colby had been intrigued by Gabrielle from the moment he'd met her, and I hadn't decided whether he truly liked her or was simply fascinated by her explosive personality and deadly magic.

Dragons don't love, Mick had once told me.

Was that true of all dragons? Or was Colby another exception—had he learned to care for people, as Mick had?

"Colby, I know you like her," I said, trying to keep my voice gentle. "I do too, believe it or not. When I first met Gabrielle, she tried to kill me, and kept on trying to kill me until we called a truce. She held Nash hostage, she tried to open the vortexes and let out our hell-goddess mother, among other things ... And still I love her, because she's my sister, and I want to help her. But I know she's not exactly stable. She's calmed down a long way in the last year, but even so, you can never tell what she's going to do."

Colby listened impatiently. "I know all that. But Emmett

the Ununculous did a number on her, and I don't think she's completely recovered. Magically yes. Emotionally, no. She needs proof she's fine, that she's strong again, if only for herself." He folded his arms, his tatts dancing on his biceps. "Don't take this the wrong way, Janet, but I think she needs to come out from your shadow."

"You mean we're smothering her, Grandmother and I."

Colby's face went redder, but he didn't back down. "Yeah, a little bit."

That stung, but he had a point. "If we were normal sisters, I'd agree with you. But Gabrielle is a messed-up, Beneath-goddess magic infused young woman with abandonment issues and an unstable temper. Who the hell knows what could happen if she stays here and plays hotel mage? I know Emmett hurt her—he hurt *me* in a huge way—and I don't want anything like that to happen to her again." I hadn't entirely recovered from the showdown either, in spite of the wonderful trip I'd taken with Mick. I'd learned things about myself during that fight I hadn't wanted to know.

"So are you," Colby said bluntly. "A messed-up Beneath-goddess magic infused young woman with abandonment issues, I mean." His scowl said it all. "But you have Mick, a family, friends. What does Gabrielle have?"

In spite of his fun-loving ways, Colby wasn't stupid, and when he made statements like this, they carried stark truth.

I'd grown up with people whispering behind my back, speculating on who or what my mother had been, what kind of freak I might be. I'd lived in a world where whose family you belonged to was everything. A mother who disappeared and left you to your dad and grandmother led to sympathy but also vast disapproval and sometimes downright hostility.

Gabrielle had grown up the same way, but she hadn't had a loving dad and watchful grandmother in her corner. When

I'd left home, determined to make it on my own in the big bad world, I'd met Mick.

My throat was dry. "She has *me*," I said. "She might not think she has anyone, but she has me. And I need to find her."

Colby watched me closely. "I understand, but I don't think you should stop her doing this."

My eyes widened. "Seriously? Let her stay here alone while the weird guy who owns this hotel exploits her in who the hell knows what way?"

"I didn't say *alone*," Colby said. "I'm not leaving."

That made me feel a little better, but I didn't calm. "I still want to talk to her."

Without a word Colby turned and walked out of the casino through the front entrance. He waved to Amos, the ever-handy limo driver who hadn't left the premises.

Amos brightened and strode to us. "I heard you found Gabrielle. My intel was good, then."

Amos had located a maid who knew which room Gabrielle had been put into, and that maid had heard another say that Gabrielle had joined Cornelius in one of the restaurants. I'd checked out half of the dozen eateries in this hotel while Colby had taken the other half.

"She need me to drive her anywhere?" Amos went on hopefully.

Colby shook his head. "Not right now. Can you find out where Gabrielle's new office is?"

"Sure thing. Yeah, a bellman told me she's going to be working for Cornelius Christianson as his PA. Wow, I'd love that salary."

"Word travels fast," I said in surprise.

"Around here it does. You want to know anything that goes on up and down the Strip, ask the drivers, the doormen, the bellmen, and the maids. I'll find her for you." Amos started to head inside, then turned back. "I still need seventy-five from you for the ride," he told me apologetically. "I wouldn't charge you, or Gabrielle, but I have to answer to my boss."

I smothered a sigh and started to go for my credit card—Mick's actually—but Colby forestalled me and dug into his pocket for a wad of cash. "Take seventy-five out for the fare and keep the rest."

Amos rearranged the bills from a crumpled mess to a smooth stack with the ease of an expert. "Thanks, Colby. Appreciate it. Be right back."

———

FIFTEEN MINUTES LATER, COLBY AND I EXITED AN ELEVATOR on the top floor and went through to an office suite presided over by a receptionist. Guards lingered in the halls—I suppose Cornelius kept money and other important things in the offices, as I did at the Crossroads. I didn't have three beefy, suited guys to protect my meager earnings though.

"Ms. Massey isn't taking appointments yet," the receptionist said, pleasant but immovable. She was in her forties, well groomed, and quite pretty. She touched a small keyboard on her desk. "I can schedule you for tomorrow."

"I'm her sister," I said impatiently. "Can you tell her I'm here?"

The receptionist gave me an emotionless look. "Ms. Massey is seeing no one today."

In other words, the woman didn't care if we were family, clients, or ax murderers. Gabrielle had said to keep us out, and the receptionist was obeying orders.

I admired her for sticking to her guns, but at the same time ...

I called up a small crackle of magic—which was tough, because I was exhausted—to push the guards back if I needed to, and started around the desk.

And stopped as though I'd run into a wall. Nothing was there, only empty air, but I couldn't budge it.

"Holy shit, she's warded it," I said in amazement.

"Against dragons too," Colby said, sounding hurt. He touched the air, pushing against the pressure that kept him out.

"Against everyone magical," the receptionist said coolly. "As I say, you must have an appointment, and she isn't seeing anyone until tomorrow."

"Kind of sucks to be on the other side, doesn't it?" Gabrielle's voice floated to me down the short, chocolate-painted hallway. She leaned against the doorframe of the office at the end. "It's all right, Shelly. I'll make an exception, just this once."

She waved her hand, and the barrier vanished so rapidly that I lost my balance and fell forward. I caught myself and marched down the hall to Gabrielle, who grinned in enjoyment, Colby on my heels.

CHAPTER TWELVE

Janet

Gabrielle's office looked out over the west side of Las Vegas with a view of the vast mountains beyond, their tops brushed with snow. The office itself was smaller than mine at the Crossroads, but held simple luxury. A framed painting hung on a wall, a spotlight illuminating it. The only furniture was black—minimalist desk, a padded desk chair, and one metal framed chair for a visitor, only one.

I glanced around the room but my eyes returned to the painting, the art major in me coming alert. "Holy crap, is that a Hockney?"

Gabrielle glanced at the red and gold depiction of a fold of the Grand Canyon, done in an unusual but beautiful way. "I don't know. Pretty, isn't it?"

"I thought it was in a museum." Could be a copy, but I had the feeling it was an original.

Gabrielle slung one hip on the corner of her desk, her

dark blue dress businesslike but showing off her long legs. She tried to appear nonchalant, but I saw the sparkle in her eyes, her defiance, anger, and fear.

"Have you come to spoil all my fun and tell me to run home like a good girl?"

I folded my arms. "What exactly does this Mr. Christianson want you to do?"

"Protect the hotel. Keep the baddies out. Eject them personally if I have to." She swung her foot in a dark blue, high-heeled pump that matched the dress. "It's something I can do."

She could, I had no doubt. "What I mean is, why would you want to? You can do the same thing at the Crossroads. I like having the extra power around."

Gabrielle gave me an annoyed look. "No you don't. At the Crossroads, I'm crazy Gabrielle who might do anything—*and for the gods' sake, don't let her near the vortexes.* Here, I'm Ms. Massey, respected magic woman, the one they'll rely on to keep them safe. Cornelius is giving me a job. *You* give me a place to stay—reluctantly."

I felt a twinge of guilt, which irritated me. Gabrielle truly was dangerous and slightly insane, and we'd be foolish to trust her near the vortexes.

Plus I worried about what Cornelius really wanted from her. Gabrielle wasn't the best judge of character.

She was right, though, that I didn't always show her she was welcome in my home. Her motives were never clear, and I'd learned to watch her with caution. I probably didn't hide my dismay whenever she showed up at the Crossroads.

Colby was no help at all, settling in against the doorframe to watch us argue.

"Can you blame me?" I asked Gabrielle. "You've only

recently stopped trying to kill me. I'm sorry we haven't sister-bonded as much as you like, but you can't make that all my fault."

The flash of rage in Gabrielle's eyes usually meant a slap of magic would follow, but I saw her control her instinct to strike.

"You can't make it all *my* fault, either," she said hotly. "Your grandmother treats me like I'm a live grenade. Your bratty nieces get away with far more than I do. You think I wear your clothes because I need to be like you, don't you? Have you thought that maybe it's because I don't have any money of my own, and no one will let me out to go shopping for more? Cornelius knew I was strapped and gave me unlimited credit at his store."

"I've bought you clothes," I began, but she cut me off.

"When you wanted to, where you wanted to, and what you wanted to. I had to practically beg you for that party dress and then the stupid dragon slayer ruined it." I saw her look of vast anger, my sister more upset that her dress had been destroyed than that the dragon slayer had nearly killed her.

I softened my tone. "I'm sorry, Gabrielle. I didn't come here to fight with you."

"Yes, you did. You came to tell me to stop being an idiot and go home, or at least that I'm stupid for wanting to stay." Gabrielle stood up, her high-heeled shoes letting her tower over me.

She was a beautiful young woman, and at the moment, with her midnight hair flowing back from her face, wearing a color that brought out the gloss in her skin, her dark eyes nearly black, she was stunning. Maybe crazy Gabrielle had grown up.

But Gabrielle, despite the power as she had, was in many ways still naive. Good and bad were confused in her world.

"I'm worried about you," I tried. "You know we've heard weird things about this hotel and its owner."

"About *John* Christianson and the hotel in Los Angeles, sure. Cornelius isn't like him. He doesn't approve of his brother or what he does."

Since I hadn't met Cornelius I had no way to judge whether he'd told Gabrielle the truth or was putting one over on her. The brother of an evil man could very well be a liar and just as bad.

We continued to stare at each other, Gabrielle beautiful in her fine clothes, me in jeans with my unwashed hair tucked into a sloppy ponytail.

I had no idea what to do. Put my foot down and have Colby carry Gabrielle home? Or let her remain here, possibly in danger—possibly endangering all those who stayed in or worked at this hotel?

Grandmother would expect me to throw a rope around her and drag her back to Many Farms, no matter how much Gabrielle protested. So would Mick. Drake would say the same.

My father, on the other hand ...

My father would do what he'd done with me all my life. Loved me and stood by to help me when I needed it.

I felt Colby's tension as he watched us. He'd given me his opinion downstairs, that I should leave Gabrielle to do what she wished. I wasn't sure if Colby would try to prevent me from taking her away, or if he'd help me. He liked Gabrielle and clearly wanted to protect her, and that might include protecting her from me.

"Do you trust Cornelius?" I asked Gabrielle, looking her straight in the eye.

She glanced around, as though scanning the room for listening devices, then she faced me again. "Do you trust *me?*"

Something in her eyes made me pause. Gabrielle gazed at me with a quiet confidence I hadn't seen in her before, one different from the arrogance she hid her fear and anger behind.

I also saw a gleam of intelligence. Gabrielle was canny enough to know something was going on with Cornelius and the C, and she'd decided to take the position to find out what.

Her argument about wanting respect and a job of her own wasn't feigned, but I realized in a humbling flash that Gabrielle wasn't as foolish as I'd painted her. She'd taken the job not simply from pride but because she knew, like I did, that the best way to investigate was from the inside.

I understood, and admired her for her reasoning, but at the same time grew more worried than ever. If Gabrielle suspected something bad was going on in this hotel, I didn't want to leave her in the thick of it.

I lifted my hands. "All right, all right. I'll get out of your way, let you live your own life. But if you need me you *call* me, all right?" I slid a chammy bag out of my pocket and laid it on the desk. "Any time, day or night."

Gabrielle glanced at the bag with some dismay but also perception.

Neither of us said out loud what was in it. Gabrielle was right to suspect listening devices, and neither of us wanted to let on to any other mage that we had a magic mirror. The last mage who'd tried to take it from us had nearly destroyed us, and hurt Gabrielle most of all.

Gabrielle slid open a metal drawer under her desk, plucked out a new small black purse, stuffed the chammy bag into it, and snapped the purse closed.

"I also have one of these." Gabrielle slid a smartphone out of the drawer and waved it at me. "I can text you now. Oh, wait, you always break or lose your cell phones. That's okay; I'll text Mick."

"Probably best," I conceded, my face warm. I was notoriously hard on my phones.

"Or me," Colby rumbled. "Janet's heading back to the Crossroads. Me, I'm staying in Vegas. You need me, I'll be only a few floors away."

Gabrielle's face softened. "Aw, Colby, that's sweet."

I made a noise of exasperation. "Sure, be happy *he* won't let you out of his sight."

"If you were a big, hot, dragon-man I might feel differently about you," Gabrielle said. "But you're my nosy older sister—not the same thing."

She dropped her purse and phone into the drawer. "Run off and save the world, Janet. If you need me, you know where I am."

I had a lot of misgivings turning around and leaving her. But I did it. I had the dragon slayer to worry about, and I had trust Gabrielle sometime, or our relationship would never move forward.

Could a relationship between two women whose only tie was a seriously evil goddess mother ever move forward?

I hoped it could, and I hoped that by walking out of this office, I wasn't making one of the biggest mistakes of my life.

Gabrielle

MY FIRST CALL CAME IN AROUND MIDNIGHT. I'D SPENT THE

afternoon and evening after Janet finally left settling in and getting to know the hotel and its staff.

I was surprised to find that many of the maids, bellmen, and maintenance guys not only believed in dark magic but knew how to tell when guests were using it—they weren't magical themselves and so couldn't sense when magic was in the air, but they knew how to spot the accouterments of conjuring, spells, and the like. They didn't confront the magic users but alerted security, and now me.

There were monitoring cameras all over the hotel, which I saw when I was showed into the security room—a little creepy, but some people came to Las Vegas to scam their way to riches, the head of security told me. The monitors caught mundane criminals, however, not magical ones, which was where I came in.

Cornelius had said I could make my own hours, as long as I kept a diligent eye out and agreed to remain on call. I decided to give myself time to sleep in the mornings, time to enjoy myself in the afternoon, then I'd watch the hotel at night, when most dark magic was likely to happen.

Colby moved into the hotel, in a different room from mine, of course. He wasn't the sort of clientele the C liked, but I persuaded Cornelius that he needed to stay to lend his muscle. I fully intended to spend my enjoyment time with Colby, seeing the sights, letting him take me to lunch and then dinner …

I still hadn't gotten over the kiss he'd given me, but I decided not to let on to him about that. The last thing I needed was a possessive dragon in my business—if Mick was anything to go by, dragons could be *seriously* possessive. When I caught myself touching my tingling lips, I'd quickly jerk my hand away.

Anyway, I was lounging in my office in my new blue

dress, my feet propped on my desk so I could admire my new shoes, when my phone rang.

"This is Gabrielle," I said cheerily into it. "What do you need fixing?"

The breathless and frightened tones of one of the room-service waiters came to me. This young man had brought me a heaping bowl of ice cream an hour ago when I'd grown bored and hungry.

I was by myself—Shelly, the receptionist, worked eight to five, like a normal person, and I had the feeling Cornelius wouldn't approve of Colby up here with me—but I wasn't afraid to be alone. The offices of this hotel must be the most securely locked and warded places on earth, and besides, there wasn't much villainy I couldn't handle.

"Something going on in room 4235," the room-service waiter said in a voice just above a whisper. "I delivered a bottle of wine to them. Guy who told me to come in was scary looking, with yellow eyes. I didn't go far inside, but I'm pretty sure he had a woman penned up in there. Front desk says a lady checked into that room by herself, the reservation for only one. You said to tell you if I saw anything suspicious —so I'm telling you."

"Thank you, sweetie," I said, swinging my legs off the desk, my elation rising. "You stay safe in your kitchen, and I'll check it out."

"Want me to alert security?" he asked.

I'd told the staff today that if they saw anything dark magic-y, or that even looked dark magic-y, they should contact me first. The goons with the earpieces were for ordinary bad guys, but I was first response for magical problems.

"I'll call them if I need them," I assured him. "Otherwise, they might get hurt. 4235, you said?"

"Yep."

"All right. Thanks, Steve. I got this."

I hung up, logged the report into my computer as Shelly had showed me, grabbed my purse and universal keycard, and left the empty office suite.

They'd given me a card that would open every guest room in the hotel. How cool was that? At Janet's hotel, I didn't even have a key to my own room. The maids or Cassandra always had to let me in.

Cornelius had already put a lot of trust in me, and I was determined not to betray that trust.

The hall in front of room 4235 was quiet, but the nasty magic oozing from the crack under the door made my fingers itch. A demon was in there assaulting one of our guests.

I swiped my keycard through the slot and the door clicked open. "Housekeeping!" I called as I charged inside.

The naked demon with yellow skin, yellow eyes, horns, and a magical aura that nearly blew me back into the hall was on top of the woman on the bed. She turned her head to me when I banged in, her eyes pleading.

Gabrielle to the rescue. I reached through the demonic aura, wrapped a snake of crackling magic around the demon's neck, and hauled him off the woman.

She sobbed, and he gibbered, and then I noticed a few things.

First, something, not the demon, was sucking at my magic, as though trying to siphon it off.

A moment of watery panic tore through me as I flashed back to the shallow desert canyon, where Emmett Smith stood over me and ripped my magical self away, the diamonds on his glasses gleaming in the starlight.

I shoved away the memory with a gasp. The drawing-off

wasn't the same—nothing ever would be as terrible as what Emmett had done. This felt like an opportunistic magical being taking in power where it could find it.

Second, there was a circle on the floor, with the bed in the middle of it. The bed was against the wall, but the circle continued up the padded headboard and onto the wallpaper in an unbroken line. The marks were chalk, easily erased, but the magic that flowed through them turned the marks blood red.

The demon glared at me and snarled, but I knew no demon would draw a chalk circle in a room to contain a human victim. They didn't need anything but their own strength to subdue their kill.

Which meant this demon had been conjured.

The woman was giving me a look of pathetic gratitude, but I sensed the erotic joy inside her, her triumph as she absorbed the demon's magic.

"Eww," I said, wrinkling my nose. "Can't you just read tarot cards and light candles like other witches?"

I took a step forward. The demon hung in midair by my noose of magic, and now *he* sent me a terrible pleading look.

The witch sat up in panic. "No! Don't break the circle!"

She was beautiful and voluptuous—at least, that was the glam she projected. Underneath, I saw an ordinary-looking woman trying to be irresistible to the netherworld.

"Why not?" I stopped with the toe of my shoe just outside the chalk line. "Oh, that's right. Because if he's no longer bound, he's free to kill you. I'd kill you too, if I'd just been violated."

"What are you talking about?" The woman tried to sound scared. "He came, he—he—"

"Nice circle," I said admiringly. "I have a friend, she does

circles, but she's not stupid enough to conjure a demon in
them, well, not for sex at least. Of course, she's a good
enough witch not to have to feed off other beings' magic in
the first place."

The demon stared at me. I have no idea whether he
understood us, but I could taste his need for vengeance. All I
had to do was erase one mark, and he'd be free to annihilate
the woman who'd tried to suck him dry—plus anyone else in
this hotel, including me.

"Don't take this the wrong way," I told the demon. "But go
to hell."

A blast of my power sizzled through the markings,
burning them bright orange and then blue-white. The
demon shot me a grateful look before he vanished in a flare
of light.

"You stupid bitch!" The woman was up and off the bed,
her glam falling away to show her sagging belly and breasts.
She was stark naked, which was something I really didn't
want to see. "He's a *demon*! Evil."

"Depends on your point of view, sweetie. Even evil beings
have feelings." With a sweep of my hand, I blurred the chalk
markings into white powder, which poured down from the
wall onto the pillows. "How about I send up a vacuum, you
clean this place, and then you get the hell out of our hotel.
You'll owe us for the night."

I felt her glaring at me as I turned for the door. I also felt
her gather her magic, laced with whatever she'd been able to
imbibe from the demon, ready to strike.

I spun on my heel and blocked the wave she threw at me,
shards of her spell hitting my wall like sand on glass.

The witch snarled in rage. "Your time is coming." She
pointed a pudgy finger at me. "You will be obliterated from
this world, and clean magic will pervade. I've waited for this

moment for centuries, and finally, it is upon us." Her triumph blazed, her smile wide.

She sounded like the dragon slayer. I wished I knew what they were going on about, but I didn't want to give her the satisfaction of asking.

"Are you saying your magic is clean?" I asked. "Seriously? It stinks of demon from where I'm standing."

"Not like the evil I smell on *you*."

I put my hands on my hips. "Now you're pissing me off. Everyone knows better than to do that."

The witch frowned, her cockiness abating, but part of my power was my unpredictability. You never know what unstable Gabrielle is going to do.

She lifted her hands and began chanting words I didn't recognize. Her fingers bent into claws, her eyes went dark, and inky smoke issued from her mouth.

I watched with interest as the smoke slid into my barrier and tried to destroy it. It failed, of course. I saw the witch's frustration when she couldn't budge my wall, but I definitely did not like the sensation of her Earth powers against mine.

She wasn't stronger than I was—very few mages were— but I smelled a damp dirt odor, similar to what I'd sensed when I'd fought the dragon slayer, felt the same pressure as when I'd faced him at the pool.

I made a grabbing motion, squeezed the witch's magic into a small, dense ball, and threw it at the window. The glass shattered from the impact, the magic dispersing in a draft of cool October air. The witch's eyes widened, then she hissed.

"Now you owe us for the window," I said. "Pack up and get out. If you're still here by the time I send up security, I'll have to get *really* unfriendly. And tell your friends that dark magic isn't welcome in my hotel."

The witch's glare didn't wane, but I was so done with her.

I stalked out, a waft of my magic slamming the door behind me.

I laughed. I liked my new job.

As I turned the corner to head for the elevator, a wave of something so dense and dark it blotted out all sight and feeling hit me and sent me to my knees.

CHAPTER THIRTEEN

Gabrielle

W hat the fuck?

It wasn't so much a blow as a slow, inevitable pull that took me down to the carpet, as though something tried to drag me down through the layers of the hotel into the ground. I again smelled damp earth and tree roots, had the sensation of being smothered with dirt, crushed alive by it.

I'd left my cell phone in the office, arrogantly figuring I could handle anything without having to call for backup. There were panic buttons in the halls for those in the know, in case employees were threatened by guests or intruders. They went straight to security, but security wasn't what could help me. In any case, I couldn't summon the energy to stand up and reach one of the buttons.

I heard a step behind me in the hall. "You see?" the witch said with mean glee. "It is a beginning. Abominations like you will pay."

The witch, dressed and with a shoulder bag slung over her arm, walked past me as I struggled to stand, barely able to see her.

I expected her to let loose her magic or at least kick me, but she continued down the hall, pushed the button for the elevator, entered it, and disappeared.

The crushing sensation didn't leave me once she was gone, which meant the witch hadn't instigated whatever this was.

I tried to call up my Beneath magic, delving into my most hidden reserves, but I could barely move through the sludge. I managed one lone spark, which did nothing but glitter in my hands.

An answering glitter came from my purse. As I closed a shaking hand around it, the clasp came undone and a shard of glass spilled out and fell to the carpet.

No, not glass—mirror.

I'd forgotten about it. The magic mirror had been unusually quiet since Janet had handed it to me, but it wasn't awake all the time. Now it lay on the floor and winked up at me, showing my wide brown eyes and blotchy face.

"Oh sugar," it said. "You do *not* look good."

"Colby," I croaked. "Get Colby." My breath left me.

"I belled him," the mirror said. "Hang on to your knickers, darling. Looks like you're caught in a bad Earth-magic sink, like the kind that made me. Not good for Beneath-goddess beautiful women. Don't die Gabrielle, okay? You're too hot to die."

I didn't even have the wherewithal to tell it to shut up.

The elevator dinged and the floor shook with Colby's heavy tread. *"Gabrielle."*

He caught me as I collapsed all the way. His dragon magic burned me—his magic was Earth magic, but so was whatever was attacking me. I wanted to scream, but smothering weight began to crush me.

Colby rubbed my arms with his big hands. "Stay with me, Gaby. Come on, sweetheart."

"Take me out of here," I tried to say, but nothing crossed my lips.

Colby lifted me to his lap as he sank to the floor and cradled me against his chest. He was trying to reach me with dragon magic, but the fire he slid into me was snuffed out by the deep weight of the Earth magic.

"Shit." He lifted me closer, burying his face in my hair, and I felt him shaking. "Hang on, Gabrielle. Don't leave me yet."

I had no intention of going anywhere. I wanted to take this dragon out to dinner, flirt like hell with him, go dancing with him, then end up in my sumptuous hotel suite and make love with him all night. I bet he was good in the sack, could teach me so many things, first and foremost to not be ashamed of my own passion.

Colby kissed my neck, his breath warm, then he freed one of his hands to push buttons on a cell phone. "Get over here," he said to whoever answered on the other end. "Weird shit is going on, and you're the only one I can think of to fix it."

Colby

I HELD ON TO GABRIELLE AS THOUGH I COULD SAVE HER WITH sheer willpower.

I didn't know what the hell was wrong. I'd never seen Gabrielle down except for when she'd fought that bastard the

Ununculous, and then she'd been physically fine, just magically drained.

Now she lolled against me, her hair spilling warmly down my arm, and I didn't know what to do. I'd vowed to take care of her, and here she was, dying on my watch.

Nothing was attacking her as far as I could tell. The corridor was empty, silent, the antique furniture undisturbed and the thick pile carpet clean and well vacuumed.

The mirror in my bathroom had started screaming, *Help! Help! She's dying!* And I'd followed its hysterical directions to the fourth floor. The elevator had opened to show me Gabrielle lying in a tangle of limbs, blue fabric, and silky hair.

"Don't leave me, sweetheart," I said as I gathered her closer. "I want to get to know you, find out what you're all about."

I knew there was more to Gabrielle than the crazily dangerous half human, half goddess everyone made her out to be—she was smart, funny, adapted rapidly to perilous situations, and she had more courage than anyone I'd ever met, including dragons.

Gabrielle fought every day of her life. I wasn't about to let that fight be for nothing.

The elevator made a soft ding and someone got off. Not the man I'd hoped to see but a black-skinned woman in a colorful shirt and dark pants.

She knelt next to me, concern on her face. "What happened?"

I recognized her as Chandra, the nurse who'd taken care of Gabrielle. I'd met her earlier today when Gabrielle had been introduced around.

"Don't know," I said. "She called me, and I found her like this."

Chandra touched Gabrielle's face then took her wrists, checking her vitals or whatever humans did to figure out what was wrong. Her touch was firm, competent, professional.

"Physically, I think she's fine," Chandra announced, to my relief. "Though scans might tell us something different. She needs a hospital."

"No, she needs the guy I just called. This is a magical attack."

I didn't feel weird telling this woman about magic, because I sensed it in her. Deep inside her, like she kept it buried—so buried I couldn't tell what kind it was.

Chandra looked at me sharply. "What guy?"

The elevator's door rolled back once more. "Him."

Sheriff Jones barreled out, followed by Maya. He didn't bother to ask what was going on before he crouched down next to us.

Chandra gave him a startled look but moved aside. Maya, in a bright red dress—they must have been out on the town —leaned over Nash, her eyes holding worry.

Nash studied Gabrielle with a frown before he put his broad hand on her shoulder.

Gabrielle jerked under his touch. I held her steady, knowing more or less what was happening, but Chandra scowled at Nash. "You're hurting her."

"No he isn't," I said, then sent Jones a dangerous look. "Are you?"

"I don't know," he answered. "Do you know what happened?"

"No," I began, but Chandra interrupted.

"It will be in her log. She must have been answering a call."

A call Gabrielle hadn't bothered to alert me about, which meant she'd thought she could handle it.

I'd been respecting her space, agreeing not to hover around her and get her fired on her first day. I should have ignored her, damn it.

Nash continued to frown. "This is weird. I usually feel nothing, but …"

He drew an abrupt breath, while Maya leaned closer. "What?" she asked anxiously. "What do you feel?"

"Like a wall …" Nash closed his eyes, sweat beading on his face. "Pushing me out."

Chandra's lips parted as she watched him, her eyes growing wider. "What kind of witch are you?"

Nash didn't answer. Gabrielle jerked again. I tried to still her, but she began jolting and lurching like she was having a seizure.

"No, you don't," Jones said under his breath. He closed his hand on Gabrielle's shoulder and touched the other to her gray and perspiring face.

I heard a groan, which came from none of us—a sound of defeat but also rage. Something dark sprang from Gabrielle and smacked Nash right in the chest.

Maya reached for him in alarm, but Nash shouted, "Don't touch me!"

The darkness sank into Nash. He kept his hands firmly on Gabrielle, not flinching as the inky blackness shoved its way into his body. Another groan sounded, louder this time, vibrating the walls as Nash folded in on himself.

Nash's face was slick with sweat as he fought whatever invaded him. Maya balled her hands, and Chandra stared in alarm and some fascination.

I felt as helpless as the two ladies did—for all my dragon

might, I could only hold Gabrielle while Nash silently fought whatever had attacked her.

The final bit of darkness streamed reluctantly from Gabrielle's chest, stretching like an elastic band. But Nash not only had training that made him a ruthless soldier and cop, he had a will of iron. The fact that he was a weak human in the middle of dragons, demons, goddesses, Nightwalkers, and witches never fazed him. I don't think he noticed.

Nash abruptly let go of Gabrielle and pressed his fists into his stomach. "Get out, you son of a bitch."

Whatever he fought, whatever tried to best him, didn't win. Nash gave a final growl and tore at his chest, lifting his shirt from his body. Then he closed his fists and slammed them together.

A last groan sounded, this one ending in a wail of pain. Finally Nash lowered his hands, sat back on his heels, and uncurled his fists.

"Everyone all right?" he asked.

Gabrielle's chest rose with her breath, but easily as she relaxed. Her eyes fluttered open, and she looked blearily up at me.

"Hey," she said. "Did you come rescue me?"

I gathered her closer, my heart banging in relief. "Any time, sweetheart."

Gabrielle turned her head and looked at Nash, who breathed hard but otherwise looked unhurt from his battle.

"Nashie," Gabrielle said, her voice a croak. "Lovely to see you again. Were you who Colby called? That was smart. Don't tell Maya. She'll be jealous." She looked past Nash to Maya, and winked at her. "Hey, Chandra. The gang's all here. I say we party."

"No, you get yourself to bed and rest," Chandra said in a stern voice.

"What she said." I gave Gabrielle a no-nonsense look. "What was attacking you?"

"I don't know." Gabrielle tried to sit up and collapsed onto my lap instead, leaning against me while I held her, which was fine with me. "I banished a demon and sent a witch packing, and then something hit me. Horrible spell or ... something." She shuddered. "Like being buried by a ton of dirt."

Nash nodded as he sat back, his arms resting loosely on his knees. "That's what it felt like to me too. I had to push my way out."

Chandra frowned at Nash. "What are *you*?" She poked a tentative finger to his shoulder. "I've never felt anything like you before."

"He's a county sheriff and my boyfriend," Maya told her in a hard voice.

"He's a magic null." Gabrielle gazed at Nash with admiration. "That's what Janet calls him. He negates magic. He was hit with some kind of spell when he was in the army."

Nash scowled. "That's need-to-know information."

"Chandra's fine," Gabrielle said with tired assurance. "She's a doctor, and I think she has some magical ability, though I don't know what it is."

Chandra fixed her attention on Nash. "It's more than a spell. This one is special." She turned from him and looked at Maya. "Very special. You must take good care of him."

"I always do," Maya said glumly.

CHAPTER FOURTEEN

Mick

D rake, Titus, and I surrounded the dragon slayer in the basement of the Crossroads hotel. The binding spell nearly smothered him, but I watched the man with diligence.

I knew from experience how powerful he was—I'd fought him as a young dragon, before he'd come into his full powers. If he hadn't thrown off the spell by now, he had some reason for retaining it.

The basement was the best place to confine a magical prisoner. Not only was it dark and intimidating, but one end held a pool of shaman magic that could destroy cities, and the other end held a Nightwalker. While the slayer had segued into a demon centuries ago, blood still beat in his veins, blood he needed for life, and a hungry Nightwalker could divest him of that.

We also had Cassandra, Janet's cool and pale-as-ice manager, whose power I had yet to understand the depth of.

The dragon slayer didn't look worried as he sat cross-legged against a brick wall, three dragons he'd nearly defeated hovering over him and happy to tear his heart out, Cassandra, one very competent witch, looking on. She'd let us rip his heart out, and he must know that.

Titus filled his hands with fire. "Talk. The longer the conversation, the longer before you die, so tell us everything."

The dragon slayer gave him a contemptuous look. "This doesn't end your contract."

"It will if you're dead."

Titus had always been too sure of himself. He'd gotten into the fight with the dragon slayer in the first place, because he'd been certain he'd win, and I had to dive in and try to save his ass. I'd probably been just as arrogant, neither of us realizing how powerful this guy was.

Titus and I had grown since then—mature dragons were a hell of a lot stronger—but our arrogance had grown with us, I guess.

What the slayer would do to us now for ending his games prematurely, I didn't know. He rarely came to the arena to watch his matches, not obviously anyway. He knew dragons would honor a contract, because we had too damn much honor. He just liked his power over us.

Would he try to kill us or make us finish the games another time? In the passing years, he'd become more and more powerful, like Emmett, but as a demon, not a mage. We might be able, all three of us, with a boost from Cassandra and Ansel, to kill him. And we might not.

"Speak," Drake said, more restive than I'd ever seen him.

The slayer had almost killed Drake, from what Colby had said, which I could see had pissed Drake off. Most people didn't understand how strong he was—until he got mad.

"What is this danger you speak of?" he demanded of the slayer. "And how do we defeat it?"

"*You* don't," the slayer said. "It is old, older than time. It is Earth magic from so deep inside the planet that it will erase all in its way."

"Deep inside the planet is molten rock," I pointed out. "Volcanoes are caused by geothermal incidents, and earth-quakes happen when plates shift. The gods take advantage of those things to create or destroy, but the events themselves aren't magical."

The dragon slayer smirked. "Smirk" is a word I hate but it is the only way to describe his expression.

"You are wrong," he said. "I have learned Earth magic from the dawn of time, and the forces are caused by an entity. Every thousand or so years, that entity rises and goes in search of abominations that pollute it. And it wipes them out. Why do you think we aren't overrun by demons and old gods, and wielders of bright magic like that girl I almost drowned? The Earth devours. It will not rest until it is appeased."

By "abominations," I figured he meant Beneath-magic beings, the gods and other creatures that had been shut into the world before this one. Dragons had already existed when the present world rose to dominance, and dragons and gods like Coyote had let the good emerge from Beneath but sealed the evil inside.

Evil got out from time to time, though, like the skinwalkers, demons, and goddesses like Janet's mother. Then Earth-magic wielders—me, Janet, Cassandra—shoved them back in and closed the way.

But I knew that Earth-magic beings could only do so much against the tide of demons and evil gods who tried to crawl out to this world and claim it for their own. It had taken all my effort, and Janet's and Coyote's and Nash's, to shut off the vortex behind Janet's hotel, and I wasn't certain we'd done it permanently.

I realized the dragon slayer might be right—our meager efforts couldn't possibly have kept the demons at bay for millennia.

From the looks Titus and Drake gave the slayer they thought what he said was plausible too.

Cassandra leaned over the man. She did nothing overtly threatening, but the slayer regarded her worriedly.

"You need to be more specific," she said. "Everyone in this room has Earth magic. By your definition, we don't need to be concerned."

"It is old," the slayer said. "So old it is almost mindless. It will devour everything magical, including Earth-magic beings in its need to be thorough. But I, my slaves, *I* know how to fight it."

Gabrielle

Not the best start to my job to answer one call, get trounced by an invisible assailant, and be banished to my bed by Chandra and Colby.

Chandra wanted to tell Cornelius what had happened, but she gave in when I begged her not to. I didn't want to admit to him that I'd gotten hurt on my first assignment. He might have second thoughts and send me away.

Once I was tucked up with a pot of tea on one nightstand —Chandra's recommendation—and a stiff drink on the other—Colby's prescription—I asked Colby to bring me the shard of magic mirror.

Chandra had gone. I'd made her leave me so she could get some sleep, and she reluctantly went, not looking tired at all. I wanted to ask her why she'd been up and quick on the scene, and why I felt some magic from her when I hadn't before, but I didn't want her around when I pulled out the mirror.

I stared into its depths, seeing that my eyes were sunken and red-rimmed and my hair a total mess. I resisted the urge to reach for a hairbrush and pinned my stare on the mirror.

"What did you mean?" I asked it. "I heard you say I was caught in an Earth-magic sink, like the one that made you. I thought a witch made you, a powerful one a couple hundred years ago. That's what Janet told me."

"Sort of, honey," the mirror said. "A witch did put me together, but she got lucky. The magic that infused the silicon she heated came from a deep magic sink, where I was born ... *early one frosty morn*."

I cut it off. "Where?"

Colby, who sprawled in a chair at the foot of the bed, his feet on the bedspread asked, "And how did an Earth-magic sink suddenly form in the hallways of a Vegas hotel?"

"You know all those sand dunes?" the mirror said. "The ones in Southern California, south of the Salton Sea, near the border with Mexico? Yep. Lots of sand, Earth-magic sink. Put it together—ta da! Magic mirror."

"Plus a witch who knew what she was doing," Colby said. "What does that have to do with what happened to Gabrielle?"

"Beats me," the mirror chirped. "But she asked."

"I don't see a lot of sand dunes around here," I said. "Maybe the Earth-magic sink travels?"

"Don't think so," the mirror said. "But it could grow, maybe."

"Three hundred miles?" Colby asked. "How could it spread that far?"

I didn't have a clue how far it was from Las Vegas to where the mirror was talking about, but I took Colby's word for it.

"I dunno," the mirror said. "It's the Earth, so it's all connected, right?"

A shiver went through me. If the entire world became this Earth-magic sink that had tried to bury me, what could I do against it? Did it sense I didn't belong here, that my magic was other-worldly, and so had attacked me?

The Earth is rising, the dragon slayer had said. *You woke it from sleep.*

Mick and the other dragons had taken the slayer back to the Crossroads, Colby said. Janet should be there too, by now. I needed to call her and tell her to beat out of the dragon slayer what he was talking about.

But later. I was weak and sick, and at the moment I didn't want to explain what had happened to me. Janet would probably freak if I told her I'd been attacked and rush back here to sit on me. Or, demand I return home.

There was one person who usually had answers, or at least annoying, cryptic hints, every time weird shit was going on. I hadn't seen Coyote around in a while, and I didn't know exactly how to get hold of him, but I could call Fremont Hansen. Fremont was the font of all gossip in Magellan, and if Coyote was anywhere in town, Fremont would find him.

I started to sit up, but damn, I was wiped. Dizzy, I fell back to my pillows, to find Colby at my side.

"Stay still," he admonished. "You almost died twice in the last couple of days. I don't need to be rescuing you a third time because you raced out of here and fell over."

I had the feeling I was in mortal danger whether I stayed here or not.

I didn't like the freezing fear that ran through me. I tried to console myself by thinking that Coyote would know what to do, and Janet, with her kick-butt storm magic could help. Janet flailed around a lot trying to figure things out, but once she did, she was unstoppable.

I should be comforted. I had people I could turn to.

But I wasn't. I was scared shitless.

"Colby," I said in a small voice. "Would you lie down next to me? You know, like we're a couple or something. I'd like to sleep with you around me."

I expected Colby to yell, "Yes!" do a fist pump, rip off his clothes, and dive full-length on the bed. But he went quiet, his cheeks flushing as warmth entered his eyes.

Without a word, he rose from the chair, came around the other side of the wide bed and sat down on it. He looked at me, his black hair falling in a braid over his shoulder—he wore it long, like an Indian.

He quietly unlaced and took off his boots, then rolled onto the bed, landing on his side next to me and snaking his arm around my waist.

"How's this?" he asked in a near whisper.

I laid my head on his shoulder, imbibing his warmth, his strength. The tatts on his arm were silken soft.

"I like it," I murmured.

"You go to sleep," Colby said. "I'm watching over you."

"Thank you," I said in all sincerity.

"Oooh, girlfriend." The mirror's tinny voice came to us. "Can I see?"

Colby plucked the mirror shard from my fingers, reached across me to jerk open the drawer of the nightstand, dropped the shard inside, and slammed the drawer shut.

Janet

I MADE IT HOME TO THE CROSSROADS TO FIND EVERYONE IN the basement with the dragon slayer.

At least this is what Elena, my cook, told me when I walked in, exhausted, and dropped my bags on the lobby floor.

She followed me ponderously down the stairs. "That man is disturbing me. I can't cook with him here."

"He hates dragons," I said over my shoulder. "You have a lot in common."

"I do not *hate* Firewalkers," Elena said indignantly. "They are nuisances. I hate no one. It is a useless waste of energy."

I didn't argue with her as we reached the basement. She might not hate anyone, but she didn't *like* that many people either.

The dragon slayer lay slumped against a wall, surrounded by dragons, a purple bruise on his face that looked new. His eyes were closed.

Ansel, his hands on his lanky runner's legs, gazed down at the slayer.

"What happened?" I asked him.

"I believe he is unconscious," Ansel answered in his smooth voice, looking like the affable young Brit he'd been in the 1940s. "Likely the result of this dragon hitting him." He gestured at Drake.

Mick moved to me and slid his arm around me, giving me a half hug to welcome me home. "The slayer called us his slaves," he said, pressing a kiss to my hair. "Drake took umbrage."

Drake gave us an annoyed frown. "I feared he was about to break the binding spell. I struck him as a precaution."

Mick grinned. "The expression on your face didn't say 'precaution.' It said, 'Fuck you.'"

Drake dipped his head. "There might have been a bit of anger in my reaction."

"He didn't tell us much anyway," Titus put in. "He said that you and your sister woke something whose time was coming." His eyes, which turned golden, pinned me in an unnerving way. "That the abominations would be erased, that we—dragons—were his slaves. Never mind the binding." He gestured to the dark, magical threads that engulfed the dragon slayer like a chrysalis.

Drake did not look contrite. "I felt him fighting the spell. We'll make him explain when he wakes up."

I let out a sigh. I was tired from the long drive home in Maya's truck—she'd be coming back with Nash—and I was hungry. I needed a hot meal and coffee. "Any dinner left?" I asked Elena hopefully.

She shook her head, assuming a mulish look. "The kitchen is closed for the night."

"There must be something ..."

More head shaking. "The kitchen needs many repairs. I can barely cook in there as it is. And I don't want you eating all my ingredients."

I opened my mouth to remind Elena who owned the hotel, but I prudently closed it again. Elena was an amazing chef, and when she said she could "barely cook," she'd meant she'd turned out a five-star meal my guests would rave about for years. Besides, if she got mad and walked out, my grand-mother would never let me hear the end of it. She and Elena had become BFFs.

"I'll go to the diner," I said, averting that crisis. Magellan's diner was open twenty-four hours and did a surprising amount of business late at night.

"Not alone," Mick said quickly.

Fine by me. I didn't mind dinner out with Mick, and besides, I wanted to grill him about the dragon slayer.

"What about *him*?" I pointed at the slayer.

Drake folded his arms. "I will remain here."

"With me," Titus put in. "Maybe I'll get a few questions in before this one shuts him up again."

Drake, again, didn't look offended. He settled against the wall, stoic, still in the jeans and T-shirt he'd acquired in Las Vegas.

"I will also question him," Elena said. "He is strong. And strange."

"Be careful," I said. I directed my words mostly to Ansel.

He gave me a boyish grin. "Never fear, Janet. I have sated myself with cow's blood, courtesy of Elena. I will not go Nightwalker and end the dragon slayer—unless he tries to kill someone. Then I will not be held accountable for my actions. He's not quite human anymore."

I had to leave it at that. Upstairs, Cassandra, who had also been in on the interrogation, Mick said, but had resumed her duties once the dragon slayer had been put out of commission, barely glanced from her computer to give me a nod. She was checking in a couple who looked like ordinary tourists, but who held a faint whiff of magic. Low-level mages, I guessed.

Pamela, Cassandra's girlfriend, lounged on a sofa in the lobby, her long legs stretched out. She was a Changer and always wore the look of a watchful wolf, even in her human form. A boy of about twelve sat on another sofa, regarding her with awe.

Mick and I departed on his bike for the diner in Magellan. It was full when we reached it, but Mick managed to snag us a booth from someone who was just leaving.

The whole town must be here. There was Fremont, squeezed into a corner with Flora, one of the hotel's maids. Emilio Salas, out of his police uniform, ate with his two brothers.

Jamison Kee, my oldest friend, sat in a booth in the back with his wife, Naomi, and his daughter, Julie. The three had been avoiding me, because they guessed I'd had something to do with Julie's restored hearing, and none were comfortable enough to talk about it with me yet.

A large man swung around on a stool at the counter. He wore jeans, a denim jacket, shiny gray cowboy boots with pointed, roach-killer toes, a long black braid bound with a silver ring, and a hefty amount of silver and turquoise jewelry, including an old-fashioned squash-blossom necklace.

"Janet!" Coyote's roar cut through the heavy throb of voices. "How are you? Ready for the end of the world?"

CHAPTER FIFTEEN

Janet

Coyote rose from the stool, the bulk of him filling the crowded space, grabbed me off my feet, and hugged me hard.

Mick watched from two inches away, pretending to smile affably, but I felt his tension. He didn't trust Coyote. They had a past.

I hugged Coyote in return, happy to see him. He'd been evasive since the big fight with Emmett at my hotel, and I missed him. I'd seen him in town, playing the storyteller for the kids and charming the tourists, but he'd only waved to me in passing and never sought me out.

I wasn't surprised. Coyote usually only talks to me when something bad is going on.

Coyote signaled to Jolene, who worked behind the counter, walked straight to our booth, and sat himself down. Jolene, just emerging with his food, followed him and deposited a huge plate of chicken-fried steak with a mountain of mashed potatoes, everything smothered in gravy, in front of him. A freshly opened bottle of beer followed, Jolene delivering the order with a wide smile before she retreated.

Mick guided me into the seat opposite Coyote and sat down tightly next to me, knowing Coyote didn't always keep his hands to himself. Coyote's excuse is that he's the trickster god, a thief, and a womanizer. Of course he'd snuggle up to a pretty woman.

Whenever he tries that bullshit on me now, I remind him that I know his wife. Makes him contrite real fast.

I wished she was here. Bear was a goddess of deep wisdom, who might know a) what evil was coming, and b) how to defeat it.

As Coyote ate, Mick filled me and Coyote in on what the dragon slayer had said before Drake hit him. *The Earth devours. It will not rest until it is appeased.*

"I wouldn't know how to fight the Earth itself," I said. "How is that even possible?"

"He didn't say the Earth, specifically," Mick, ever practical, responded. "He said an entity, which to me means a god of some kind. Maybe one so old it doesn't have a name anymore."

Jolene returned and gave Mick and me an expectant look, her pen poised to take our orders. Mick asked for two burgers with all the works, coffee for me, and beer for himself.

I used to chafe when Mick presumed to order for me, as though I were his sub, or something, but I had to admit he did know what I liked. We always got our food faster and cooked especially well when he charmed the waitresses, so I let it go. Jolene melted under his smile and moved back to the kitchen.

Coyote took a large bite of steak and potatoes. He was a

god, one of the oldest, and he did not have to nourish himself with human food, but he seriously enjoyed it.

"How do you think the world formed?" he asked us after he swallowed.

Mick shrugged. "Accretion. Matter blasted from an exploding star got caught in the gravity of the sun and eventually formed planets."

Coyote threw back his head and laughed. "Accretion? That's hilarious. You mean rocks ran into each other until they stuck together? And the Earth was created? With all its water and trees and animals?"

"That came later," Mick said, unoffended. "Primordial ooze and amino acids. That whole thing."

"No gods involved, huh?" Coyote bashed at his potatoes, mixing them with the gravy. "You don't have time for gods, do you?"

"I'm a dragon," Mick said, keeping his voice quiet, not that anyone could hear in the madness of the diner. "I'm realistic. Gods might have pushed at things and directed them here and there, but the universe is an amazing place without them."

Coyote shook his head, the diner's lights gleaming on the gloss of his hair. "You are looking at only the outside. Gravity, the weakest force in the universe, might have stuck planets together and had them revolve around the sun, our sun around a galaxy, our galaxy clustering with others. See, I read books too. But—you know about the Beneath world, the shells of worlds inside shells. You've been there. So have I —I was born there. Janet has been there too. Good times, right, Janet?"

"If you mean horrible, terrifying times, then yes," I said. "Mick lost his magic when we went Beneath—he barely remembered who he was."

Mick nodded, then paused to accept his beer from a waiter, one of the vast Hansen clan, who also thunked down my coffee. The diner's staff was being run off their feet tonight.

"I figured Beneath is not a physical realm inside the Earth's crust," Mick said calmly. "But another dimension entirely. The multiple universes idea. When Beneath was spent and evil beings were taking over, gods like yourself found a way to bridge into this universe. The vortexes are like wormholes, which is why they don't all lead to one specific place Beneath—each vortex leads to a different dimension, or a different aspect of that dimension."

Coyote listened, his smile broad. "So the dragon believes in quantum physics." He lifted his beer bottle and tapped it to Mick's.

"It has nothing to do with belief," Mick said good-naturedly. "The physical world is what it is. Whether I believe it or not."

"Good answer. But you weren't around when I found the way up from Beneath, eons before you were born. We only made it to this layer of the world because the Earth allowed it. In time, it didn't like the creatures that escaped with us, objected to being invaded, and tried to obliterate us."

I locked my hands around my coffee cup. This didn't sound good. "So what did you do?"

"Hid," Coyote said. "A lot of beings were lost, though, the good as well as evil. The Earth didn't distinguish. I don't think it knew how."

"Kind of like the flood in the Bible," I said. "Expunging creation and starting again."

"Exactly like the flood in the Bible. That story is ancient, repeated in many cultures, with only slight variations. In each, the gods are displeased with what has become of their Earth and wipe the slate clean to start over."

Something cold clenched in my belly. "Are you telling me we have to go up against God?" I tried to speak lightly. "My grandmother would not be happy about that."

"Your grandmother is a wonderful woman, if too quick to smack a helpless coyote with a broom." Coyote winced at the memory. "She could probably teach the gods a few things. Never tell her I said so."

"I draw the line at fighting God." I smiled, knowing—hoping—he was joking.

"Nothing like that," Coyote said, to my relief. "This is not an unseeable god of all the universe. It's one that grew inside the Earth—grew with it, you could say, became a part of it. Earth magic comes from it, or it caused Earth magic to manifest. Not sure which. It is why *he* exists." He pointed at Mick. "And why your storm powers formed, and why Night-walkers ... walk."

Mick took a placid sip of beer. "How do we fight it?"

"I don't know," was Coyote's comforting answer. "I don't know if it can be fought."

"Thanks," I said. "Very helpful."

"Everything has a weakness." Mick folded his hands around his beer bottle, the general in him coming out. "Where did you hide the last time? Might be a place we can send Janet, out of harm's way."

Coyote shrugged. "Beneath." He lifted his beer. "Not sure that's where Janet should go."

No, I should not. My mother was there, for one thing, waiting to kill me. Even if I didn't go to her exact dimension, the skinwalkers and other demons wouldn't be to happy to see me either.

I gave Coyote a level stare. "One day, I'll come to you for help, and you'll actually *help*."

"Now, that wouldn't be any fun." Coyote lost his grin and leaned closer to me, his expression serious. "I know one thing, Janet. You can't hide from this. You'll have to face it. Will you be strong enough?"

"I don't know." I sighed. "But I'm still recovering from the mess with Emmett."

"You mean when you absorbed all that power and became the strongest magical being in the world? For ten minutes?" Coyote looked thoughtful. "Maybe you could do that again."

"Not anytime soon." I shuddered. "I can't explain what that felt like."

Horrible. Glorious. I'd believed—no, I'd *known*—I could fight anything, kill anyone, do whatever I wanted. All emotion had gone out the window—love, hate, joy. I hadn't cared for anything but my power. It had been awful.

Mick's hand found mine, and he gave my fingers a squeeze. I'd almost killed him, had wanted to kill him, had known exactly how to. And he'd stood there and loved me anyway.

I swallowed. "I never want to do that again."

Coyote shrugged and took a sip of beer. "You probably wouldn't be able to, in any case. Had to be a specific set of circumstances. You returned all the power to all those people, let them find peace. Your choice." He scooped up a snowball-sized portion of potatoes with his fork. "I was proud of you."

His words warmed me—Coyote wasn't lavish with praise, at least not with me. I basked in it, and Mick's hand on mine, until Jolene came out and slammed burgers and a huge basket of fries down in front of us.

"Oh, one thing," Coyote said as we dug in. "Watch over Gabrielle. She's going to need you."

I nearly choked on my first bite of cheeseburger. I set it down hastily and gulped water. "Shit, why are you telling me this *now*? I left her alone in Las Vegas. Well, with Colby. And Nash."

"Good," Coyote said. "As long as she has guardians. She's fine for now, but there will come a time when she'll need you."

"You mean to fight this Earth entity, or whatever it is?"

Coyote only gave me his best cryptic *You'll figure it out when you need to, Janet,* look.

I let it go. Pressing him for details would only make him speak in more riddles.

I made myself relax and enjoy my burger, which was tasty. For a while, we simply ate, three friends meeting for dinner at Magellan's diner. Normal—if anything in this town could be called normal.

Coyote had scraped his plate clean and drained his beer when a twelve-year-old girl with honey-brown hair and blue eyes halted by our booth.

"Julie!" Coyote bellowed. He rose, caught Julie in a hug, and lifted her up to rest in the crook of his arm. Julie was getting taller every day, but Coyote held her easily, and she looked content to hang in his arms.

"How's my favorite lady?" Coyote asked, kissing her cheek.

"Just fine," Julie said. "I came to talk to Janet."

Everyone in the diner was watching, overtly or covertly, a few blatantly staring.

The news that deaf Julie could now hear had made it around town with lightning speed. Most assumed Jamison and Naomi had saved up for surgery and implants for her, and all were pleased the procedure had been successful.

Those who believed in Magellan's magical aura knew some kind of spell had gone on, maybe one to enhance the surgery. Either way, the town rejoiced with the family, and few but Jamison and family connected Julie's restored hearing with me.

Coyote gave Julie another hug, set her down, and invited her to sit with us. Julie complied, sliding in next to him and resting her arms on the table. Her limbs had taken on the lankiness of early teen years, but I could see a softness in her, the budding of beauty.

"I'm sorry Mom and Jamison won't talk to you," Julie said to me. "They're a little freaked out."

I couldn't blame them. I hadn't been anywhere near Julie when she'd woken up able to hear, but Jamison, who was a shaman and a Changer, had known that immense magic had found its way to Julie and figured I was the cause.

"It's okay," I said, but Julie shook her head.

"No, it isn't." Her words were a bit slurred, and I saw her pause, try to listen to herself, and change the movement of her tongue. "I told Mom you were my friend, and I won't let anything stand in the way of that." She made a dismissing gesture with her slim hands. "They'll get over it."

"I'm sorry." I closed my mouth, feeling stupid for apologizing—I would never take back what I had done, even if I knew how.

Julie laughed. "What, that you cured me? Yeah, I'm all broken up inside. All the noise kind of gives me a headache, but I'm getting used to it. I cried for almost a whole day, but not because I was sorry." She gave me a twelve-year-old wide-eyed stare. "Because I knew this time it would stick."

Once before, a spell had restored her hearing, but the

magic had been temporary, lasting only until the object that helped make the spell disappeared, taken by a goddess who knew where. Julie had been resigned about the whole thing, as though knowing the healing had been too good to be true.

Julie looked different now, vibrant and excited, like a kid should.

"All right," I said, squaring my shoulders. "I'm *not* sorry." I'd do it again, I decided, even if I had to experience that raw, all-consuming, terrifying power to heal her. Julie was worth it.

"I like your voice, Janet," Julie said, cocking her head. "It reminds me of how velvet feels."

I flushed, too pleased to answer.

"You know what I like best, though?" she went on. "Being able to hear my mom. And listening to Jamison play his flute. He's teaching me how."

I reached for a napkin from the dispenser and wiped my eyes. Julie grinned at me. "I keep making people cry," she said. "It's so easy."

Coyote rumbled a laugh. "That's my girl."

"Coyote sounds like thunder," Julie observed, and wrinkled her nose. "Really *loud*."

"We love him anyway," I said. "What about Mick? What does he sound like?"

I glanced at Mick whose eyes were suspiciously moist. "Yeah, what do I sound like?" he asked in genuine curiosity.

Julie regarded him closely, assessing. "Sexy," she concluded.

The three of us burst out laughing, and Julie joined in.

Julie glanced across the diner. "Have to go. Looks like Mom and Jamison want to leave. They didn't try to stop me coming to talk to you, don't worry. They're not *really* mad at you. Just, you know, confused." She gave me a sage nod, a kid who had long ago realized that adults were slow.

She rose, bent to give Coyote a warm kiss on the cheek, fluttered her hand to us, then trotted to Jamison and Naomi, who waited at the diner's door.

Naomi caught my eye. Instead of looking away as she had for the last month, she flushed and met my gaze. It was a neutral look but with a touch of wistfulness, as though she wanted to talk to me but couldn't for the life of her think of what to say. I gave her a little nod to show her I understood.

Jamison, on the other hand, underwent a transformation. His stolid quietness shattered, and he broke from Julie and Naomi as he strode down the aisle for me.

Mick was on his feet, ready to stop Jamison if he shifted into his mountain lion and attacked me. *That* would be an interesting news story for the tiny local paper.

At the last second, Mick stepped aside so Jamison could haul me into his arms. My face squashed against his hard shoulder, the scent of wood smoke, stone, and outdoors filling me as his long hair tickled my cheek.

Jamison, my oldest friend, the man who'd rescued me when I was crying on a ledge in Canyon de Chelley, terrified of my storm magic, Jamison who was calm and sensible, and definitely not demonstrative in public, now squeezed me in a breath-stealing hug.

We stood this way for a long time, while people around us either laughed, or said "Awww," or "Not right in front of your wife, Kee," or "Watch it, Jamison, her boyfriend's tough."

Jamison ignored them and when he pulled away, his dark eyes swam with tears. "You ever want anything, Janet —*anything*, you got it, all right?"

"As long as we're still friends," I managed, my voice not working.

"We are." Jamison squeezed my shoulders with his

powerful artist's hands, then turned around and did the same to Mick. "Hell, yes, we are. Anything you need. I keep my promises."

Jamison broke away from us and joined Julie and Naomi waiting at the diner's door. Naomi smiled at me, and Julie waved, then they departed under the delighted stares of the rest of Magellan.

I turned to see what Coyote had made of the scene, surprised he hadn't peppered us with his smart-ass comments.

He was gone. Coyote, the trickster god, had vanished.

Mick reached for the crumpled twenty-dollar bill that lay beside Coyote's empty plate.

I sighed, shaken by Julie's frankness and Jamison's gratitude, and pretended to be nonchalant. "At least he didn't stick us with his check this time," I said.

Gabrielle

Janet woke me in the morning to ream me out. Colby, the traitor, had called her as soon as he got out of bed, and told her what happened.

Of course I'd planned to call her myself—Janet needed to know about dangerous shit—but at the same time, I hadn't wanted to listen to her fussing and telling me what to do.

"Colby can fly you back to the Crossroads," Janet said in her big-sister voice. "I don't want you in Vegas if there's a magic sink—and you'd better believe I'm going to ask the mirror why it didn't alert me."

Because it was in a drawer, I didn't say. *Because I didn't want it commenting while Colby and I snuggled.*

Not that anything happened between Colby and me. I'd slept hard, and when I'd awakened, he'd been gone. But it had been nice lying against him, aware of him in the night, even as I'd slept.

"I told the mirror not to say anything," I said. "No need to bother you when I was fine."

"But you weren't fine! You almost died. Thank the gods for Nash."

"He came right away, so nothing to worry about," I said quickly. "Colby knew exactly what to do. I've got a good team. There's shit going on here, and I need to stay and find out what."

"I know there's shit going on. You need to come back *here* so we can figure this out, and decide how to fight it if we have to."

I pretended to consider. "No, don't think I will. I'm going to check out the arena where Mick was fighting—if there's anything left of it—and see if there's a connection. Besides, I have a job, remember? What would Cornelius say if I ditched out on my second day? I can't let him down."

"You can—" Janet broke off suddenly and started arguing with someone in the background. There was a rattling, then a voice I didn't expect came over the line.

"Gabrielle, you will stay there," Grandmother Begay said. "I will be coming to watch over you."

"What?" I jerked upright, pillows scattering "No, no, no. You know where I am, right? *Las Vegas.* Not really your scene."

I pictured Grandmother Begay, gray-and-black haired, wrinkled, and stubborn as hell, leaning on her cane and glaring at everyone in the C's casino. She'd scare away all the customers.

"Everyplace in the world is my *scene,* as you say," was her reply. "Janet must stay here and interrogate the dragon slayer, but you must not be in Las Vegas alone."

"I'm not alone," I said, my voice rising. "Colby's here, and Nash, and Chandra ... What are you even doing at the Crossroads, anyway? What about Pete and Gina's wedding?"

"Gina was happy to see me out from underfoot. She does not say so, but I know. My son feels the same, though he is ashamed at his relief. I am a commanding old woman. Janet cannot leave, and so I will come to be with you. Do not argue."

"Are you going to fly?" I demanded, unable to keep the tremor from my voice. "Long way for a crow. What will you do for clothes when you arrive?"

"I will be there," she said, not amused. "And then you and I will have a talk. A very long talk."

CHAPTER SIXTEEN

Gabrielle

I did not want to wait around for Grandmother Begay to show up and tell me what to do—or more likely, what not to do. I took my free time after I ate my breakfast-slash-lunch and headed out.

My outfit today was a multicolored dress in vivid primary colors like Chandra wore, which I ordered from the gift shop while I ate. The skirt was short and swingy so I could fight in it if I had to, and it looked cute if I didn't.

I called Amos—I had his card—and asked him to pick me up out front. Colby came with me, hulking and dangerous, and also, to my surprise, Chandra.

"You keep getting hurt," Chandra said as she slid into the limo next to Colby, forcing him to move closer to me on the seat. "You need me."

"And me," Colby said. "Same reason."

"Fine by me," I said without hesitation. "How can I lose?"

I understood now why Janet liked to surround herself

with friends—there was strength in numbers. With Colby's muscle, Chandra's smarts, and Amos's loyalty and wheels, I felt powerful. Alive.

I took a long breath, expanding my chest, grateful for air. The sensation of being buried by crushing dirt had scared me more than I wanted to admit.

Amos drove us up the Strip to the hotel where Janet, Maya, and I had so optimistically begun our girls' weekend. I didn't think the hotel security would be in a hurry to see me again, so Amos drove around to the loading docks and sneaked us in through a back door. He vouched for us with the guys working there—Amos truly knew everyone—and we walked right in.

The delivery docks hadn't been touched by our magical hijinks, but the maintenance halls we'd first traversed in pursuit of Mick were a mess. Workmen busily shored up walls and ceilings, their electric saws, nail guns, and hammers making a racket.

Amos found a bellman who showed us a way around the destruction to the lower floors of the basement. He was good-looking and kept glancing at my legs.

"We'll take it from here," I said to Amos and the bellman when we reached the floor with the arena. I gave them a big smile as Colby and I blocked the way farther down the hall. I didn't want the two humans following us and getting hurt.

Amos took the hint and ushered the bellman back upstairs. Colby waited to make sure they were gone before we started looking around.

The electricity had been jury-rigged back on, the bellman had explained, so repairs could commence. The lighting hadn't been the brightest in the first place, but we could see the entrance to the arena, which hadn't been destroyed, and the pile of rubble blocking the way to where Janet, Maya, and I had come down to find Mick.

"You did that?" Colby asked, studying the impenetrable mound of concrete, pipes, and wires.

I started to say, *of course I did*, but that wasn't quite the truth. "Janet and I did it together. We sent all those poor little demons back home."

Chandra regarded me thoughtfully. I couldn't decide how old she was—if she had a medical degree, that meant many years in school, plus time interning, so she wasn't in her first youth, but she had a smooth, unlined face and young energy. I sensed wisdom in her eyes that came from long experience. But maybe she'd had to grow up fast, like me.

"You envy your sister," Chandra observed.

I started at her words, and suppressed a dart of anger. "Well, of course I do. She has superpowers. Janet can take a storm and make it do her bidding. Her Earth magic is far stronger than my Beneath magic, though I'd never tell her that. If she could work her storm magic all the time, she'd be unstoppable. *I* couldn't stop her."

I realized from the way Chandra and Colby regarded me that a simple *Yes* would have answered the question.

I closed my mouth, my face growing hot.

Colby discreetly turned away. "Arena's in here?" His voice echoed as he disappeared under one of the arched doorways.

The darkness inside lit up as he tossed a ball of dragon fire into the air. I entered the arena as the flame rose to the high ceiling and spread out, lighting the room in a brilliant red-orange glow.

Chandra stopped beside me. "My, my," she said softly.

Stone arches lined each level of the spectators' area, which was about fifty tiers, as far as I could count. Either a very clever design or some kind of magic made it reach that high without bursting into the hotel above it.

The room was a semicircle, not a full oval, but the architects had designed it to be similar to the famous Flavian amphitheater in Rome, known these days as the Colosseum. Each keystone in the arched openings was carved with leaves and grapes, or heads of gods, or cavorting nymphs.

I'd noticed a trend in Las Vegas to base hotels and casinos on European models, maybe to make them seem more classy. That explained the small-scale representations of Paris, Venice, Monte Carlo, Ancient Rome, and in the case of the C, Versailles.

There were no seats in this arena—those who came to watch the combat had to stand. The first row hung twenty feet above the arena floor, which was covered with sand.

I moved down to the front row and leaned over the stone wall that kept the spectators from falling down to the combat area. Arched openings below let the competitors enter, but I saw that those keystones were decorated with demons rather than nymphs, many of them stabbing one another with pitchforks.

Why were demons so often portrayed with pitchforks? I'd never seen a demon actually wield one. Pitchforks are farm tools for lifting and spreading hay—maybe artists back in the day couldn't think of anything more evil than a symbol of backbreaking work.

I needed to go down there. I could look for the elevator we'd used to descend to the cells, but I was pretty sure the way to it would be blocked by rubble. Janet and I had been zealous.

I didn't want to wait to find Amos and ask his friend to show us another way around, so I vaulted over the balcony and used a burst of magic to slow my descent to the ground.

Both Chandra and Colby called out when they saw me leap, but I landed easily and brushed off my skirt.

I looked around, though there wasn't much to see. The arena floor was covered with about a foot of sand, which rippled out to lap the walls. The better to soak up the blood, I supposed.

I was proud of what Janet and I had done. We'd stopped the dragon slayer and sent the poor beasties he'd coerced back home. I hoped my snake demon had found her way to her children.

When I turned around again, Colby and Chandra were next to me. I blinked at them in surprise, but Colby pointed to one of the dark arches opposite the one we'd come in through. "Stairs."

"Sure, do it the easy way." Warmth suffused me as I studied him, remembering how fine it had been to lie against him last night.

"Place gives me the creeps." Colby shivered. "The dragon slayer must have chosen it for a reason."

"I wonder what ..." I mused as I looked around again. "The Earth-magic sink? Is it here too? Hang on." I opened the tiny red purse that went with my outfit and extracted the shard of mirror.

I glanced at Chandra, who'd moved to the far wall in the huge arena, examining it on her own, before I held up the mirror and turned in a circle to show it the entire arena. "What do you think?" I whispered to it.

"Ooo, hot guy. Love those tatts."

Colby scowled as a glint of reflected firelight fell on him. "Do you have to let it talk?" he rumbled in a low voice.

"Unfortunately, yes. Focus, Mirror. Whatever your name is."

"You can call me Sexy. In fact, sweetheart, you can call me *anytime.*"

I growled under my breath. "I know why Janet keeps threatening to melt you. Do you sense anything?"

The shard moved in my hand. "Deep magic. Strong." Its usually obnoxious voice went somber. "I haven't felt anything like this since ..."

It fell silent, while Colby and I waited. I was about to shove it impatiently back into my purse when the mirror let out a piercing scream.

"What?" I whispered frantically at it, but it continued to scream without pause.

Colby was cursing, and Chandra clapped her hands to her ears and doubled over. I stared at Chandra for a stunned moment then marched to her and dangled the mirror in front of her face.

"You can hear it," I said over the shrieking. "You can hear this. Loud and clear."

"Loud." Chandra kept her hands over her ears. "Yes, that is a good word."

"*Why* can you?" I demanded. "I know you have a little magic in you, but you have to be *very* magical to hear more than a hum."

The mirror's screams finally died to sobs, and Chandra straightened, gingerly lowering her hands. "Yes, I have much magic," she said in her quiet voice. "But as with my medical degree, I do not use it anymore."

"Magic isn't like a degree," I snapped. "It's part of you, what you are. So what are you?"

Chandra shook her head. "Nothing you would understand."

"Because you're from Africa? Try me. What kind of magical creatures do they have there?"

"Very bad ones." Chandra shuddered, something dark flashing in her eyes. "I feel safer here."

"Here in America?" I persisted. "Or here in Las Vegas? Where you no longer practice medicine, but nurse rich people in a hotel? Who the hell are you hiding from?"

Chandra wouldn't meet my gaze, or Colby's. Studying the sand on the floor, she said, "Let me say I will not bring danger upon the ones I love."

Very noble of her. I wanted to know more, much more, but I did feel a twinge of sympathy. "I understand," I said, trying to soften my tone. "I have family I want to protect too. At least in my case, I have to protect them from *me*. I don't know anyone more evil than I am, so I make sure I don't hurt them."

Chandra raised her head and looked at me, her eyes holding surprise. "You are not evil, child. Who has told you this?"

"Everyone." I flapped my hand at Colby. "Even he thinks so. That's why he likes me."

Colby's cheeks reddened. "Hey, now, I never said that."

"It's all right. I know exactly why I'm intriguing. My mother is a goddess so evil there isn't a name for how horrible she is. I'm half human, but all her crazy Beneath magic went into me. Janet and her grandmother are trying to help me control it, because we all know what will happen if I let it get out of hand." I made a big circle with my arms. "I'll destroy everything in sight."

Chandra continued to watch me in amazement. "They have said this? These people who are your family?"

"Sure." I spoke brightly. "They're right. I'm unpredictable and dangerous. Have to be kept in check at all times."

Chandra gave me an allover look as she had when she'd checked me for injuries. "I sense nothing evil in you,

Gabrielle. You are very powerful, yes, but the magic in you is neutral—neither good nor bad. It just *is*. Some magic is dark, as in what runs through Nightwalkers or skinwalkers, but not you. The magic you have is only as good or evil as you make it."

My hand closed tightly around the magic mirror, and I winced as it made a tiny slice in my palm. "So the magic isn't evil—*I* am?"

Chandra actually laughed. "When I say there is no evil in you, there is none. I'd know it. If you are dangerous, it is because you believe you are a destructive force. You have not put a rein on what you can do because others have made you believe it will do no good to try. That you are hopeless." She shook her head. "They are fools. Do not listen."

The cut on my hand drew blood. Colby came to me and gently took the shard away. He dropped it back into my purse then extracted a package of tissue from it and started to clean my palm.

I stood there and let him, unmoving. *I wasn't evil?* What was she talking about?

Chandra didn't know me. She didn't know how I'd wished my father dead and then watched him die without stopping it. How I'd hated Janet because she'd usurped me, how I'd tried to kill her, how I'd tried to capture Nash and take him to my mother, because she wanted his null magic. How much I'd wanted to destroy everything in the world because I hated it, and myself.

Of course I was evil. I didn't want to be, but I was my mother's daughter.

Crap, now I was starting to cry. I yanked my hand out of Colby's grasp and swiped at my eyes.

"We can't be standing around talking," I said, trying to sound stern, like Grandmother Begay. "We have a lot of work to do. Does this place have anything to do with that weird Earth magic? The kind that makes me feel like I'm being buried alive?"

Chandra ignored me. "If you are so evil, Gabrielle, then kill us. Right now. We are alone with you here—who would know what you did? You can bring down the walls on us, and it will be a long time before anyone finds our bodies."

My mouth popped open.

I expected Colby to say something like, "Speak for yourself," and get ready to fight, but he folded his arms and regarded me calmly. His tattoos were vibrant under the light of his fire, his black braid a streak of midnight against his gray T-shirt.

"I could do it," I said in a shaking voice. "Easily. You couldn't stop me."

Chandra only gave me a wise look. "I know. Colby knows. If you are truly evil, you will need no reason to kill us. Or maybe it would be for the enjoyment."

"Killing isn't fun," I said in amazement. "It's awful. I fight to kill only when I'm afraid. You know, like when demons and Nightwalkers and other nasties attack."

"As would most people," Chandra said. "This is known as the fight-or-flight response. In your case, instead of running away, you stay and face the danger, knowing it is your best chance of survival."

For some reason, her calm explanation made me very angry. No, not angry, scared—worried she was right. It was much easier to believe I did the things I did because I was evil incarnate, made so by the evil goddess who'd hatched me.

"You don't know me," I yelled at her. "You don't. I don't want to talk about it."

I spun away, my skirt swinging.

"I do know you, Gabrielle," Chandra said. "Better than you think."

I don't know what she meant, and at the moment, I didn't care. I skulked around the walls scanning for auras, trying to focus on the business at hand, but I couldn't. I kept hearing Chandra saying, *You are not evil, child.*

But I was. I'd stalked Nash, studying everything he could do, then burst into his house and chained him up. Maya had tried to shoot me for it. I'd made up for it by helping save him and bring down a murderous witch, but all my good deeds couldn't erase how bad I was. Grandmother Begay reminded me of that every day.

I stood in the middle of the arena and tried to put the disturbing conversation out of my head. I couldn't sense any auras other than the lingering ones of the demons, dead and alive, but they were faint, days old.

The mirror had said it sensed something immensely strong, something that scared it into screaming. But I felt … nothing.

I went to Colby and took back the shard from him. "You're malfunctioning. There's nothing here."

The mirror sang in a whisper, "You're wro-ong."

"Let's go," I said angrily, stuffing the shard away, and I walked out, this time using the mundane method of the stairs.

CHANDRA, COLBY, AND I RODE IN SILENCE BACK TO THE C. Amos, who'd missed the drama, shot me puzzled looks in the rearview mirror, but no one enlightened him about what we'd found or not found.

When we reached the C, I ran inside before Chandra

could even get out of the car. I didn't want to face her anymore. Colby followed me but headed for the gardens, cell phone in hand, saying he had calls to make.

So it did not help my mood as I strode through the casino to catch sight of a small woman at a slot machine resolutely punching its button. The C didn't have many slot machines, and the woman seemed very angry with this one.

I almost hadn't recognized her in the black pants and deep blue top she wore, looking like any other retiree who'd come off a tour bus to do a little gambling.

I marched up to her, but she didn't cease smacking the button, even when I stopped next her.

"There is something wrong with this machine," Grandmother Begay growled while she pinned the spinning wheels with her glare. "It is not paying me any money. You must tell them to fix it."

CHAPTER SEVENTEEN

Gabrielle

"There's nothing wrong with it," I tried to explain over the machine's electronic notes. "Slots won't pay out because you punch the buttons harder."

"Gambling is evil," Grandmother Begay said, switching her glare to me.

"Then why are you doing it?"

She jabbed the button again. The wheels went around and lined up, three identical symbols in a row. Lights flashed and bells rang.

"You see?" I said. "You won."

Grandmother Begay stared at the empty coin tray. "Why is no money appearing? It is broken."

She reached to hit the button again, but I caught her hand. "The slots here don't give you coins—you get a credit slip." I touched a smaller button and snatched the paper the machine spit out. "You take this to the cashier, and she gives you the money."

"No one explained." Grandmother Begay scowled at me as though the casino's policies were my fault.

"What did you use to start playing in the first place?" I asked her.

She pointed to a slim opening in the machine. "It said to put in my cash."

I swallowed. "How much cash?"

"Twenty dollars."

I relaxed. "Well, that's not so much to lose. How long have you been playing?"

Her dark eyes glinted. "An hour. Waiting for you."

"I was busy. I was investigating …" I trailed off. Why could she make me feel guilty about every little thing? I understood why Janet was so jumpy after growing up under that watchful stare. "Anyway, I'm here now, and you only lost …" I glanced at the slip. *A thousand dollars?*

"I lost a thousand dollars?" Grandmother Begay's voice rose in outrage.

"No, you won!" I waved the slip in front of her face. "You won a thousand. Let's go cash in."

"You mean I won nine hundred and eighty dollars," she corrected me. "I lost twenty."

My eyes narrowed. "You didn't cheat, did you?" I wiggled my fingers at the spinners. "No shaman magic?"

Her outrage grew. "Of course I did not cheat. I would never do such a thing. I am ashamed enough that I was tempted to wager." She grabbed at the paper. "I will tear it up. Twenty dollars is enough to teach me, and you, a lesson."

I held the paper out of her reach. "No, no. No sense in throwing away money. You can spend it on the wedding."

Grandmother Begay lowered her arm. "That is true." She gave me a grudging look. "I will entrust it to you. Now, tell me *everything*."

Mick

We didn't get much more out of the dragon slayer that afternoon. Titus and Drake had him beaten down, making him too weak to wake up enough to try to break the binding spell.

I didn't like to kick a man who was down, but on the other hand, it was arguably good that we kept the slayer physically incapacitated. Janet, with her usual dry humor, said she thought that was a good excuse for Titus and Drake.

I stuck close by her when we emerged from the basement to the ground floor of the Crossroads hours later. Janet halted in surprise, and I stopped before I ran into the back of her.

The lobby was packed. It was nearly check-in time, one of the busiest parts of the day, but I'd never seen the lines like this. Cassandra tapped at her computer, quick and efficient as ever, but she looked exhausted.

"What the hell?" Janet's unease came clearly to me, like a buzz through my blood.

The hotel had twelve guest rooms, which were rarely all filled. In a pinch, guests could use an empty room on the third floor, or Janet could give up her bedroom, but even with that, we'd never house the dozens of people that crammed into the lobby. I saw more outside the open door.

Elena came out of the kitchen and waded through the crowd, her face like the thunderclouds now building on the horizon. The saloon was still being renovated, and she'd been making and serving buffet meals in the lobby.

Janet held up her hands as Elena joined us. "I don't know

what's going on. We must already be full—Cassandra will turn them away. You won't have to do any more cooking."

Elena raised her brows in surprise. "Of course they must stay here. They are magical, and afraid. I will feed them—I will send Fremont for more groceries."

"Fremont is here?"

Elena nodded. "He stopped to see Flora, but he can make himself useful. Flora is being a great help."

High praise from Elena, who liked so few.

I scanned the room, the dragon in me sensing magic the same way Janet could sense auras. Many of the people were witches and mages, low to medium level. A few had demon magic, but they were mostly human, and I scented their fear. Changers roved among them, restless and beastlike even in human form. Pamela, who lounged near the check-in desk like a bodyguard, kept a keen eye on them.

None were very powerful. My wards, which I'd reinforced after we'd dragged the slayer here, would have told me if anything dangerous had entered.

Janet looked around again. "They've come for protection," she said softly.

I nodded. "The weak seeking the strong. Word has gotten out."

"Where the hell are they all going to sleep?"

Elena answered. "Anywhere they can. We will have Fremont round up blankets and pillows." She sniffed the air. "There is a storm coming."

October was one of the drier months in the desert, the monsoons of summer having petered out. But October could still bring storms, violent ones sometimes, as the cooling air let in the wind and water.

Elena turned and stared directly at Janet. "Will you be strong enough?"

Janet's shoulder tensed under my hand. Coyote had said a similar thing to her in the diner. *You can't hide from this. You'll have to face it. Will you be strong enough?*

It was my ongoing dilemma. I wanted to protect this woman with everything I had—it killed me to see her hurt, and she was hurt so often. On the other hand, she had power unlike anyone I'd ever met. If I cocooned Janet as I wanted to, I'd have been dead, or if alive, enslaved, and much of the world destroyed, years ago. The first day I'd met her properly, she'd blasted me with lightning. I'd felt her phenomenal magic and known there was nothing I wouldn't do for this woman.

The best I could hope for was to fight by her side and lend my dragon strength to hers.

I bent down to her, breathing the scent of her hair. "We'll get through this." I kissed her cheek, like satin under my lips. "I'll be right next to you."

Before Janet could draw breath to answer, Elena said, "Of course you will be. We need all the dragons here. You must summon them from the compound." She scowled. "As much as I dislike the Firewalkers underfoot, we will need them. Tell them."

She turned on her orthopedic-shod foot and stamped back toward the kitchen.

Gabrielle

I spent some time explaining to Grandmother Begay all that had happened, while getting her checked into a room she didn't find fault with.

Took us five tries, she not liking the odors—no one else

could smell anything—the placement of the furniture—
pretty much identical in every room—the pictures on the
walls—specially commissioned from famous artists.

The staff of the C was patient with her, but even they
were grinding their teeth by the time we finally found a
room she said would "do."

She sat herself down in an antique chair and didn't move.
She didn't want me to leave her, no matter how much I
argued I had a job to get back to, until she met Chandra, who
came to see how we were doing.

The two women looked at each other, both with long
assessment.

Then Grandmother Begay said, "I will sit and speak with
this woman. Go on, Gabrielle. No reason for you to hover
over me. I am not feeble."

No, she was not. She played the frail old woman only
when it suited her.

I heaved a sigh, left her to Chandra's care, changed into a
black skirt and top, and returned to my office.

I said hello to Shelly, who was on her way home. She said
it had been quiet, but I knew that would change once darkness fell. People liked to work magic at night, though I could
tell them spells worked perfectly fine twenty-four seven.
Many witches swore they needed the moon to do their
magic by, and didn't listen when I argued that the moon is
always up in the sky, even if you can't see it.

Colby hadn't returned, and I had to wonder what he was
up to, but I figured he'd check in when he was ready. I
pretended to myself it didn't matter whether I saw him or
not, but the little voice inside me knew that was bullshit.

I sat down, pattering my fingers on the desktop, thinking
about the arena and Chandra's words to me. Not evil,
she'd said.

But how could she know? She'd met me a day ago, when she'd nursed me back to health and helped me shop. I'd been on my best behavior and grateful to Cornelius.

Chandra hadn't seen the things I'd done when I was a kid and hating my so-called dad, such as throwing him across the room for hitting my stepmom. We'd had to take him to the hospital more than once, and police and child services had been called. I think they made my stepmom take me back home because they didn't know what to do with me. Anna Massey, my stepmom, had covered for me—a lot.

I pushed Chandra's assessment aside, no matter how hopeful it made me feel. Once she got to know me, she'd change her mind. People always did.

The phone rang. "Gabrielle, here," I said listlessly. "What's the problem?"

"Dark magic in room 2384," came the breathless tones of one of the maids. "I delivered some towels—lots of people in the room, black candles, a pentagram. They invited me to stay, but I ran."

"Good choice," I said. "You might want to leave the floor and take yourself a break."

"Sounds good to me," the maid said in relief and hung up.

Repeating the procedure from the night before, I logged the call, snatched up the key card, grabbed my purse, and headed out.

I stepped off the elevator on the second floor to find myself shaking. I'd managed to push the attack last night out of my thoughts, but it had scared the shit out of me. If not for Colby and Nash, I'd be dead, without ever seeing who'd tried to kill me.

The elevator doors slid closed behind me, leaving me alone in the long, silent, hall. Unlike the generic sameness of most hotel hallways, the ones at the C had walls of rich color, little niches with furniture and artwork in them, and chairs to sit down on if you were tired from walking from the elevator to your room.

The corridor bent around a corner, and the lights—lamps or sconces—were out there, creating deep pools of shadow. The room I wanted was around that bend, of course.

I'm not afraid of the dark. The terrible things that come out of the dark are mostly me or beings like me, and those I could handle.

So why did I not want to walk into that blackness? I knew that around the corner was a similar hall—the hotel was a square that went around the vast casino below, with a roof garden on top of that. You could get your workout running laps in the hallways.

I squared my shoulders and marched onward, my black skirt swinging. The top had peek-a-boo shoulders, and my exposed skin grew ice cold.

When I stepped into the shadow, the world abruptly went dark. I couldn't see the hall beyond, nor where I'd come from.

As I stood there, my feet strangely unable to move, I heard a breath, one from something immense. An inhale, an exhale. Silence.

I saw nothing, sensed nothing, smelled nothing, which was weird. Evil beings tend to stink.

A heroine in a horror movie might call out timidly, "Who's there?" instead of running for help or turning on a light. Who did she think would answer? *It's me, the ax murderer. Nice to meet you.*

I conjured a ball of Beneath magic.

"Are you looking for me?" I said into the darkness. "If so, it's your *un*-lucky day." I shot the orb of magic high, letting it burn like a magnesium flare.

It illuminated nothing. I mean, I saw the hallway with its carved wooden chairs, heavy tables with glass art on them, the brown and black carpet, the paintings on the walls, but nothing else.

No heavy breather, no evil creature, nothing.

"Don't mess with me," I told the empty air. "I'm serious."

No answer. My feet started moving again, and I had a strong impulse to run like hell.

My fear pissed me off. I strode onward through the hall to room 2384, my ball of magic following me, and slammed my keycard through the slot.

"Room service," I shouted as I stormed inside. "You ordered a bottle of stop-doing-that-shit-in-my-hotel."

A woman screamed. A man said, "What the fuck?" Another woman cried out, and I heard more curses.

I halted, my magic light dying into a fizzle. I took in the foursome on the bed, the chalk marks on the walls and the herbs on the floor, the candles burning around the beds in total violation of our fire code, and the woman who sat in a chair on the other side of the room, candles on the table next to her.

"You gotta be kidding me," I said.

"How dare you interrupt our sacred ritual?" the woman in the chair demanded.

She was the only one dressed, and she wore a terrycloth robe that came complimentary with the room.

"Sacred?" I asked, hands on hips. "Is that what you kids are calling it these days?"

They were practicing Tantric. The theory was that an orgasm produced a lot of energy, which could be used to do some nifty magic. If you held it off and built up the release, the explosion of that energy could be harnessed and used to work spells. Two people might do it together, or several couples or triples or whatever could feed that power into one person who collected it and worked the magic.

"Are they having sex?" came an eager voice from my purse. "Let me see. *Please.*"

No one in the room reacted as though they could hear the mirror. Which meant they were ordinary humans, or low-level mages at best.

The woman in the chair rose to her feet, her frizzy hair tumbling across her shoulders. "Nonbeliever!" she said imperiously. "You have destroyed our work."

I glanced at the four on the bed, none of them wearing a stitch. They stared back at me in dismay and growing anger. "I wouldn't say that," I said. "I can see you're having a good time, but you're upsetting the staff."

The head woman sneered. "This is a holy place. Only those of our brethren are chosen to perform the rites. It is cleansing magic that will bring benefit to everyone in this hotel. You toy with what you do not know."

"Oh, please. Talking in pseudo-medieval phrases doesn't make anything sacred. My sister and her boyfriend do Tantric all the time. They strengthen their wards and protection spells with it, which, trust me, is stuff I don't want to know about. Thank the gods I don't have to watch."

"You understand nothing," their leader said. She fumbled with the knot of her robe, and I took an alarmed step back. Please say she wasn't about to flash me. "Our magic will change everything."

"Honey, you haven't conjured enough to light a candle." I gestured, and all the candle flames in the room leapt high, and then extinguished themselves. "Now wrap it up, take cold showers, and settle down. Don't make me send security to throw you out. That would be so embarrassing."

They glared at me through the smoke, the room smelling of warm wax and the acrid odor of burnt candlewicks.

The woman raised her hands from her robe's belt, to my relief, and began to chant. I didn't understand a word—the language could be Latin, could be Celtic, could be made up. I knew English and Apache, a smattering of Spanish, and a few words in Diné that Grandmother Begay muttered at me.

"For real magic, you don't need words," I said. "Unless you're feeling whimsical. Like *Presto*." I squashed the candles beside her chair into wide pools of wax. "And *Abracadabra*." Her chair flew up to the ceiling.

"And now for my big finish," I went on. The couples on the beds had untangled themselves and were watching me, openmouthed, one of them modest enough to cover herself with a sheet. The head witch stared at me in sudden and abject fear.

I raised my hands. Before I could speak or whirl my Beneath magic around the room and scare the crap out of them, all the lights went out.

I mean *all* the lights, including the little emergency ones that were supposed to come on as backup. Out the window, I saw glittering electronic signs marching down the Strip, but all lights in and around the C hotel had been extinguished.

"What the fuck is that?" one of the men cried. He was on his feet, naked body silhouetted against the Strip's glare, pointing shakily out the window into the darkness.

That was a whirling mass of something I couldn't identify, heading straight for us.

It hit the hotel with an enormous blow, the walls bowing inward, and then dirt, mud, and tree roots smashed through the windows, like a hurricane composed of the Earth itself, intent on burying its children.

CHAPTER EIGHTEEN

Gabrielle

I stood for a frozen moment while clumps of soil and shards of glass littered the floor. Then the wind caught up the glass and whirled it into the deadly mix.

"Out!" I yelled at the witches. "Into the hallway."

"No!" Their leader cried. "She's a dark mage! She's trying to kill us!"

"For fuck's sake." I flung open the door and raced out.

The darkness in the corridor was even more solid. The hotel swayed from the attack, which smelled of the bowels of the Earth.

"Let me see!" the mirror shrieked. "I'm scared! Oh, honey, I'm so scared!"

I yanked the mirror from my purse at the same time I sent up a flare of Beneath magic.

The light barely made a dent in the gloom, like a candle lantern in very dense fog. But I had to get through, had to find Colby, or Chandra, or call Nash—someone to help me.

"I'm not afraid of the dark!" I shouted at it. "The dark is afraid of *me!*"

A huge form came out of the blackness, towering over me like hell itself, reaching a claw to rake me open. I screamed.

The claw landed on my arm and resolved into a hand, the bulk into the shape of a large man.

"Colby!" I nearly sobbed. "*Shit.* Don't *do* that."

He jerked me close, wrapping solid arms around me, his strength cutting through my panic. One swift, hard kiss, and he pulled away.

"What the hell?" he demanded.

For answer, the building shuddered again, accompanied by the sound of windows breaking, bricks popping, people screaming. Colby swung around in the dim light of my smothered magic, and smashed his hand to the fire alarm.

Nothing happened. "Great!" I yelled.

Regardless, people began pouring out of doorways in various stages of undress. I tried to light the corridor as I herded them toward the fire exit, but my flare of magic wouldn't expand.

A stream of dragon fire poured along the ceiling, cutting through the darkness and filling the hall with brilliant red-orange light. Now the guests screamed and dropped, thinking the building was on fire.

Whatever. As long as they got out.

I ran back into the Tantric witches' room, they having finally come to their senses and vacated. Damp dirt and roots continued to stream in through the windows. Dodging the flying glass, I brought up the hardest magic I had and threw it at the mess.

The roots drew back as though from a sudden blast of herbicide, but they quickly regrouped and came at me, more determined than before.

Colby grabbed me around the waist and yanked me away, then slammed the rain of roots and dirt with fire. I heard an unholy shriek, and the roots retreated out the window.

"You can fight it," I exclaimed to Colby in surprise. "Why can't I?"

"Not the time for pondering." Colby's hands held flame, his face and arms covered with dirt and sweat. Another deluge of mud and roots poured in through the window, and Colby sent ball after ball of fire at it.

The roots withdrew, but more dirt pounded on every wall of the hotel. I heard screaming in the street, the wail of sirens, the babble of scared voices elsewhere in the hotel.

"This is *not* going to look good on my quarterly review," I growled, ducking out of the room.

The darkness in the corridor was heavy. Colby's fire dampened as soon as the emergency exit door thudded shut a final time, the hall now empty of people. My breath fogged in the air, eerie in the light of Colby's last flames.

Colby drew ragged breaths. "I need space."

I knew what he meant. "This way." I led him at a run in the opposite direction from the fire exit, gritting my teeth against the icy blackness. Colby's small ball of fire helped but couldn't banish the darkness entirely.

One of the hall's niches held a door marked *Employees Only*. My keycard opened it, and I led Colby up a cement staircase, which shook and cracked as we ascended.

At the top was a steel door, solid and locked. Again, my universal keycard came in handy, and we stepped out onto the hotel's roof garden.

Las Vegas spread around us. The *C* wasn't tall, but it stood relatively alone, positioned on a manmade rise, so I could look straight down the Strip.

I saw the bright lights of Caesar's Palace, the fountains of the Bellagio beyond it, the fake Eiffel tower of Paris Las Vegas, the giant high rises of the City Center behind the Bellagio, and far in the distance, the laser show from the Luxor.

Nothing wrong with *their* lights. Only the *C*, set apart and elegant, was being attacked, with a rain of rocks, mud, dirt, and roots that seemed to come from utter blackness. The trees in tubs, flowers in boxes around a walkway swayed and shuddered, as though they wanted to join the fun.

Colby scooped me close and kissed me again, then he sent me a grin and ran across the roof. Darkness shrouded him and then burst away as he spread the wide wings of his dragon.

He took off, a streak of red against the night. Black dust and roots rose around him, and Colby sent a line of fire straight at them.

The wall of dirt parted for him, but poured at me, the indestructible Gabrielle, battering me until I fell to my knees.

The previous attack had crushed me with magic, like a mind battle. This was the physical manifestation of whatever strange entity I'd fought before, and I was just as helpless against it. I swiped ineffectually at the earth and tree roots around me, my Beneath magic like a crackle of nothing.

A sting bit my hand, and I jumped, remembering that I clutched the mirror. I raised my head, barely able to see with all the dust in my eyes, and directed my words to its glimmer.

"Janet!" I called. "Can you hear me? I need dragons! Colby can't do this alone."

"Gabrielle?" Janet's voice came to me like the tinny sound from an AM radio. I saw her reflection jaggedly—she must be looking into the original mirror, the one with a hole in the middle and spiderweb cracks radiating to its frame.

In a half crouch, I retreated to the door of the hotel, batting away rocks that came at me, my hands bloody. I wanted to weep.

"Colby's fighting it," I said, my voice dry. "But he can only do so much."

The shard in my hand trembled. "Yeah, Janet, babes, this is *scary*. Send in the dragons."

Mick's face appeared next to Janet's. His curly hair was wilder than usual, as though he was starting to go dragon right there. "Hang tight, Gabrielle. We're coming."

The shard went dark. I felt slightly better, but it could be hours before the dragons arrived. Even as fast as they flew, they had to cross miles of open desert.

I could be dead by then, Colby along with me.

I climbed to my feet, wiping water and dirt out of my face, peering around to locate Colby. I heard his bellows, saw flames cutting across the monster of a dust storm, but wind, dust, gravel, and more roots obscured him.

The door behind me burst open. Nash ran out onto the roof, Maya after him. Nash took one look at the storm, seized me, and pushed me at the door and Maya.

"Gabrielle, get in here," Maya yelled from the doorway as I evaded Nash and turned to keep Colby in sight.

Nash strode past me to the edge of the roof and spread his arms.

He was trying to absorb the spell. I watched him waver as the magic streamed into him, he closing his fists and bunching his shoulders against the deluge.

Boulders manifested from the whirling madness and dove at him, real rocks that could crush him. Magic couldn't hurt Nash, but he could be beaten down physically.

Maya screamed. She shot toward him, ducking and dodging across the roof. I headed for them both, but balls of dirt and mud that missed Maya slammed into me. I stumbled and fell, splattered with slimy black ooze.

"You bastard!" I yelled at the storm as I climbed to my feet. "This is a new outfit!"

A rock came at me. I tried to deflect it with Beneath magic, which didn't work, and the rock smacked into my palm, making it bleed.

Maya had hold of Nash, who was being pummeled by the storm. I managed to reach them and hauled up Nash. He glared at us, but didn't argue as Maya and I towed him to the door. Maya rushed inside with him, but I turned back, the wind whipping my long hair around me.

Colby screeched as he flew past, his fire dancing. Boulders and roots pummeled him, knocking him back and forth, tearing at his wings. He snarled and flamed, swirling to fight on.

But how could he fight a storm of the Earth itself? How could any of us, even Janet?

I peered out across the city, longing to see the dragons manifest—the black and red terrifying bulk of Mick, the midnight darkness of Drake, the orange and red beast I'd sensed in Titus.

Dust, rocks, and snakes of roots was all I could see. Too bad I'd sent all those demons home, I thought. They'd be a great help right now.

Then again …

An image of the rubble outside the arena came to me, the great hole Janet and I had dug from the casino down, down, down to the demon worlds beyond. I laughed. I might not have the power to fight the storm directly, but I was still a Beneath-goddess.

I gazed along the Strip, past the rows of glittering lights to the hotel where Janet, Maya, and I had stayed—I'd tagged along like an annoying little sister. Janet and Maya hadn't wanted me there, and I'd known it.

But good thing I'd come along, right? Or Mick would still be there in the arena fighting for his life, maybe dead by now.

How long would it take me to get down the street? Even with Amos driving?

Too long. I reached toward the building with my senses, hoping I could, from this far away, blast open the hole with my magic and summon the demons to me.

Of course I couldn't. I had a lot of magic, but I couldn't be in two places at once, and if I tried to open a vortex to Beneath here, it might tear apart the hotel I was trying to save.

If I could even do it. Opening a way was difficult, and I'd needed Janet's help to succeed—best to start with a way already partially unlocked.

Lights wavered beyond the storm, beyond my reach, mocking me.

Lights.

I held up the magic mirror. "Hey, can you bounce light all the way to the hotel where Mick was fighting? Maybe use the mirrors there? Help me blast open my hole to hell?"

"Can I?" The mirror snorted. "The question is *will* I? Say the magic word, sugar."

"*What?*" I shook it. "What the hell are you talking about? What magic word?"

"You know. *The* magic word. The P-word."

"You mean *Piss off?*" I growled. "That's two words. Just do it."

"Aw don't be like that. Say *please.*"

"Oh, for the gods' sake. *Please!*" I yelled. "Hurry up. Colby can't last forever." A rock hit me on the cheek, and blood spattered the mirror. "Ow! I can't either."

"Now don't get all agitated. I can't concentrate if you're upset."

Another rock sent me to my knees. "Come on," I pleaded.

"Don't worry, honey," the mirror said, suddenly all business. "I got you."

A beam shot from it, eye-killing light in the darkness, but the mirror didn't generate the light—it reflected it.

The mirror reached through the gritty sand for the flashing sign of the next hotel over, and then grabbed a beam from the next one and the next one, creating a series of arcs all the way down the street.

I didn't know whether the humans below could see the light, but my curiosity about that was in the back of my mind. Let them think it part of a Vegas show.

I held up the shard and piggybacked a snake of Beneath magic along the reflections, picking up electric bulbs, the digital flashes, the old-fashioned neon and brand new LEDs, infusing the beams with my magic.

Light, if I remembered from my science classes in high school, was a stream of photons that moved at a speed nothing could surpass. I'd always thought it cool that time would slow for you if you approached the speed of light, but only for you, while the rest of the universe continued at its normal pace. When you returned from your light-speed journey, everyone you knew would be dead, but your age wouldn't have changed all that much. I had tried to figure out how I could make that real and so escape my dad and my misery of a life.

I don't know if photon-infused magic worked any better than my power on its own, but lights flared as the mirror bounced it past them, illuminating the sky in a warping dance. The mirror sent my magic in jumps down the street, heading for the hotel and the rubble-filled hole in its floor.

"Hey, my friends," I said as the light drilled down past the debris to swirl to life the vortex Janet and I had created. "I need a little help. Come out and play?"

If Janet knew what I intended, she'd stop me. Colby turned his great dragon head and winged toward me, no doubt to do the same. Nash came out of the hotel again, running at me to—guess what? Stop me. I whirled from both of them, and Colby had to sail on past, fighting the renewed pounding of dirt and rocks.

I didn't dare let myself dance on the air as I liked to when I was working hard magic, because I couldn't trust the wind in this storm. Keeping my feet solidly on the rooftop, I called the creatures of hell to rise and do my bidding.

They came. Flying creatures that resembled dragons but weren't, gruesome skeletal beings, ethereal beasts with human faces twisted into terrifying screams, and other hell-monsters flew up out of the vortex and streamed down the street to where I waited, my arms outstretched. They swirled around the rooftop, shrieking in the foul wind.

They were obeying me, their summoner, but I knew that if I lost control they'd dive at me and devour me. Their gratitude for releasing them from death in the arena only went so far.

I didn't worry about losing control though—I wasn't stupid enough to summon any demons I couldn't handle.

"Fly, my pretties," I cried, spinning in a circle. "Stop that bad storm and send it home."

How they would, I wasn't sure. The storm was a manifestation of power, not the actual entity that powered it. We were fighting a spell, not a person.

Colby winged past me, his eyes filled with fiery rage. He rolled from the path of a glowing white demon and spewed fire directly into the wind.

I watched the fire spin into a swirl that flew into the heart of the storm like a javelin. "Nice one!" I shouted at him.

My demons fought with their own kind of weapons— acid, streams of dark magic, brute strength. They kicked rocks and roots away from me, formed a protective circle around me. The storm raged, building, trying to beat me down.

Pretending I wasn't terrified, I laughed as the storm increased its fury. It might squelch my unconquerable Beneath magic, but the beings I'd summoned to do my bidding, many of them from Earth-magic hells themselves, could fight for me.

The storm whirled into a black tornado, obscuring the sky, the rest of the city, Colby. He screeched and flapped away from the hotel, his cries growing fainter.

Nash headed for me, determination in his eyes. He was going to try to pull me to shelter.

"No!" I screamed at him. "You'll kill me!"

He hesitated, working through the logic of my plea. If he drained my magic, I'd lose control of the creatures, and we'd all be demon fodder.

Nash figured it out and circled around me, but he faced into the heart of the storm as he had before—I guess he liked boulders crashing at him. Maya, wisely, stayed inside and looked out the window in the door, hands cupped around her face.

Rocks bashed at Nash, but I saw the darkness of the storm enter him and be snuffed out, little pieces of it at a time. He was brave—I gave him that. And powerful. No wonder my mother had wanted to make a child from him.

I was tiring, even my stamina waning. The dragons needed to get here soon, or I'd be a puddle of steaming goo.

Would Janet miss me when I was gone? Or breathe a sigh of relief?

A large rock smacked me in the head and I crashed to the rooftop. I tasted blood, felt the sting of scraped flesh on my hands and face. The mirror spun out of my grip and landed facedown on gritty cement.

My magic flickered, faltered. *Shit.* Well, I'd tried.

I heard wings, then my body was jerked from the roof. I was too tired to fight, and dangled helplessly in the claw closed around me.

The talon was warm with life, not cold with demon death. I patted it, the claw black as soot on an equally silken black leg.

"Drake," I said tiredly. "Nice to see you."

CHAPTER NINETEEN

Gabrielle

The battle wasn't over. Drake had lifted me to safety, but both demons and the storm swirled around *him*.

Drake winged high, rolled, dove, and winged again until I was dizzy. *Dragon flight. A delight of motion sickness.*

The demons respected Drake's strength and fire and gave him a wide berth. They continued to kick at the storm, having fun, but I didn't know how long this could last. The entity controlling it might have vast stores of power, and we were only so strong.

Colby passed us, his fire bellowing. Whether he saw me in Drake's talon or not, I couldn't tell. He kept fighting, sweet guy. He could have run for it, but no, he stayed and did what he could.

The colossus of orange and black must be Titus. He was bigger even than Mick, and flame roared out from him, exploding rocks from the sky.

At Drake's next pass, I saw Grandmother Begay totter out

onto the roof. She supported herself with her polished walking stick made from strong cottonwood, its turquoise-studded handle shimmering with magic.

Maya hadn't held her back, but then, no one stopped Ruby Begay when she decided on a course of action. Beside her was Chandra, her red, blue, and gold shirt and matching scarf a fusion of color in the dark sky.

Grandmother planted her walking stick in front of her and threw back her head, the threads of gray in her black hair moving in the wind. Superimposed upon her was the figure of a feathery crow with a gleaming dark beak and a bad-tempered glitter in its eyes.

I knew Grandmother Begay could take the form of a crow, or project herself into one—I was never sure which—though I'd never caught her at the transformation.

But maybe there wasn't a shift. Maybe she *was* the Crow, and could become it whenever she wished, or maybe Crow became her. Explained why I, with my super-powerful goddess powers, didn't argue when she told me to take out the trash.

Grandmother rested both hands on her cane and began to sing. I didn't know the language of the words, but I *understood* them.

Her voice rose, wavering syllables calling to the Earth beneath us and the gods that inhabited it—the gods of places and sky and storm. She told them to gather, to calm the beast within the Earth, to appease the spirit that whirled in rage.

Chandra stood next to her, arms at her sides, her body swaying with Grandmother's song. Her mouth moved, as though she chanted along or perhaps spoke an incantation of her own.

Looking at Chandra through the magic-infused haze, I

saw another figure superimposed on her, one that made my
heart stop.

Couldn't be. Could. Not. Be.

I must be mistaken. Holy crap, I *had* to be. Fear gripped
me so hard I nearly lost my hold on what power I had left.

Grandmother continued to sing. The storm softened. Not
perceptibly at first, but then I noticed the wind had receded a
bit, fewer rocks smacking against Drake.

Grandmother's song changed, her voice stretching out
the words, beautiful tones like crystal in the night.

She was calling the Earth entity itself, invoking the gods
to bring it forth to answer for its deeds. I shook my head, as
though she could see me—not that she'd take my advice if
she did.

"No," I said, my hoarse words lost to the wind. "Too
dangerous."

The wind groaned, and in its note, I thought I heard
words.

Give me a vessel.

Near Grandmother's feet, the mirror flipped over,
reflecting a beam so bright I had to slam my eyes shut.

I heard the mirror's cry above the wind. "No!"

Give me a vessel.

"Screw you!" The mirror shouted. "I ain't no one's vessel,
honey."

I opened my eyes as it rose an inch from the roof,
shook until it rippled, and then it shattered into powder.
Grit tinkled to the rooftop, and the mirror's voice went
silent.

I beat on Drake's talon. "Down! Drake, put me down!"

He was busy fighting and didn't hear me. I clenched
Drake's claws as he did a barrel roll and flamed the spot
where the wind seemed to be coming from. I heard my

screams, felt my world spinning, my stomach rising into my mouth. Goddess, I so did not want to barf.

The wind slowed. Drake let out a dragon screech and dove for the rooftop. He winged in fast, and when I was five feet off the ground, he dropped me.

I landed on my ass, my skirt flying up to reveal my silky black underwear.

Darkness formed, and then Drake as human spun out of it, his midnight hair flying. He jerked and balled his hands to fists, as though he wrestled something I couldn't see.

Colby touched down, already forming the inky blackness for his change before he landed. Colby as human broke free of it and sprinted toward me just as Drake reached me and locked his hands around my throat.

Why did everyone try to strangle me? First the slayer, now Drake. I shot Beneath magic into Drake's hands and tore myself from him.

"What the hell is wrong with you?" I yelled as I scrambled to my feet.

"This vessel," Drake said—or at least his mouth did. Drake continued to jerk as though he fought, his eyes smoldering in fury. "Is unsatisfactory ... *Unsatisfactory.* Huh. What an understatement."

I stared. The voice was Drake's, but the words were never ones he'd speak, not in that sarcastic tone. Drake needed a video class to understand most jokes.

"Who are you?" I asked, my breath hurting.

"The Abomination speaks. I don't like that."

Drake started for me again, but Colby jumped in front of Drake and punched him on the jaw.

Drake spun, moving with the hit, and when he straightened, he shook his head, his fists opening. Colby watched him, ready to hit him again, but Drake held up his hands.

"It is gone."

"Gone where?" I asked in alarm.

Grandmother quickly raised her cane as though ready to ward off an attack. "I am no one's vessel," she said crisply to the air in front of her.

She grunted and jerked sideways, as though someone had hit her, and Chandra caught her, her dark eyes wide.

The door to the hotel was thrust open, and Cornelius exited, followed by a worried Maya. Cornelius wore his elegant suit, a diamond stickpin glittering on his lapel.

"My dear," he said to me in distress. "Are you all right?"

He took two more steps, and then his voice ... *changed.*

"Ah," Cornelius said, straightening. "*This* is a good vessel." He looked around, his eyes as cold as his diamond pin. "Dragons are much too hard to control."

Grandmother and Chandra moved to me as I faced him.

"Just who the hell *are* you?" I demanded.

My skin crawled as Cornelius fixed his gaze on me. The cruelty in his eyes was not his, and the indifferent drawl was alien to him.

"Every time I rise, I find the world changed, and always in a bad way. This time is the worst yet. I haven't fully manifested, but when I do, I will finish you all. I've tried fire and flood, even fucking asteroids, and still hell beings crawl on the Earth and pollute it. If you go back where you belong, I might spare the rest of the living things this time."

He looked up at the demons I'd called. They fluttered and spun about the rooftop, eager to destroy anything I pointed them at.

But as soon as Cornelius's focus landed on them, the demons turned tail and fled—the whole pack of them.

They raced out into the night, some streaming back down the Strip to the vortex I'd opened, some disappearing into the empty desert beyond the city. They flapped and tumbled, climbed and flew as though they couldn't get away from him fast enough.

Chandra moved a few inches closer to me, her warmth incongruous to the magical thing I'd spied inside her. Drake, Colby, and Titus drew together, three very hot men with nothing on their minds but tearing Cornelius apart.

Grandmother Begay stepped in front of Cornelius and tapped the ground with her walking stick.

"My granddaughter asked you a question. Who are you?"

"I am ... *everything.*"

His reply drifted past me, because it couldn't shake me more than Ruby Begay calling me her granddaughter.

I wasn't her granddaughter—I wasn't related to her at all. The term meant acceptance, that I was family, and even, on some level, it meant affection. A lump rose in my throat.

Grandmother wasn't finished. "You are arrogant," she said to the thing inside Cornelius. "That will harm you in the end."

"Doesn't matter, old woman. You won't be here. Because you have taken abominations under your care, you will suffer their fate." He swept a look over Colby, Drake, and Titus, and his lip curled in disgust. "I believe I will start all over again. I was thinking storms, but maybe lava this time. That way I can eliminate the dragons as well—they have become such pains in my ass."

Colby started forward, but I grabbed him. "Don't hurt him," I babbled to Colby. "Cornelius is in there. Not his fault."

"Cornelius is, indeed," the entity said. "I think I'll kill him —just to upset you."

He lifted his own, neat hands to his throat.

Nash tackled him. Both men hit the rooftop, Nash the trained army officer performing a perfect takedown.

Cornelius's head smacked the ground with an audible *thunk*. He struggled, but to no avail. Nash was in great shape —I'd seen his house, which was more or less a gym with a bed in it.

The entity grunted. "Well, shit. What the fuck are *you?*"

I punched the air. "Go, Nash! Let him suck on your *un*-power."

"Oh, you total bastard." the entity growled, then it gasped, and Cornelius's eyes went blank.

Nash ceased struggling, but held Cornelius down, wary.

Around us the storm ceased. The mud, rocks, boulders, and roots that had been part of it pelted down around us, no longer animate, and dust flooded the rooftop.

Cornelius's eyes cleared, and he coughed.

I rushed to him. "Get off him, Nash." I knelt and touched Cornelius's face. "Are you all right?"

Nash gave Cornelius a last measuring look then helped the man to his feet. Cornelius reached down for me, and once I stood next to him, he brushed off his suit with trembling hands.

"I appear to be fine," he said. "If a trifle bruised. Thank you, sir, for your timely intervention."

"What happened?" Maya wrapped her fingers around Nash's arm as Nash gave Cornelius a nod of acknowledgment. "Did you, you know ..." She made a pulling motion. "Negate him?"

"I don't think so," Nash answered. "I felt him try to go into me then sort of—get stuck. Then he—*it*—disappeared. Gone."

Drake rubbed his arms. "I too no longer feel his presence. It is interesting—the dragon slayer also said something about being a vessel. Perhaps it is the only way the Earth entity can articulate what it needs to."

Cornelius looked Drake up and down, his brows raised, then gave Colby and Titus the same appraisal. "Should I ask why you and your friends are on the roof unclothed?" he asked Colby.

Colby grinned. "Let's just say the storm blew our socks off. Me and Drakey weren't up here making passionate love or anything. He's not my type. Titus, well, he was just passing by."

Drake looked affronted, as usual when Colby talked about ... well, anything. Titus only folded his arms and looked as formidable as a naked man could. He had tatts similar to Drake's, wings that filled his back and flowed over his ass to his thighs.

I ignored them to walk to Chandra, who hadn't moved during this exchange. She regarded me calmly, her head up, knowing what I'd seen.

"You," I snarled, putting all the anger I'd experienced in my entire crazy life into the word. "I *saw* you. Liar! Pretending to be my friend and *lying* to me, you total bitch."

"Gabrielle," Grandmother Begay rebuked me in a shocked voice.

I didn't look at her. My focus was on Chandra, and the roiling betrayal inside me.

"I know what I saw," I went on. "Don't tell me you didn't notice, Ruby. She's the Beneath goddess. She's my *mother.*"

"No," Chandra said, the only word she could get out before I lunged for her, ready to rip out her throat.

CHAPTER TWENTY

Gabrielle

A blast of Beneath magic more powerful than any I'd ever felt lifted me from my feet and blew me backward to the edge of the roof.

Colby started for me, but before I could hurtle over the wall to the crowds below, another wave of magic caught me and brought me back, setting me gently on my feet.

I staggered, fighting for balance, and found Chandra in front of me, her hands on her hips.

"Now Gabrielle," she said. "Is that any way to behave to your auntie?"

I blinked at her, unsteady. I tasted blood on my lips, and a warm desert wind blew my long hair into my face. I brushed it impatiently away.

"What do you mean *auntie?*" My voice was hoarse, words clogging my throat. "What are you talking about? You're *her.* The goddess."

"I am *a* goddess," Chandra said. "Sister to the one who

caused you to be born. I knew my sister would never amount to much, but she did produce a beautiful child."

"My mother didn't have any sisters," I said, dazed, but the truth was, I had no idea. It's not like I ever had a heart-to-heart with Mommy Dearest. She hadn't wanted anything to do with me.

"She has many," Chandra said. "Brothers too."

I couldn't catch my breath. Colby and Drake moved to stand on either side of me like bookends, regarding Chandra in a wall of dragon fury.

Grandmother clenched her walking stick, her face red with anger. Apparently she hadn't known either. Chandra had been able to mask her true self well. I had to wonder why she'd chosen to reveal her identity now.

"Why were you so *nice* to me?" I demanded. "You sat beside my bed, were kind and caring. Why, so I'd trust you? So you could get close to me and kill me more easily? Or grab me and take me to *her*?"

Chandra regarded me with her night-dark eyes. "No, Gabrielle. If I had wanted you to die, I would have let the dragon slayer kill you in the pool. He was no match for me."

She didn't boast—she simply stated a fact.

"*You* pulled me out?" I dimly remembered strong hands yanking me upward while I fell unconscious. "I thought that was Colby."

"No," Colby said. "You were gone by the time I reached the pool. She must have vanished you, leaving the dragon slayer barely alive. Probably why Drake was able to bind him."

Chandra kept her gaze on me. "I did fight you away from that awful slayer, and the woman from Beneath is indeed my sister. I came to America to find her daughters, my nieces, and keep them safe from her."

"But — you're nothing alike. She's ..."

"Pale as snow? Or a ghost? She chose to be colorless, pretending she was pure. I chose to live in this world, in Nigeria, with a good family, and so I took their coloring."

I waved my hands. "Let me understand this. You're my *aunt*? How is that even possible?"

"What is possible on the Earth and what is possible in the world Beneath are different things."

"*Regardless*," Grandmother said in a hard voice. "You should have told us. Go back to the hell you came from." She raised her walking stick, the turquoise glowing in the moon-light. Power danced in her, the magic of the Crow.

"I came to help," Chandra said impatiently. "Gabrielle, you are special. You prove it every moment of every day. I can help you—teach you—"

"*I* am teaching her," Grandmother Begay interrupted. "I am teaching her how to control what is inside her, how *not* to cause destruction to everyone around her."

"Stifling her," Chandra said, scowling. "She believes that she is evil, that she must constantly be afraid of her power, her self."

"Because the magic of her mother flows unchecked in her," Grandmother said emphatically.

"The magic, yes, but her *mother* does not. I ought to know. Where is the evil in this little one? Where?"

Both stared at me until I felt like a smudge of bacteria in a Petri dish.

Grandmother answered, "She once resurrected a man who went on a killing rampage."

"Undead Jim," Maya said from Cornelius's side. "Ugh. He was awful."

True, I had found the guy dead and tried to bring him back to life. He'd gotten away from me and out of control, wreaking havoc and holding Maya hostage in her house until Janet chased him off.

Chandra pinned me with a stare. "And why did you create this zombie?"

I shrugged, my heart pounding. "I felt bad for him. I was trying to help him."

"You see?" Chandra turned on Grandmother in triumph. "She had goodness in her heart. She is simply untrained."

"She had *arrogance* in her heart, the idea that she could create life and not pay any sort of price."

"Why should she pay a price for trying to be kind?" Chandra demanded. "There is a difference between being misguided and being monstrous."

"A very fine line," Grandmother said sternly. "One you seem to be crossing. You leave Gabrielle alone."

"*You* leave her alone, old woman. You have her head twisted around so far that she doesn't know up from down."

"Don't call me an old woman. You are far older than I am, if you are telling the truth. No goddess from Beneath can be trusted. You stay away from Gabrielle."

"And leave her in your care?" Chandra asked, incredulous. "She will wither and die."

"Would *you* let her destroy the world to prove she can run about unchecked? You persuaded *this* man to be so foolish as to give her a job." Grandmother waved an imperious hand at Cornelius.

"Which she can do just fine. I think it's good training for her."

"*You* think!" Grandmother's voice rose to the volume that sent her grandnieces and neighbors scuttling for cover. Only her son didn't run—but he did walk, slowly and deliberately, out to check on his sheep when she yelled like this. "What gives you the right to think? I agree with the entity when he calls you an abomination."

"Abomination? Destroying a young woman by making her think she deserves to be destroyed is an abomination!"

The two women were nearly nose to nose. Grandmother's black eyes flashed. "You leave my granddaughter alone."

"Your *granddaughter?*" Chandra asked with a laugh. "She isn't yours. She's *my* niece. You don't deserve to call her *granddaughter,* feathered crone—"

"She is my *family.* Hell goddesses don't know the meaning of the word—"

"Stop!" I rose on a wave of magic, light crackling around me with my rage. "Both of you, stop it!"

Chandra and Grandmother Begay looked around at me, as though they'd forgotten my presence.

I had nothing to say. My words got tangled up, the English I'd learned to speak around age five vanishing. I could only think in Apache, and no one on this rooftop knew that language, except maybe Chandra. And then only because she was related to my mother and knew everything that went on in my head.

I screamed in frustration. All my life I'd been pushed and pulled, tugged between everyone I'd met—my parents who hadn't wanted me, my teachers who hadn't known what to do with me, Janet, my real mother, Mick who admonished me, Grandmother Begay, and now Chandra.

Chandra hadn't denied Grandmother Begay's accusation that she had persuaded Cornelius to hire me. I think that stung the most, which was stupid—I should be afraid of Chandra and fear that she'd come to take me back to my mother. But I'd believed Cornelius had seen something in me, trusted me.

He'd messed with me too.

I came down to the rooftop with a thump, gravel sliding under my feet. My shoes pinched and my dress chafed. I suddenly hated my new clothes, and all those who'd given them to me.

I swung around and walked away. I heard Colby start after me but then halt.

"Where are you going?" Grandmother Begay called. "You stop right there, Gabrielle Massey."

"Gabrielle," Chandra tried.

I kept marching, my throat aching, my eyes stinging. Nash only watched me, either understanding or not caring that I was leaving. *Good riddance*, he must think.

Cornelius did try to step in front of me. "My dear."

"Leave her alone." My lone defender was Maya, who shook her head at Cornelius. I'd horned in on her vacation and ruined it, and she didn't like me at all, but she regarded me with understanding.

I was too brittle even to give Maya a nod of thanks. I walked into the lovely hotel and down the stairs, emerging into the hall ruined by the dirt storm, furniture overturned from the guests who'd fled.

I moved unimpeded to the elevator, which slid open to my spark of magic—it would have ruined my exit to have to wait for it.

The hotel's electricity had come back on. I rode the elevator down to the ground floor, the casino looking odd in its emptiness. A few security guards roamed through to check out the floor, and they didn't impede me from walking out.

Guests huddled in clumps outside the hotel, beginning to laugh and joke in relief. I saw the ladies I'd met in the bathroom the first night. They stood together, their backs a little straighter as they waited to be let back into the hotel.

I noticed their husbands were satisfyingly attentive to them.

Another good deed I'd done.

Or maybe I'd done it because I was arrogant and evil. Who knew?

"Gabrielle!"

Amos came through the crowd to me, a worried look on his face. "You all right? I didn't see you out here, and I was afraid ..."

I willed English to return to my tongue. "Your car here?"

"Yeah, I parked down the block. Had to clear out for fire trucks and stuff. You need to go somewhere?"

I nodded and he led me without question to his limo, opening the door for me as though I wasn't all scratched up and bloody.

"Where to?" he asked from the front as he started up.

"Anywhere. I don't care."

Amos gave me a salute and put the car in gear. He pulled smoothly away from the curb, and I left the crowds, flashing lights of emergency vehicles, Grandmother and Chandra, and my new life behind.

WHEN WE REACHED THE FAR SOUTHERN END OF THE STRIP AND the open space of the airport, Amos halted at a traffic light and turned to me. "Seriously, where do you want to go?"

"Magellan," I said.

There was one person in all the world who would understand, who would be as freaked out about Chandra as I was.

Amos sent me a puzzled look. "Is that in North Las Vegas?"

"In Arizona. East of Flagstaff."

His brows went up. "I'll have to call that in. Our cars have GPS trackers so we don't run off with them. I need my job, not a jail sentence."

I waved my hand. "Fine. Call it in."

He did and surprisingly got the green light to take me to Arizona. His bosses must have realized it would be one hell of a fare, which Janet would have to pay. She would, I was pretty sure.

I lay down in the backseat and let the darkness beyond the city wash over me. Amos didn't ask me to talk, didn't ask what had happened. I sensed his curiosity, but for now, he left me alone.

Colby had let me go. He'd been about to stop me, but then he, like Maya, had stood aside. He understood—not long ago he'd been stuck under a binding spell, forced to do the bidding of the Dragon Council, compelled to hurt his friends. He knew all about being cornered.

Amos had to stop for gas in Boulder City, and after that, I sat up front with him. I liked the sweet freedom of being on my own, but my heart was still leaden from all that had happened on the rooftop.

I let Amos talk—I learned about his girlfriend and his dreams for the future, which didn't involve driving other people around. But right now, he needed the money to make ends meet, to save up for a life one day. He'd get a higher-paying job, and he and his girlfriend would get married and buy a house, and things would be *better*.

I'd heard this brave optimism before, from so many people. When we got to the hotel, I'd have Cassandra do some good luck magic on Amos. He was a good guy and deserved to find happiness.

Hours later, Amos turned off the 40 to drive through Winslow, then down the highway to the Crossroads and pulled into the lot beside Barry's bar, which was full of motorcycles.

The Crossroads Hotel beyond was lit up, lights in every room. People spilled out the front door into the cool night, wandered the saloon that was still missing its outer wall, and were even camping out in the parking lot.

It was just past four in the morning, and Barry's place, by law, should have been closed hours ago. Sheriff Jones didn't put up with bars in his county breaking the rules.

Of course Sheriff Jones was in Las Vegas, and his deputies were a little more flexible. In fact, Deputy Lopez was standing outside the front door of the bar, talking to Barry.

Amos shut off the engine. "I'll go inside with you."

He said it protectively—so sweet.

"Sure. Come on." He'd be safer inside anyway.

The lobby was packed. People filled the couches and chairs, sat on the staircase. Some were bunked down in sleeping bags on the floor. Cassandra sat behind her desk, looking tired, Pamela next to her. The office door next to the desk was closed, the light off.

Did I say *people*? I meant supernaturals. I saw Changers, witches, low-grade demons, and even a few Nightwalkers in their human personas.

They were all getting along. Nervous, wary, but non-confrontational. They were more afraid of whatever had driven them there than they were of one another.

A table filled with trays of food ran the length of the wall under the stairs, a huge urn of coffee at one end. As I halted in amazement, Elena came out of the kitchen with a platter of enchiladas and set it on the table, taking away an empty.

I waded across the floor to Cassandra's desk. "What's going on?" I asked her. "Where's Janet?"

Pamela gave me a fierce look from her wolf's eyes.

"Janet's in bed. Cassandra and Mick made her go. Don't disturb her."

Yep, I was back home all right.

I addressed Cassandra again. "Do all these people think the hotel will protect them?"

Cassandra's eyes were red-rimmed with weariness. "They do. The warding here is strong, though I don't know if it will be strong enough."

"Probably not," I said. "I've fought this thing a couple times now. We're going to need a lot more collective magic, plus the dragons. I'm thinking the dragons are key. Want me to add to the wards?"

"Don't you dare even touch them," Pamela growled.

What did Cassandra see in this woman? She was always crabby.

"Pamela is right," Cassandra said. "If blunt. We want Earth magic only in the wards. The dragon slayer says the entity is provoked by Beneath magic. Even Janet had to take her magic out of them. Mick and I reworked them, with help."

Dragon help, she meant. I felt the power of Drake and Titus seeping through the building. Cassandra's magic was layered in there, as well as Elena's. All powerful, all Earth-based.

"You shouldn't be here, Gabrielle," Pamela snapped. She was obviously tired, which I guess made her crankier than ever. "You'll attract its attention. I thought you were happy with your cushy new job in Vegas."

"Pamela," Cassandra admonished her gently, but I could see from Cassandra's expression that she too worried what my presence would do.

And true, the Earth entity had attacked *me*, gleefully. Me and my pure Beneath magic.

"I'm not offended," I said to Cassandra. "Pamela can't help

being a bitch—she *is* a she-wolf after all. But you don't have to worry about me. I'll grab a change of clothes, and then I'm out of here."

"Your stuff is in the attic," Pamela said. "We needed the room."

I didn't answer. Cassandra gave me an apologetic look, but she didn't chide Pamela this time. They really didn't want me around. I was torn between not blaming them and wanting to weep.

Amos was already enjoying the buffet, Elena having invited him to taste the food. Well, he was harmless, and he'd be safe here for now, if Elena looked after him.

I moved swiftly up the stairs, not stopping until I was in the storage room beyond the third-floor office. I had to step over people in sleeping bags to get to my duffel that had been tossed into a corner.

I snatched it up and went out onto the roof, using the cover of darkness to change from my ruined black dress to jeans and a top. The early morning was brisk, so I added a light jacket before stuffing the dress into my bag.

I stood up and surveyed the land, looking east to the abandoned railroad bed and the open country beyond.

The moon had long since set, and stars coated the night. Even the lights from the hotel and Barry's bar couldn't dim the heavens tonight.

Dark skies, they were called. Truly dark, without city lights to pollute the view. The canopy of night stretched overhead, filled with stars and the planets and even the faraway fuzzy haze of nebulae.

I zipped up my jacket, stowed my duffle bag, and walked down the three flights of stairs to the ground floor. I could have floated down on magic, but Cassandra and Pamela were right—Beneath magic might draw the Earth entity, and I didn't have the strength to fight it again tonight, if I even could.

No one noticed me walk back through the lobby and out the front door. In the parking lot, Fremont Hansen, sitting cross-legged near a campfire, led a circle in off-key songs. Flora, who was a pretty good Earth-magic witch, sat next to him, holding his hand.

I kept walking, moving around the hotel, past the shed where Mick worked on his and Janet's motorcycles, past the tree where Grandmother Begay liked to perch as a crow, and up the abandoned railroad bed that lay to the east of the hotel.

I stopped once I reached the top of the bed where tracks used to lie, and gazed across the open darkness. Out there, hills, canyons, and washes broke the seemingly flat land, and vortexes lay dormant. One vortex, which led down into the world where my mother lived, was now completely buried.

The goddess was cut off, sealed in by Janet, Mick, and Nash. So they thought.

I scrambled down the far side of the railroad bed and headed for my mother's vortex.

CHAPTER TWENTY-ONE

Gabrielle

W hen I reached the wash that buried the entrance to my mother's realm, all was quiet. The wash lay silent and covered in rubble and fallen trees.

Rainwater runoff had moved the rocks and piles of tree limbs a little, but there was no vortex here. She was not coming out.

So how had Chandra?

If Chandra was telling the truth. I'd sensed the immense Beneath magic in her, one that could only come from someone as powerful as my mother, but in the heat of battle, had I seen clearly?

I should have remained at the C and questioned her, but no, I had to run and cry to Janet, who, it turned out, didn't have time for me.

I climbed upon a large, flat boulder, pulled my jacket around me, and drew my knees to my chest. A streak flashed through the black sky above me, then another and another, a mini meteor shower just for me.

A coyote wandered by. He stopped and took me in, eyes glittering, wind ruffling his tawny fur.

Coyotes aren't as afraid of humans as humans think they should be, though they rarely attack, unless they're ill and need an easy meal.

This one looked healthy. His muzzle was grizzled, his forehead broad, legs strong. He stared at me for a good long time before he sauntered to the boulder and climbed up beside me.

He gave a grunting sigh as he lay down, his fur warming my side. His tongue lolled out of his mouth, and he began to pant.

"I really am not in the mood for *you*," I said.

I lied. I liked having him next to me, cutting the chill and not haranguing me for being evil and selfish.

Aw, too bad, Coyote said directly into my head. *I thought we could get snuggly.*

"Not when you smell like that." The scent of wild animal fur was pungent.

Hazards of shifting. Fleas are another.

"Bullshit. You can smell the way you want to. And don't sit here if you have fleas."

His chuckle was warm. *You can't let her out, Gabrielle.*

I glanced at the covered-over arroyo where the vortex, awash with power, had once lain. "I didn't come here for that. I came to make sure it was closed."

Hmm. You've changed.

"Not that much. But I can learn from my mistakes, can't I?" I hunkered into myself. "Not that anyone's giving me a chance."

Are you giving them a chance to give you a chance?

"Don't get preachy on me." I scowled. "I get enough of that from Grandmother Begay."

Another chuckle. *Yeah, she can really work herself up into a tirade. Ask me how I know that. But she's a wise woman, even if she likes to have the upper hand. Always.*

"When Pete gets married, he'll move to Farmington to live with Gina and her family, and leave me alone in Many Farms—you know, with Grandmother, and Janet's aunts and all their kids who like to stop by at least twice a day." Sadness touched me. "I'll miss him."

That was the truth. Janet's father's silences could soothe me, and he was the only one on the planet who didn't berate me.

Pete Begay is a good soul, Coyote said. *Not many of those out there.*

"Janet's lucky. I wish he'd been my dad." I meant that with every ounce of my strength.

Ask him.

I shook myself out of my self-pity. "What?"

Ask Pete if he'll be your dad. He'll probably say yes.

I smiled a weak smile. "I think he's afraid of me. He's seriously looking forward to moving out."

Ask him anyway.

Coyote left it at that and fell silent.

A breeze crossed the desert, stirring the brush into a whisper. The stars dazzled us overhead. I wasn't good at recognizing constellations, either the Indian ones or the Greek ones, but the patterns were familiar.

I'd always found comfort in the stars. No matter what insanity happened on Earth, the heavens were eternal. The stars had been there, just like this, for eons before we arrived, and they'd be there long after we all were gone.

"It's so beautiful," I said softly. "The sky bowing down to

meet the desert, the mountains, the woods, the canyons. Why does it want to destroy us? The Earth?"

It doesn't, Coyote said. *An Earth elemental does, one that formed and grew with the lava and the rock. It's possessive.*

"How do we even fight something like that? There's nothing to fight." I shivered. "I hate intangible enemies. Give me something I can blast."

You'll figure that out. You and Janet. Put your heads together, and you'll come up with something.

"Oh, thanks. Real helpful. What about you? Won't you be fighting with us?"

I can't destroy it. I'm from Beneath, remember? Like you. Coyote ceased panting and gave me a long look from his golden eyes. *A storm is coming. Will you be strong enough for it?*

"I'm not a Stormwalker," I pointed out.

Does that matter?

I opened my mouth to blurt, *Well, of course it does,* but I closed it again. Coyote was hinting at something, and I'd have to think about it.

"What about Chandra?" I asked him. "Is she really who she says she is?"

Coyote looked blank. *Who's Chandra?*

I hid my start of surprise. "I thought you were the all-knowing god."

Only when I'm paying attention. Who's Chandra?

I sighed and told him. Coyote regarded me thoughtfully then crossed his paws and began to pant again. Heavily. He moved the whole boulder.

Why would she make up something like being your aunt? You saw she was from Beneath as soon as she started throwing around her power.

"Maybe she's my mother playing tricks on me?"

Nope. If your mother was running around, I'd know it. That's something I'd pay attention to. Lots of Beneath gods and goddesses are related to each other. We were created by all-powerful entities. I'm probably one of your long-lost, a-hundred-times-removed cousins. His mouth widened into a canine grin. *Kissing cousins.*

"Forget it, coyote breath."

More grinning. *Give her a chance. Like you want everyone to give you.* Coyote flopped his tongue back into his mouth. *And if she truly is evil, snuff her.*

"Sure. 'Cause that would be so easy." I let out a long breath. "What do I do, Coyote? You're a wise god. Give me some wisdom."

Wisdom. Hmm. Well, if you ask Jolene at the diner real nice, she'll have the cook put jalapeños on your burger. Tasty.

"Thanks a lot. I was thinking more like, I don't have anywhere to go. The Crossroads Hotel is Janet's. Grand-mother Begay is putting up with me at Many Farms. Chandra got me the job in Vegas, so who knows what that's about? There's no place, you know, where I *fit.*"

Aw. Coyote gave me sad eyes. *Poor little thing.*

"Don't make fun of me. No one has wanted anything to do with me since the day I was born." Tears stung me.

Yeah, that's true.

Note to self: Don't go to Coyote for comfort. He'll give you unvarnished truth.

"Why am I even talking to you?" I growled.

Because I sat down here, and you wanted to whine. I said before —does it matter?

"That they'd like to see the back of me at the Crossroads, that Pete is happy about leaving Many Farms, that Cornelius had to be talked into hiring me? You're asking me if that stuff matters?"

None of those places are yours. Don't try to take them. Acknowledge that you're accepting hospitality. Be a good guest.

I stared at him while his words sank in. "You mean, *Suck it up, Gabrielle.*"

His laughter was full-blown this time. *I always knew you were smart. One day you'll be who you were meant to be, and your family will be right there with you. I know it in my bones.*

I sighed. "I hope your bones are right." I gazed into the distance, the darkness to the east tinged with the slightest bit of gray at the horizon. "Any more helpful hints on how to fight the un-fightable?"

Silence. I turned to find myself sitting next to nothing. Coyote had vanished, taking his warmth with him.

I shivered, shoving my hands into my jacket pockets. "Aren't you even going to walk me home?" I called out. "A helpless little thing like me?"

My answer was a coyote's yipping howl, which faded quickly into the darkness.

Janet

WHEN I WOKE IN THE MORNING, NOT LONG AFTER SUNRISE, IT was to find Gabrielle sitting cross-legged at the bottom of my bed.

"Morning, Sis," she said.

I rose on my elbows, every muscle aching. "Morning. Is it any use to ask what you're doing here?"

Gabrielle, neatly dressed, her hair damp and combed as though she'd just had a shower, grinned at me, her teeth even and white in her pretty face. "Helping you save the world."

CHAPTER TWENTY-TWO

Janet

I sat up, pushing my tangled hair from my face. "Are you all right?" I demanded. "Where's Grandmother? The mirror stopped broadcasting. Colby called Mick and said you won, but that you needed some space. What is *that* about?"

"You worry a lot, Janet." Gabrielle slid off the bed, as lovely and poised as ever. "It can't be good for you. You also ask a lot of questions. Get yourself dressed and come out and talk to me. We have many things to do." There was a new strength in her eyes, a determination that had me forcing wakefulness into my body.

"Hold it." I slid out of bed in my T-shirt and underwear, stopping her from sailing out of the room. "What happened to the mirror? Why did it shut up?"

"It broke itself so it wouldn't get taken over by the Earth entity," Gabrielle said calmly. "Which *did* take over my friend, and that pisses me off." She swung away, her hair a black wave. "See you outside in ten."

Ten? How fast did she think I could move after only a few hours' sleep?

Mick was nowhere in sight. He had made me go to bed by the simple tactic of picking me up, slinging me over his shoulder, and carrying me into our bedroom.

He'd also undressed me and sent a little healing magic through me so I wanted to stay on the bed. He'd done a little bit more than that to make me relax, though I'd fallen asleep just when it was getting exciting. He'd known exactly how to play me, damn him.

But Mick had been right that I needed rest. I felt less despairing as I showered and dressed, and I definitely wanted to talk to Gabrielle.

I found her and Flora chatting to guests and making sure they were well. Elena had loaded the buffet tables with more food—was she cooking around the clock? I lifted a piece of pound cake, and for something healthy, a banana, and motioned for Gabrielle to join me outside.

"Mick's down with the dragon slayer," Gabrielle said, noticing how I glanced around for him. "That guy is danger-ous. We should toast him."

"Not until we know what he knows," I said.

"Exactly. But once this is over, if we don't stop him, he'll go back to hunting Mick and Colby and all our other dragon friends."

"One thing at a time?" I put a pleading note into the words. "Now tell me what happened and why I shouldn't be worried about Grandmother."

"Because she's the Crow, and she can take care of herself. She faced down the Earth entity like it was nothing."

I shivered, the October wind bringing a sudden chill. "I don't want Grandmother to face down anything. I want her safe at Many Farms, driving Dad crazy with her wedding planning."

Gabrielle's smile flared then faded. "She won't be safe even there if we don't stop this thing. But there's more I have to tell you."

She led me beyond the hotel toward the railroad bed. Gabrielle took a running start at it, her boots digging into the red earth as she climbed. I followed less exuberantly.

From the top of the embankment we studied the land, the sun picking out pockets that were steeply cut arroyos leading to wider canyons. Clouds gathered over the mountains to the south but the plateau was bathed in sunlight under blue sky.

Gabrielle told me a long and somewhat garbled story of carrying out her job in Las Vegas, her exploration of the arena, and the battle on top of the C last night. She ended by claiming that the woman called Chandra was in fact the sister of our mother.

I stared at her. "How the hell can that be?"

Gabrielle studied the desert and its clumps of wild grasses and gnarled trees, her expression somber. "I don't know. I ran off before I asked all the questions I should have. If she'd even answer. At that moment, I'd just wanted to talk to *you*."

She slid her hands into her back pockets. We stood side by side, wind catching our hair, two children of this land connected by a mother we feared.

We were connected by more than that, I knew. We had a common struggle, an awareness that we didn't fit into patterns our families and even our magic-wielding friends understood.

We'd begun our wary relationship with a battle that hadn't ceased after we'd halted the physical fight. We'd been circling each other ever since, Gabrielle doing one crazy thing after another, me trying to stop her and tame her.

The revelation that I had a sister had shaken me, and I was still trying to deal with it. The fact that our *mother* had a sister scared me to death.

"What does Chandra want?" I asked, hugging my chest. "To drag us back Beneath?"

"I don't think so. I've been thinking about this." Gabrielle watched a hawk leave a stunted juniper and soar across the land. "Chandra dragged me out of the pool when the dragon slayer tried to drown me. She could have killed me when I was unconscious, but she made sure I was all right instead. She told me things about myself that no one else has. I liked her." Gabrielle trailed off, her mouth turning down.

"Our mother claimed she wanted to help us too."

"But this was different—hard to explain. Chandra doesn't have the brilliant beauty our mother does, like a diamond that glitters but also cuts." When Gabrielle looked at me again, her brown eyes held more seriousness than I'd ever seen in them. "But like you said, one thing at a time. First, we have to stop this Earth entity. It will go after Grandmother and our dragons—everyone trying to protect the abominations. That's us, by the way. Plus all these people who've come to the Crossroads to hide. They aren't safe here, no matter what they think."

"I know," I said glumly. "I don't know why they believe they are."

"You have a rep." Gabrielle's grin flashed. "You and Mick. When the shit hits the fan, the weak seek the strong. Everyone knows you kick magical ass and that Mick is right there beside you. Kind of like Colby and me now."

More worry stirred. "Colby? Are you still stringing him along?"

"Don't make fun. We have a thing." Gabrielle deflated. "At least, I *think* we have a thing. I hope we do. I really like him, Janet."

"What about Drake?"

"I don't know." She sighed. "I don't know about anything right now."

"Let's stick to kicking ass," I suggested. "Neither of us is very good at relationships."

Her smile returned. "Yeah, one day when it was bored, the mirror told me all about you and Mick and your rocky start."

I flushed, my face hot. The mirror had pried my entire history out of my head and watched, the nosy shit.

Gabrielle gave me her amused look but with understanding in her eyes. "We need to learn how to defeat the Earth entity," she said, back to the matter at hand. "Best way to learn? Ask it."

"Oh, sure. How do you propose to do that?"

"It likes to speak through people. Vessels, it calls them. The best candidate to be that vessel right now is sitting in your basement." Gabrielle swung to face the hotel and held out her hand to me. "Let's go."

Janet

THE BASEMENT WAS DRY AND WARM AFTER THE COOL WIND outside. Mick's blue eyes darkened when he saw me, and the ring I always wore, turquoise and onyx, tingled with his magic.

The dragon slayer lay against the wall in his prison, still bound by the dark threads of Drake's spell. I saw Mick's magic woven into the binding as well, plus a glimmer of Titus's.

Gabrielle crouched next to the slayer, grasped his sandy brown hair, and yanked his head up. "Wakey, wakey!"

The dragon slayer swam to consciousness. He glanced at Gabrielle, his eyes widening, but he wasn't cowed.

"Killing me won't help you," he said in a cracked voice.

"I have no intention of killing you," Gabrielle answered. "You told Colby you were a vessel. So be one."

The dragon slayer gave her a faint smile. "It doesn't work that way. *He* chooses. Not me. Or maybe *she* chooses. It doesn't have a gender."

"Lucky it," I said. "Can you call it?"

"I just said—it chooses—*ow!*"

Gabrielle had slapped the back of his head. "Tell it we need to talk. Now."

"Please," Mick rumbled at the slayer. "I'll even say *pretty please* if it helps."

"Why do you want to?" the slayer asked in true curiosity. "It will kill all of you."

Gabrielle poked at the dark threads the dragons had wrought. "Not when you're bound like this. When the entity showed up for a chat in Vegas, I got the idea it couldn't do much more than talk through another's lips."

The dragon slayer looked smug. "You're wrong. You don't understand what it can do. I will be happy to see you die."

"You'll likely die along with us," Mick pointed out.

"Yep," Gabrielle said. "It said it doesn't always discriminate about which magical beings it kills."

"True," the slayer said. "But I can be happy watching you go along with me."

Gabrielle turned to me, incredulity in her eyes. "This guy's nuts. I mean totally. Trust me, I know about crazy."

"I know, but we need his information." I leaned down and looked the dragon slayer in the face. "So get in touch with your inner entity and let us worry about the consequences."

"I can't," the slayer said. "Not when I'm dragon-bound."

"I'll take care of that." Gabrielle wrapped her arms around him.

I started forward to stop her but after a second I realized she wasn't trying to break the binding. White magic snaked out of her fingers into the slayer's body as she infused him with Beneath magic.

"Oh, Earth entity," she sang. "Remember me? Gabrielle? Kicking your ass with my demons on the roof? You know I'm all about the Beneath magic. So come find me."

The dragon slayer's body jerked, Gabrielle holding him tightly. The slayer sucked in a breath then gave an anguished cry and banged his head against the wall.

Gabrielle sprang up as the dragon slayer began to thrash violently. His feet drummed the floor, and he clenched his fists until his fingernails cut into his flesh.

The binding spell didn't give. The shimmering black threads squeezed him all the more as whatever was inside the dragon slayer tried to fight them off. Bindings worked like that, growing stronger the more the bound struggled against them.

Strands of the threads reached from the slayer to Mick, silver in the darkness—the magic Mick had used to contribute to the spell.

My eyes widened when I saw those strands spark. Gabrielle noticed at the same time, and the two of us sprang at Mick to shove him away from the slayer. Gabrielle swiped a crackle of Beneath magic to sever the threads between the two men.

But too late. As the sparks died, Mick jerked away from me and rose to his full height.

"So I'm here," Mick's deep voice boomed through the space. "Talk fast, sweetheart. I'm busy getting ready to destroy you and all your kind."

CHAPTER TWENTY-THREE

Janet

Mick stood over us, his eyes dragon black, but with an un-Mick-like arrogance.

I felt sick. Once upon a time, a witch had enslaved Mick and forced him to try to kill me. I remembered my heart-break when I'd seen the man I loved become someone else, turn on me, do his best to destroy me.

This situation was different—the witch had brought out the cold dragon part of Mick, the magical beast of old who'd cared for nothing but its own power. This time, only Mick's voice changed, his lips moving but his eyes holding Mick's rage.

"Yes, this one is strong," the entity said. "Better than the other. Dragons were the best of my creations."

The dragon slayer started to laugh. "Be careful what you wish for," he told us.

Gabrielle kicked him. The dragon slayer made an *oof* noise but didn't cease his quiet laughter.

"You wanted to speak to me." Mick spread his hands in a gesture so like his own it twisted pain through me. "You probably want to ask how you kill me, or banish me, or otherwise rid the world of me. The answer is, you don't. I *am* the Earth. Kill me and all else vanishes."

Fury danced my Beneath magic awake inside me. I wanted to slice it into Mick and burn the entity out, though I knew logically that would only kill Mick.

"I don't believe you," Gabrielle said before I could answer. "The Earth existed before you did. *It* made *you*."

"Is that what that disgusting coyote god told you? Doesn't matter. I'm so entwined in the Earth, so much a part of it, that you'll never separate us."

Gabrielle folded her arms. "If that's true, why aren't you here all the time? You said you disappear for centuries at a stretch and can't believe what happens to the world in the meantime. And why are Beneath magic creatures still around? Why didn't they go extinct when you last manifested and cleansed everything? Skinwalkers are everywhere these days. So are the old gods. Seems like your apocalypses aren't working."

Don't taunt the evil being, Gabrielle, I wanted to say. But I didn't trust myself to speak—I was busy keeping my Beneath magic in check.

Mick flexed and balled his hands, as though his body struggled to expel its intruder. Sweat beaded on his forehead, and the dragon tatts on his arms began to sluggishly swirl.

"I oversleep," the entity said. "Evil spawns so rapidly I can't keep up with it. Look at you. And *you*." Mick's eyes swiveled from Gabrielle to me. "A goddess nearly destroyed you, and still you didn't kill her. What were you thinking?"

I answered, my jaw tight. "We were thinking she

couldn't get out of her realm and do any more harm. She's sealed off from this world. Why are you so worried about her?"

"Oh, good point," Gabrielle said. "You seem to be fixated on Beneath goddesses."

"Please. You are nothing to me. The Earth will crush you." He pinned Mick's dark gaze on me. "It is already crushing *you*, half-Beneath, half-Earth creature, inside your own body. You know this."

Gabrielle cut in. "But you can't wait to mess with *me*. You've been after me since day one. Why?" She took a step closer to him. "Why do I scare you so much?"

Did I detect a flicker of unease? Mick's eyes didn't waver as he returned his focus to her.

"You will be dead, Abomination."

"Why am I not I already? You've attacked me a couple times now, and here I am." Gabrielle spread her arms.

Seriously, don't taunt the evil entity, I thought in exasperation.

"Yes, you are resilient." It sounded puzzled, and then the resoluteness returned to its voice. "I will simply have to crush you harder."

Gabrielle didn't move. "I'm waiting."

Mick's lips twitched into a mean smile. "You won't have to wait much longer." He looked around the basement and then up at the ceiling. The smile widened. "So many sitting ducks."

My alarm grew as he made a sudden turn on Mick's swift feet and headed out of the room, fire flaring in his hands.

Gabrielle and I leapt after him. Gabrielle, in front of me, reached Mick first. He casually swatted her aside, and Gabrielle let out a shriek as his fire bit into her.

I sensed her Beneath magic welling up in response as she

clutched her seared arm. If she let it fly, she'd stop the entity all right but kill Mick in the process.

I thrust my left hand into the air, touched the ring on my third finger, and whispered the musical notes of Mick's true name.

He turned around, his eyes changing from black to deep blue, then to black again. The entity within him snarled.

Mick closed his hands around his fire, his face streaked with sweat. "Again," he whispered in his own voice.

I sang the syllables Mick had taught me, the words that weren't words but music made manifest. His name, the one thing no other being could break, the power he had entrusted to me. No one knew a dragon's true name, not even other dragons.

Another snarl and a wash of cold air blasted past me. Mick staggered and fell against the wall.

I was next to him in an instant. "Mick! You all right?"

He drew a long breath, his eyes shifting once more to dark blue. "Thank you, Janet." The words were low, hoarse, and came from his heart.

"What the hell?" Gabrielle stared from me to him. "What happened? How did you do that?"

No one could hear the name when I sang it except me and, fortunately, Mick. "I called him back to me," I said softly.

Gabrielle's brows drew down. "This is a lovey-dovey, dragony thing you're not going to tell me about, isn't it?"

"You might learn of it one day," Mick said, giving her his warm look. "Let me see your arm. I'm sorry about that."

Gabrielle winced as she held it out, her skin red and burned. Mick let his fingers hover over her as he whispered a word, and a gleam of healing magic trickled into her.

"I don't blame *you*," Gabrielle said, drawing a breath as

her skin turned whole and bronzed again. "I blame that full-of-itself entity. Did he spill any secrets when he was inside you? What did you learn?"

"That I never want to do that again." Mick brushed his thumb over Gabrielle's wrist, imbibing her with a last glint of healing magic. "It's powerful. More powerful than anything we've faced."

"And yet, it can't just show up." I curled my hands, my relief at seeing Mick back to himself making me weak in the knees. "It needs to speak through someone, and it couldn't do much when it was inside you. Otherwise, we'd all be dead."

"Same thing happened in Vegas," Gabrielle said, absently rubbing where she'd been burned. "It started to talk through Drake, didn't like him, and went for Cornelius. I think when it looks for a 'vessel' it tries to find the weakest one it can. Because they're easier to possess, maybe?"

"Now my ego's taking a hit," Mick said with a faint grin. "You're saying I'm the weakest being in this basement? I didn't let that thing into me willingly."

"No, but it didn't go for me or Janet," Gabrielle pointed out. "You are connected to the slayer by the binding spell. The binding spell stymied it from going into the slayer, I'm guessing, and it traveled across the threads to the next best thing. I made it admit it's fixated on Beneath magic wielders, which means it's afraid of us."

"But we knew that," I said patiently. "It's Earth magic, which hates Beneath magic."

"Yes, but why?" Gabrielle persisted. "Most Beneath-magic creatures don't like being on Earth, and stay near the vortexes. So why is it so worried about us? If you don't poke at Beneath, it leaves you alone."

"Sort of," I said. "Skinwalkers and demons usually don't need a reason to attack. Sometimes, neither do you."

Gabrielle spread her hands. "What can I say? I have a short fuse. What I'm getting at is, this entity preys on the weak. You saw that it wanted to go upstairs and blast the witches and things gathered here. The hotel is less like a sanctuary and more like a trap."

I shook my head. "Only if we let it come here. I can't send all those people back home to wait to be picked off."

"Exactly," Gabrielle said with determination. "Which is why we need to choose the place and the time—*us*, not it— and finish this."

She was right. My beautiful, crazy, baby sister was looking at me with serious eyes and speaking wisdom.

"Yes," I said slowly. "And I think I know just the place." I looked at Mick, and he nodded, guessing my thoughts.

"Yep." Gabrielle held up her hand, high-fiving a now-grinning Mick. "Let's go kick some Earth-entity ass. And then we finish the dragon slayer, and go out for pizza."

Gabrielle

THE ARENA UNDER THE HOTEL IN LAS VEGAS WAS QUIET. AMOS had let me off outside and now was having a meal upstairs with his friends while I wandered the arena. He'd loved the Crossroads and enjoyed camping out under the stars and singing songs with Fremont.

I walked the arena alone. Mick and Janet had stopped at the C to confab with Grandmother Begay and the dragons and Nash, while I'd gone on with Amos.

Well, that's the official version. The truth is, I had sneaked away from the C when no one was looking and told Amos to drive me here.

I agreed with Janet that the arena was the logical place to meet the entity. It was far from the Crossroads and far enough from the C to ensure that Cornelius and my new friends on the staff would be safe, plus far enough underground to keep the violence away from the denizens of Las Vegas.

Janet and the dragons and I would meet the entity, destroy it, and save the world. Again.

Except that I knew we couldn't.

We couldn't fight an unfightable creature, one with no substance, who could bury me alive while I was above ground. It didn't like Beneath magic—fine, but how to use that to snuff it out forever?

Or would we only be able to banish it, where it would bide its time before breaking out and endangering future generations of Stormwalkers and Beneath-magic wielders?

I could think best about the problem alone, where I wasn't confused by the feelings my friends and family had recently brought out in me: confusion, anger, need, love, the desire for acceptance.

I was a three-year-old child all over again, trying to figure out what I'd done to make my parents not like me.

Answer—I existed.

When I'd met Janet and her family—okay, so it was more like I tracked her down—same problem. I was alive in the world. What were they going to do with me?

Janet's family couldn't kill me, because they were too kind, and they played by the rules. So they tried to bring me in and form me into their mold.

Though, that wasn't quite right. Coyote had tried to

explain this to me. They'd decided to be family, and family extended hospitality. He'd told me to be a good guest.

So I was doing what good guests did—left before they brought trouble raining down on the people who'd been nice to them. While Janet, Mick, and Colby were safe at the C, I was here, figuring out how to save them.

Here in the arena, I could summon the demons again. I could tap into the Beneath magic to lure out the Earth entity, and then we could obliterate it. Somehow.

The magic mirror had talked about an Earth-magic sink that had been in the sand dunes that created it. I pulled out the new shard I'd taken from the original mirror before we'd left the Crossroads and unwrapped the cloth napkin I'd folded around it.

"Here we are again." I lifted the shard and flashed it around. "What do you think?"

"I think it's cold and dark and really scary, and I don't want to be here, sugar."

I ignored this. "Is the arena connected to the Earth-magic sink? You said it ran deep and had spread far. Could you tap into it?"

"You don't want to do that, sweet thing."

Interesting—it hadn't said it *couldn't* tap the Earth-magic sink. "Do you have a better idea? Should we sit around and wait for the entity to rise? Make some popcorn?"

"Maybe it will find something else to do," the mirror said in a small voice.

"I'm thinking it won't. But fine with me. If it wants to fight Beneath magic, I'm going to let it. Oh, one more thing. If you can tap into this Earth-magic sink, can you also conjure a storm?" From Coyote's hints, I knew we'd need one. "Or at least make sure one comes here, so Janet can be at her full strength? The weather has been obnoxiously nice lately."

The mirror let out a breath. "I'm going to point out that you can't make me do anything. I belong to Mick and Janet, brought to life by their fabulous sex magic. *They* command me, not you."

I brought the shard close to my face. My eyes were dark in the gloom, and the crease between my brows made me look as stubborn as Grandmother Begay. "Do you want to save them so they can go on cuddling with each other? Or do you want to watch them die? The entity is going to get me in the end, so I might as well go out saving my sister's life. You want to help me? Or let them be wiped out? Your choice."

"Oh," the mirror said. "Well, if you put it like that ..."

"I do put it like that. First thing, find the magic sink."

"I don't have to *find* it. It's right here. All around us. Why do you think the dragon slayer likes this place?"

"Figures," I muttered. Also explained why Janet and I were able to open a vortex as easily as we did. Took a lot of Earth magic plus Beneath magic combined.

The dragon slayer had come with us on our journey, bound physically with ropes in the back of Fremont Hansen's plumbing truck, borrowed and driven by Titus while Drake sat with the slayer and kept the binding spell topped up.

Mick had ridden his Harley, and Janet and I had luxuriated in the back of Amos's limo. The only way to travel.

"So what do you want me to do?" the mirror asked.

"Storm," I said. "Bring one here, then we'll jump up and down and call for the entity."

The mirror heaved a long sigh. "Girlfriend, you really are insane. But all right. Here goes."

Because I was deep inside a basement, I wouldn't know if

the weather was cloudy or sunny or foggy or snowy. But I felt a pressure in my ears, as though the atmosphere outside changed.

"One powerful thunderstorm, coming up," the mirror said. "You know, Janet will catch on that someone manipulated the weather. And if she asks me, I'll have to tell her the truth. She won't be *happy*," it finished with a singsong note.

"By that time, it won't matter." I took up a stance in the middle of the arena, my heart pounding. I tried to press my fear aside, or at least ignore it.

I could do this. The entity hated Beneath magic, was afraid of it. Therefore, it must be afraid for a reason. If I could save Janet and Mick so they could canoodle the rest of their lives, and Grandmother Begay, so she could fuss over Pete and Gina, and the dragons ...

I almost cried. With Colby and Drake I'd found guys I could be with, without worrying about hurting them. They took my teasing and my craziness and shrugged it off, seeing me more as an interesting challenge than a weird, scary woman to avoid.

They had no obligation to me, unlike Janet and Grandmother, and even Mick. Colby and Drake hung out with me because they wanted to.

The warm fuzzies that thought conjured made me want to rush away from here and grab on to Colby and not let go.

I made myself stand still, go through what I'd come here for. Fighting the entity would save Colby's life.

If I lost mine in the process, no big deal. Janet and Grandmother would be saved the bother of me, and maybe they'd remember me with fondness rather than eye-rolling exasperation.

None of those places are yours, Coyote had told me when I'd whined that I didn't belong anywhere. *Don't try to take them.*

He was right. I'd been trying to take over, make Janet and her family acknowledge me—first by fearing me, and then by putting up with me.

I was finished with all that. If I survived, I'd thank Janet and Grandmother and all for their attempts to help me, and return to the *C* and do my job—if Cornelius wanted me back, that is. I'd show him I could be good at what I did, even if he'd only hired me because Chandra told him to.

Sometimes you have to grow up and move out of your family's back bedroom.

"What are you doing?"

The rumbling voice belonged to Titus. He stood above me on the first tier of the spectators' area, resting leather-gloved hands on the railing.

"Getting ready for a fight," I answered lightly. "What do you think I'm doing?"

"I have no idea." His eyes glinted gold then shifted slowly to light gray. "I haven't made up my mind about you."

"Well, make it up fast. Is it raining yet?"

"Sprinkling as I was coming in."

"Good." I spread my arms. "Let's get this party started."

CHAPTER TWENTY-FOUR

Colby

I knew something was wrong as soon as I realized Gabrielle hadn't followed Janet and Mickey to her grandmother's suite where they explained what the Earth entity had told them.

I barely heard them, expecting Gabrielle to run in and join us at any moment, saying she'd been caught up in a quick baccarat game or saving someone's life, or something.

Any moment now.

I knew in my bones she wasn't coming, but no one else seemed to notice. They were too focused on Janet's tale, too worried about what to do.

I saw Titus slip away once he'd taken in the gist of Janet and Mick's story. I followed, but lost him when the elevator doors closed on him before I was halfway down the hall.

Didn't matter. I could guess where he was going.

Thunder greeted me as I stepped out of the C. No one

looked worried, or even reached for umbrellas. In this dry desert, thunderstorms didn't always bring rain.

The skies had been bright and clear all day, with no hint of clouds. Now they boiled up over the mountains and streamed across the desert, blotting out the sun and sending cold shadows over the city.

Again, no one panicked. Storms blew up fast out here.

I grabbed a taxi and told the driver to take me as fast as he could to the hotel where Janet and Gabrielle had first stayed. I knew Gabrielle had gone there, to the arena, to scope it out for a reason.

I reached the hotel, throwing twenties at the driver as I raced out of the taxi, and charged inside.

The casino was full of people, but they were milling about, focused on finding a slot machine that paid out or heading for the spa or one of the fine-dining restaurants. The rubble-filled hole in the floor had been cordoned off, and guests and staff went about their business as usual. Las Vegas rolled on.

I strode straight through the casino to the maintenance corridors Amos's friend had showed us and to the stairs leading down to the sub-sub-basements.

I passed through an archway to the arena floor just as Titus vaulted down from the first row above and Gabrielle spread her arms, white light emanating from her hands.

"Stop her!" I yelled at Titus—I was too far away. "Gabrielle, no! You can't fight it alone."

She smiled at me through the radiance. "I won't be alone."

The light swirled around her, faster and faster, until they became a whirlwind—a vortex.

"Shit," Titus said, dancing back.

Gabrielle raised her arms, her dark hair flying, as she channeled the whirlwind straight down her body and through her feet. The sands spun away with a grating hiss, the Earth groaned, and a hole opened beneath her.

I snarled and hurled myself at her, but Gabrielle rose out of my reach, the opening beneath her spreading as she floated over it. I knew exactly what she was doing, and the little smile on her face confirmed it.

There was a sharp, cracking sound, and then a maw to Beneath opened.

"Hey, Earth entity!" Gabrielle yelled to the ceiling. "Come and get it!"

The impact of the vortex flung Titus and me to the far wall. As soon as I gained my feet, I shucked my T-shirt and scrambled out of my jeans. This arena was massive—plenty of room for a dragon, maybe two.

Gabrielle was dancing on light. The building shook, but I wasn't sure if that was because of the hole or the storm outside.

A piercing scream cut the air, but it hadn't come from Gabrielle. A flash of light emanated from her hand, one so brilliant I had to screw my eyes shut against it. I pried them open again in time to see her throw something into the air, a piece of glass—or a mirror.

"Catch, Titus!" she called.

Titus, his eyes blazing black, reached out to grab it. I leapt forward, shoved him aside, and caught the shard in my hand.

Gabrielle's eyes widened. "No! Colby, throw it down!"

The instant before I'd decided to make the catch, I'd realized her plan, and why she'd wanted Titus to grab the shard of magic mirror.

She wanted the Earth entity to manifest, to choose a vessel so she could break it. Titus was a powerful dragon, she figured, able to handle the forces, but she could best him.

But I knew she couldn't. Titus was old, one of the first

dragons. If he channeled the power of the Earth entity, he'd be unstoppable. He'd crush Gabrielle like an eggshell.

Gabrielle had a chance, though, if the entity empowered *me*. And if I had to die to save Gabrielle and the world, well, what a hell of a way to go.

"Colby!" Gabrielle's eyes held anguish. "Get out!"

Too late. Darkness crawled over me along with the decaying odor of ancient dirt, and I became dragon.

Titus got the hell out of my way. I saw his eyes change to dragon black. He understood what had just happened, and knew that he had to join forces with Gabrielle to take me down.

Especially as Gabrielle hung there, unwilling to act.

"I *like* this one." The words came out of my mouth—interesting, because I couldn't speak in human words when I was a dragon.

"No," Gabrielle whispered.

"Then it will be easy," the entity sneered.

I struck. Or, rather, the Earth entity did, through me.

My reason and cognition didn't go away. I was fully me, Colby, Colbinilicarium, the dragon shit who liked to party. But at the same time, the entity's awareness flowed through me from head to tail.

I felt like I'd swallowed acid mixed with brimstone, and that after a three-day bender. It burned me, pounding at my head and twisting my stomach.

The entity was mindless, a formless being with a burning need to devour. The Earth had created it, and it had been born deep inside magma, burbling to the surface whenever it could.

Miners died when it emerged—they were buried alive as the entity made shafts explode, or they dropped after inhaling poison gas the entity caused the rocks to release.

The entity exhaled itself through lakes, destroying entire villages, or pulled down buildings as it shook the Earth apart. It didn't always cause earthquakes or volcanoes, but took advantage of them to emerge and do as much damage as it could.

It enjoyed destruction, and it wanted to burrow into the previous world, the Beneath world, and destroy that too.

Dragon fire—not mine—exploded around me. I blinked away the relentless fixation of the entity to see that Titus had changed to his dragon and streamed flame at me.

I batted aside the fire with a flare of my own. The Earth entity was getting the best of both worlds with me—its resolute, catastrophic force, coupled with the agility of a wily dragon.

I didn't for a second try to fight the entity inside me and break myself free. I knew I couldn't. Simple as that. Why waste the energy?

What I could do was force Gabrielle, stunned and uncertain, to act. She had the power to take this thing down, and she knew it. She'd figured out why the Earth entity hated Beneath magic, and I understood as well from its half-insane thoughts.

Beneath magic could devour it. The entity hid itself deep in the Earth, but by doing so, it encountered the occasional cracks to Beneath that stung it, woke it from its happy slumber. The gods and demons from Beneath, ready to feed on anything that got in their way, hacked at it until it had to flee.

Thus, the entity woke itself every millennia or so and went on a rampage to destroy any Beneath magic that threatened it. If other magical beings got killed along the way … Oh well.

And I know my brain's been jacked if I'm using terms like 'thus.'

I swooped from Titus's fire and faced Gabrielle.

Come on, sweetie. Give me your best shot.

Her eyes widened. She was so beautiful, my lady, all long legs and silky black hair, dark eyes I could gaze into for days.

She wasn't a simpering, brainless fool either. Gabrielle could go toe-to-toe with any dragon I'd ever known and then slap down a demon or two and go out for breakfast.

"Get the hell out of Colby!" Gabrielle shouted. "Face me, you coward!"

For answer, the entity made me suck in a breath and spew flame all over the woman I loved.

But she wasn't where I aimed. She'd zoomed upward the moment I'd focused on her, slamming a wall of Beneath magic in front of her to deflect the fire.

Gabrielle was smart—she knew she couldn't fight the entity, but she could fight a dragon.

Dragons had been born of hottest Earth magic—we were probably the closest thing to the entity that any living creature could be. If Gabrielle forced the entity and dragon to fuse into one being, she could defeat it, or at least cripple it enough to send it into hiding for another millennium.

Titus had been a good choice, strong enough to stand the entity taking him over, but not a good choice for Gabrielle. Like I said, he'd have killed her.

I was powerful enough for the fucking entity, but I had a vested interest in keeping Gabrielle alive. I'd rather let her kill me and go party with Janet than fight her.

The mirror was screaming and keening from the floor where I'd dropped it. Gabrielle had used it to bounce the Earth entity into me, the mirror having been forged from the same kind of magic.

I created it, the entity whispered in my head, *at the dawn of time.*

No, the mirror had said someone living at the Salton Sea had done it. Or, wait—it had said its *sand* came from there, in an Earth-magic sink.

I remembered sitting at the foot of Gabrielle's bed, watching her in worry, while she'd interrogated the mirror. The mirror had been forged from ancient sands, which now the Earth entity was taking the credit for forming. That both unnerved me and gave me ideas.

Meanwhile, I was made to fly and roll and stream fire at Gabrielle and Titus. Titus had launched himself to the top of the arena and hovered there, as though hanging out and waiting to see how things went.

No you don't, you bastard.

I banked and went for him. The arena was big enough that two dragons could circle around each other but if I kept a little below Titus, I had much more room to maneuver. It also let me flame him in the belly.

My fire swatted him there, and Titus screamed, rolling to dampen the flames.

Dickhead. He should be protecting Gabrielle, not saving his energy to fight me once I killed her.

"Abomination!" the entity shouted through my mouth. "Destroy it!"

I didn't have a choice. As when Drake had made me burn down half Janet's hotel, my lungs inflated with air that would pump up the fire in my flame sacs and stream it out hotter than any fuel a human could make.

Dragons didn't breathe fire, or belch it, which would be, frankly, gross. Just as the digestive and breathing systems in our human bodies were separate but used the some of the same space, a dragon's fire mechanism was a series of separate organs.

Sacs around the stomach stored the fuel, which in theory

was harmless until ignited. We mixed the fuel with oxygen and used lung power to flush it through pipes outside the corners of our mouths, and the fuel lit when it hit the outside air.

That's why we can't spit fire in human form—human bodies don't have the flame system. The fire we shoot from our hands is nothing but cool magic.

The entity put me through this explanation, fascinated even as I was doing my best to singe the hell out of Titus.

Titus finally rolled down from his refuge at the top of the arena and started to fight me for real.

We circled each other, dropping or rising to get a bead on each other, Titus's dragon a black and red colossus of fury.

"No!" Gabrielle screamed at me. "You fight *me*."

"Sorry, sweetheart." The entity said, "You don't get to choose. The point is to kill *me*, remember? This dragon I'm in is collateral damage."

That was so not the right thing to say to Gabrielle. I started to feel sorry for the entity.

Gabrielle rose on her magic, surrounded by white lightning. "My boyfriend is *not* collateral damage. Get *out* of him!"

Boyfriend? When did that happen? And why did it make me, the free spirit, so pleased?

Titus didn't wait for debate. He swooped, flamed, and caught me in the side.

Dragon hides are tough and thick—have to be. We live with the equivalent of plastic explosives inside us, which, like I said, are harmless until ignited.

But fire still hurt, and if my skin burned away enough to let any flame inside, I'd explode like a bomb.

I bellowed as Titus's fire melted scales and cracked the webbing on my wings. I folded them and dropped—wings are vulnerable, and a dragon with burned-off wings is a sitting duck l'orange.

The fall put the fire out, but my hide smarted, which pissed me off. I soared up to Titus again, shooting flame, catching the length of his tail. See how he liked it.

Gabrielle watched in agitation, surrounded by shimmering silver magic that kept her safe from stray flames. She wasn't moving on with her plan. She didn't want to kill me.

I was touched, but there was a bigger picture here.

I flew at her, fire streaming. *Come on! Do it, Gabrielle. Kill it.*

"You can't win, little girl," the entity said. "Your boyfriend is my slave. He is finished, and so are you and your kind."

Oh, please, can you come up with any more lame villain speak?

The arena rumbled again. Gabrielle lost her stricken look and actually laughed, though the laugh was strained.

"You want to finish my *kind*? You wait until my sister gets here. You know, she's your kind *and* mine, all mixed up, and she'll trash your ass."

"Then we shouldn't wait," the entity said, and struck.

I barreled at Gabrielle with all my dragon speed, strength, and fire. She barely dodged in time, and her magic shield wavered under my onslaught. I went for her again, the Earth entity enhancing my natural dragon power.

Gabrielle's eyes ignited with rage as I knocked her off her feet, and I saw her realization that she'd have to strike back.

She came for me, my girl, dark eyes sparkling and beautiful. Beneath magic streamed from her, lighting up her body, her hands coming together as she directed all she had at me.

I met the attack with a wash of fire, which was split by the Beneath magic. We lit up the arena, flame and white light bouncing off the stones. Titus zoomed upward and behind

me again, taking advantage of Gabrielle's frontal assault to
hit me in the ass.

My tail went up in flames, and I beat the air with it, trying
to put it out. Titus, not waiting, sent another stream like a
swift arrow at my haunches.

The fire never reached me. A sudden beam of light
reflected from the tiny piece of mirror below and batted the
flame aside.

Titus flapped quickly backward. I blinked in surprise and
realized that Gabrielle had defended me, bouncing a point of
Beneath magic through the mirror to intercept Titus's attack.

Mistake. The distraction left me free to fly right at her.

I didn't bother with magic this time, I simply ran my
dragon bulk into her. Her Beneath lightning stung me all
over, but I took her down.

Gabrielle's body was human, never mind her mother was
a goddess. The Beneath goddess had manifested inside an
existing woman in order to do the deed with the human man
she'd chosen to impregnate her. Gabrielle wasn't a demon—
she was a human being.

Being tackled by a dragon would break all her bones and
crush her to death, which was what the entity wanted.
Wanted me, as dragon, to eat those bones too.

I infused myself with as much of my own will as I could,
and changed to my human form as the pair of us went down,
landing on the sands beyond the hole Gabrielle had opened.
The darkness that swathed dragons when they changed
enveloped us—the cold magic force that allowed a huge beast
to stuff itself into the narrow shape of a man.

Gabrielle squirmed under me, her body warming mine
even as we fought.

"Colby." Her eyes filled with tears, her magic dropping
away.

"You have to finish it, sweetheart," I said. "He'll never stop until you do."

"Why?" She balled her fists and pushed at me. "I wanted you to stay out of it."

"To give you a chance, baby." I kissed her lips, lingering a moment to enjoy her warm breath, the taste of her, her softness. She looked into my eyes, and I knew I'd found what I'd been looking for all my life.

But no time to savor. I rolled from her and dragged her to her feet. "Now, do it."

Gabrielle spun away from me in rage, balling her fists and raising them to the sky. "Come on out! Let's finish this!"

The ground trembled. A bolt of lightning shot straight through the ceiling, breaking open the roof and sending Titus spinning.

Sand whirled. White light streamed upward from the opening in the floor to meet the bolts streaking down.

Hell rose and boiled forth. At the same time, Janet the Stormwalker strode in, her hands full of lightning. Behind her came Mick, fire encasing him, and then Grandmother Begay and the woman called Chandra.

The entity looked through my eyes, and I saw what it saw.

Ruby Begay no longer hobbled, but strode with head up, wrapped in black feathers, an ancient Earth being made dangerously unhappy. With her was Chandra the doctor, except she shone like silver, too bright to look at. I felt the entity's fear rise.

It feared even more the next being who arrived, Nash, who appeared to be a pillar of emptiness. But the nothingness wasn't passive—it sought, and the entity didn't like that.

Maya followed barely a step behind Nash. The entity recognized she was human and dismissed her.

Idiot. She carried a pistol of some kind, holding it competently.

Then there was Drake, his huge black dragon superimposed on his human body. He led the dragon slayer on a rope of binding magic, and I saw the double nature of the man—human and demon—the melding of the two and something beyond that.

I also saw that the binding spell wasn't binding him anymore. He must have recovered his full strength—but then he'd had days lying in Janet's basement to heal.

"Drake!" I shouted, and then something hit me and knocked all the air out of me.

CHAPTER TWENTY-FIVE

Gabrielle

Colby yelled over the noise of my demons bursting into the arena from below. They knocked him over just as the dragon slayer jerked his head up, gave Drake an evil smile, and snapped his arms open.

The black threads fell away, and the dragon slayer stood free.

Drake, without missing a beat, started the spell again, sending tendrils to wrap the man. The dragon slayer threw them off with ease, jumped over the balcony to the dirt floor, and prostrated himself in front of Colby, who'd climbed to his feet.

"I brought them, master. I serve you."

"Good," the entity said with Colby's voice. "Keep the dragons away from me."

I hated hearing Colby talk like this. I wanted to reach inside him and strangle the asshole monster who'd taken him over.

What scared me was that I suddenly knew I could do it. But I'd kill Colby in the process.

"This wasn't *his* plan," I snapped at the entity, waving my hand at the dragon slayer. "It was *my* plan. He's been stuck in a basement. I want the credit for bringing us all back here, understand?"

Colby raised his fists to strike me, but I shoved him away with a burst of magic. I had to get the entity out of him without damaging him—maybe by knocking Colby out? Worth a shot.

"Take him down!" I shouted at the demons, pointing at Colby. "But gently."

They moved in, way too fast, teeth and claws striking. Colby spun away from them. He gave me a look of understanding, cloaked himself in darkness once more, and became a dragon.

The demons—flying ones, crawling ones, man-shaped ones—attacked him, trying to force him to the ground. Demons are hard to control, as the witch who'd summoned the one in the C had discovered, but I had so much more power than she did. The demon that witch had conjured was here, in fact, racing to attack Colby.

"No!" I waved at him frantically. "You! Get the dragon *slayer*."

The slayer was trying to escape through one of the arena entrances, but Mick stepped in front of him, grinning dangerously.

The mirror continued to scream, the keen of it grating on my nerves. I kicked the shard out of the way, and it ended up against the wall. A bright light shot from Colby to it, and its scream wound to a thin, piercing wail.

"I'm soreeeeee," it sobbed, and then the Earth came.

It was like the attack on the rooftop, except this time, we were already underground.

Clods of dirt, sheets of mud, and the snakelike roots dove out from the arches at all of us—demons, dragons, Earth goddess, Beneath goddess.

Janet drew down the lightning from the storm outside and struck back. She was beautiful with her power—both kinds entwined in her, balanced and whole. She'd struggled with that for a while, and now here she was, honed and terrifying.

I'd been struggling for similar balance, but I couldn't worry about that right now. I was Gabrielle, goddess of Beneath, and I wanted to kill.

So did the demons. They surrounded Colby, braving his fire, striking with acid, claws, teeth, venom.

Titus went for him too, the fury in his black eyes telling me he'd give Colby no quarter.

Mick and Drake and the red-eyed, horned demon stalked the dragon slayer, while Janet fought the suffocating Earth with her storm. Rain washed away the dirt, wind blew back the roots, and lightning pulverized the rocks.

And Grandmother and Chandra? They watched. Their heads turned as they observed the demons flying around, the dragons fighting, the Earth itself attacking us.

Nash was in the arena, trying to get close to Colby, probably with the idea of sucking out the entity as he had from Cornelius. Even Maya tried to help, though she mostly hid behind a pillar, looking to see where she could point her gun.

I had to get to Colby. The demons would hold him down, and Titus would rip him apart if the Earth entity didn't eat him from the inside out first.

I blasted a path to him. The demons melted away, afraid of their goddess, and I walked through them.

"You want to mess with Beneath?" I yelled at the entity in Colby's dragon eyes. "Then you got it!"

I spread my arms, willed the sands of the arena to surround me, twisted the storm into the vortex, and called forth the world of Beneath.

I became it. The liquid light from below swallowed me, my goddess magic twining with it to let the light rise and have substance. If the Earth entity could attack with all the power of the Earth, then I could fight it with all the power from the world of Beneath.

I'd never entirely control what flooded me—I knew that. But as the magic filled me, I had a sudden insight as to why my mother had wanted nothing to do with me.

Not disappointment in me, as I'd thought. And not because Janet had Earth shaman magic, inherited from her father's family, the power to control the storms, when I did not.

It was because I had too much Beneath magic. My mother would never have been able to bend me to her will, and she'd known it.

Maybe I had a reason to be so crazy and unpredictable. Self-defense.

The Earth entity in Colby didn't like what I'd done. Colby spread his wings, driving aside the demons, and came for me.

This was our first dance, and our last.

I flew toward him on a wave of Beneath magic, my body catching the brunt of Colby's sudden stream of flame. The flame and white light wove around each other and haloed us.

The Beneath magic that I'd become opened like a gigantic maw. The Earth entity screamed, and then I devoured it, dragon and all.

"Colby," I whispered as the world went away and there was nothing but magic and death. "Give me your true name."

"Give me yours," came his response, tinged with laughter.

I didn't even have to think about it. I closed my eyes and slid the syllables of it to him on his fire.

In return I heard music, pure, crystal notes mixed with Colby's rumbling bass, swelling in my heart.

The Beneath magic swallowed Colby, and crushed the Earth entity inside him.

I CAME TO MYSELF KNEELING ON SAND, THE ROOM CAVING IN around us. Colby's body, broken, his tatts smeared with blood, lay in my arms. His eyes were open, filmed over, sightless.

The moan that tore from my throat was inhuman. I'd never heard a sound like that before. It broke through the chaos of demons, dragons, and the sudden laughter of the dragon slayer.

The sound was my grief, an emotion I'd never experienced, not truly. I'd been sad when my stepmother had died, but her life had been hell. The afterlife was surely better for her.

Colby was dead. In my embrace, gone. He'd died so he could save me.

This was why he'd intercepted the mirror's beam when I'd wanted the entity to take over Titus. I'd figured I could fight Titus, kill him if I had to, and be sorry but resigned.

Not with Colby. We hadn't had a relationship, not really. Not yet. It had only been budding.

But I grieved. For Colby's laughter, his friendship, the way he could infuse the direst situation with humor, breaking tension and making me feel less afraid. He took all kinds of shit cheerfully, had even put up with punishment by the Dragon Council because Bancroft, the head dragon, couldn't keep his dick in his pants.

I grieved for what could have been. If I'd been a person instead of a confused, half-insane, half hell goddess, I could have given myself to him without hesitation, without worry.

Colby didn't deserve this. He'd sacrificed himself. For me, for all of us.

I'd wanted to sacrifice *me*, and he'd stopped me.

I wailed, my grief too strong to hold inside. I'd never controlled my emotions in my life—never had to, never understood how to.

Hands settled on my shoulders. I recognized the touch, the scent of lightning mixed with dust. My sister Janet sank beside me, tears spilling down her cheeks.

I continued to wail, the hurting tearing at me like a live thing. I couldn't make it stop.

"Shh." Janet put her arms around me, the only person in the world who dared to. "You did it, Gabrielle. You saved us."

I couldn't breathe, could barely see, but I became aware of the quiet. The demons were gone. The way to Beneath had vanished, the vortex closed.

The roots and boulders had disappeared, and the floor beneath me was still. Lightning had torn the roof open to the desert sky, and a gentle rain pattered to the sand.

I didn't care. Colby was dead, his body already growing cold. He was gone, and I could never have him back.

"It's not quite finished," came a voice.

Janet jolted up and around, but I could only dash tears from my eyes and rock Colby, my fingers on his beautiful face.

The voice was the dragon slayer's. Janet went rigid as he marched our way.

I had no interest in him and didn't look up when his

dusty boots stopped a few feet away. Janet's smaller but no less dusty motorcycle boots faced his.

"I will use this host to hold me while I recover," the dragon slayer said with the Earth entity's voice. "And then you will pay. All of Beneath will be wiped away."

"You killed our friend," Janet said, her voice shaking. "Not gonna let you get away with that."

"*I* did not kill him. *She* did. Of her own accord and her own desires."

"Wrong answer," Janet said, and she reached for the rain.

"That won't work," the dragon slayer said softly. "The storm has played out. Your witch sister doesn't have enough strength to sustain it or to call the Beneath entity again. Why don't you—"

Maya shot him.

I'd seen her come out of the shadows behind the dragon slayer and aim her dark pistol at him. An explosion of sound —then blood and gore took the place of the top of his head.

He toppled. Janet leapt the hell out of the way even as Mick grabbed her and pulled her to safety. The dragon slayer fell over, blood spraying in a semicircle to land hotly on my arm.

Half demon, half human, Mick had said. The dragon slayer had managed to extend his lifespan for hundreds of years, but he was still mortal.

Nash sprinted forward. He put his hands on the dragon slayer's shoulders, and I heard a scream of protest as the entity streamed into Nash.

Nash let go of the inert slayer and balled his fists over his gut.

Could Nash's null-ness cancel out the entity? Or would it kill him before he could? Or would it try to leap into another body—Maya was standing behind Nash, wide-eyed, the pistol pointed downward, her finger well away from the trigger.

The entity liked the weakest person in the room, as I'd said in the basement of the Crossroads, which was why it had so readily jumped into Colby, a less powerful dragon than Titus.

"Now," Grandmother Begay said.

She hobbled quickly to Nash. I no longer saw the Crow, but only a small, slightly bent Diné woman leaning on her walking stick. Behind her came Chandra, taller, younger, more robust.

Grandmother held out her hands. "Give him to me, Sheriff Jones."

Nash looked at her in puzzlement from his half crouch. "You ladies need to back away," he said.

Grandmother Begay didn't listen, of course. She touched his chest with her hand and the head of her cane. She pulled, scowled, pulled harder, then set her feet and yanked.

Nash blew out his breath as darkness shot from him and spun once around the walking stick. I heard a howl as the entity touched the turquoise in the cane's handle, and then tried to flee from it.

Grandmother Begay shoved the stick under her arm and caught the darkness between her hands. She began to press it together, as she did when she gathered up dough to make her fry bread, compressing it into a small ball.

Chandra watched, hands on hips, the loose sleeves of her top fluttering over her wrists. Grandmother gave her a nod, and Chandra smiled.

She reached out her hands, palm downward, and let white light flow from them to the ground.

I heard an inhale and an exhale, exactly as I had in the hallway of the C the night the entity attacked.

Not the entity I realized. The Earth itself.

A hole opened in the arena floor. Not the frenzied vortex I'd wrought, but a neat hole with straight sides that let directly into the ground. From it came a breath of heat, and red light mixed with white.

"The Beneath world is necessary," Grandmother said to the ball of struggling darkness in her hands. "From it came all life. The Earth understands that. The two places are not entirely separate, but you have been too obsessed in yourself to understand. So now we will teach you."

While Chandra held the hole open with her steady stream of magic, Grandmother lifted the dark ball above her head.

"Janet," she said calmly. "Help me."

Janet moved to her, bewildered. "How?"

"Just touch it."

Mick didn't like that. He was next to Grandmother in a heartbeat, but he didn't interfere when Janet put her hand on top of the ball. She gasped as though something was dragged out of her, and then Grandmother Begay hurled the ball downward.

A scream, a white light and a red one, and then Chandra clapped her hands together.

The hole sealed, the white light faded, and the sands ran over where the hole had been. I heard another deep exhale, and then all was silence.

CHAPTER TWENTY-SIX

Gabrielle

Chandra looked at Grandmother Begay. "You didn't need to give it a lecture," she said. "You only had to throw it into the hole. I was getting tired holding the way open."

Grandmother set her cane to the floor with a thump. "Beneath goddesses are so impatient."

"How did you know how to do that?" Janet asked them, mystified.

"Coyote told me," Grandmother said. "It was perfectly fine, Mick Firewalker," she said to Mick, who hovered near Janet. "I needed Janet's combination of magics to send the entity to the space between Earth and Beneath. It will be absorbed there and not bother us again."

I heard conviction in her voice, but for my part, I wasn't so sure. Then again, at this moment, I was aware of nothing but Colby, lying dead on my lap.

He wouldn't be coming back to me, and I couldn't stand

that. I rocked him, my sobs unceasing. It was as though someone else controlled me, but I knew they did not. This was me, finally realizing what it was to lose someone.

Chandra's scent of cleanness and lavender touched me. She knelt beside me, resting her hand lightly on Colby's unmoving chest.

He lay motionlessly, his dark hair, loose from its braid, spreading across my arms. His colorful tatts were beginning to fade as death robbed him of everything.

"We can't have this," Chandra said softly. "I will need you whole."

I didn't know whether she meant me or Colby.

Grandmother stumped to her. "No," she snapped. "That is forbidden."

"By whom?" Chandra asked. "Gabrielle is my niece, my family. She is too young for this grief."

"It is the way of the world," Grandmother said in a hard voice, but she didn't sound as assured as usual.

"Not in my world." Without further word, Chandra closed her eyes and sent an incredible amount of magic into Colby. She withdrew her hand after a moment and sat back, watching.

I caressed Colby's bare chest, searching frantically for signs of life, but I found none. His eyes remained empty, his body inert, his heart not beating.

I started to break all over again. Death was too powerful, nothing to stop it, didn't matter how much I willed it. Chandra was a goddess, with immense magics, like Coyote and my mother. If Chandra couldn't save Colby, no one could.

Chandra took my hand, hers surprisingly cool for all the magic she'd just worked, and held it with mine over Colby's heart.

"Call him," she said.

I stared at her in confusion for a few seconds, then understanding penetrated my fogged and pain-numbed brain.

Call him. The notes of Colby's true name drifted through my head, the sounds he'd given me just before I'd killed him.

They were many and complex, like steps in an intricate dance, and I was surprised I remembered them all. The music wove through my thoughts, gleaming and clear as glass but with a deep tone that reminded me of Colby.

I heard another whisper, that of my own name, my spirit name, given to me at my birth by a god. I hadn't realized until this moment which god.

I lifted my head and saw him standing at the top of the arena, in coyote form, his golden eyes still. No one else noticed him—maybe he wasn't really there. But Coyote locked his gaze with mine, and after a moment, he winked.

Colby coughed. His true name surged through me in a brilliant crescendo, and then it dispersed, a sigh on the wind.

He coughed again.

"Colby?" I scooped him against me.

I was surrounded—Mick, Janet, Drake, Titus, Nash, Maya, Grandmother, and Chandra. All bent to Colby, all praying, I felt, to their own gods in their own way.

Colby's eyelids flickered and his opaque eyes turned dragon black. They remained that way a moment, then like the sky scattering clouds, his eyes resolved to light blue. He opened his mouth and emitted a groan.

"Colby!" I gathered him up, reckless in my joy, kissing his face, his lips, his hair. He brought up weak hands to me.

"Did we get him?" The words were slurred, cracked, broken. Colby moved his tongue around his mouth as though trying to remember how it worked.

Mick answered, leaning to him, hands on blue-jeaned knees. "We got him, my friend. Or *you* did. And Gabrielle, and Ruby and Chandra. And Janet. And Maya with a great assist. The dragons owe a huge debt to Maya, actually."

"It's good to have friends." Colby met my gaze, his smile tired but full. "And more than friends. Gabrielle's a good kisser. Don't stop, sweetheart."

"Sounds like he's all right," Janet said, her thankfulness clear.

I did kiss Colby. A long, heartfelt kiss as tears poured down my face. His lips could barely move in response but his hand pressed hard on mine.

When I let him up for air, Colby's grin was stronger. "I'm liking this." Then his eyes softened. "Are *you* okay, baby?"

I managed a nod. I had no idea if I was all right or not—if I tried to stand up I might pass out or throw up, and who knew how injured I was—but I knew what he meant. I was alive. And whole. At least for now.

Colby blew out a breath of relief. "Then I guess that means we go out for pizza."

He wasn't going anywhere soon, but I laughed and kissed him again, warmed by the laughter of my friends and family.

I sensed Coyote, high above us, turn and go.

Two weeks later

Janet

MY DAD MARRIED GINA AT HER FAMILY'S HOME OUTSIDE Farmington, in a hogan that had been built and blessed specifically for them. I held Mick's hand as we entered the hogan, the groom's family keeping to the north side, Gina's family spread across the south.

The small space under the wood and mud roof was crowded but blissfully cool. The October air was mellow but warm in the sun, the hogan's shade welcome.

Mick watched the ceremony in fascination, his eyes going dragon dark as Gina scooped up water with a dipper and washed my father's hands, and then my father did the same to Gina.

I heard a sniffle somewhere to my left—Grandmother, her chin stuck out, surreptitiously wiped her eyes.

A feeling of great peace came over me as the rite continued—Gina's sister set a basket of cornmeal mush in front of the bride and groom, and Gina's father sprinkled white and yellow pollen in two circles over the mush. He then crossed the lines to symbolize Gina's and Dad's joining.

My dad, resplendent in his velvet shirt and silver and turquoise jewelry, took a pinch of the mush and fed it to Gina, and she did the same to him. They both laughed when the crumbly cornmeal got everywhere, my father showing a relaxed mirth I rarely saw in him.

My eyes filled, and I squeezed Mick's hand. Gabrielle, on my other side, started to clap. Not really what she should do, but it caught on, and soon the entire hogan was cheering.

After the bride and groom fed each other, we all were invited to eat the mush and the mountains of food piled in the other baskets. We streamed out of the hogan to finish the feast, the picnic tables outside laden with food. Gina's family had been cooking day and night.

My father flushed as his friends teased him, but I saw his happiness, and whenever he looked at Gina, his eyes betrayed his love.

I was touched by how many people had come to wish

Dad well. I figured my large, extended family would fill out
the crowd, but they were joined by most of the population of
Many Farms and a large number from Chinle, Round Rock,
and other communities, as well as Gina's friends and family
from Farmington and surrounding towns. My shy father
had cultivated the respect and warmth of many over
the years.

Grandmother stood ramrod stiff at the end of a picnic
table. Her mouth had moved along with Gina's father's
during the blessings, as though she willed him not to get
anything wrong. Next to her was Chandra—Grandmother
had been certain the hogan would fall down when a goddess
from Beneath walked into it, but it hadn't.

That convinced me more than anything that Chandra
was not the embodiment of evil my mother was. Blessed
ground is a powerful tester.

Gabrielle wandered to us, alone for the moment. She'd
been plastered to Colby's side since the two had arrived
together.

She wore a colorful print dress in blues and reds, her hair
falling in a silken wave over her shoulders. The high heels
she navigated with ease made her tall and stately. I wore a
traditional long skirt, velvet blouse, and silver jewelry at my
grandmother's insistence, but I felt graceless in them and
kept tripping on my hem.

Gabrielle planted herself in front of Chandra. "Where
have *you* been? I thought you'd be at the C when I went back
to work, but no."

Chandra shrugged. "Here and there. Maybe I was putting
things in place so I can take up my medical practice again."

"Why do you need to? You're a goddess."

Gabrielle's directness was rude, but I wondered the same
thing. "I like to stay busy," Chandra said, shrugging. "And I

need something to do while I keep an eye on you. I am a good doctor, and I like to heal people."

"I don't trust doctors," Grandmother said darkly. "They take perfectly functional bits out of you and too late realize they didn't need to after all."

Chandra broke into a smile. "I said a *good* doctor. Whenever you need looking after, old Crow, you come and see *me*."

"Humph," Grandmother said.

Janet

THE FEASTING LASTED WELL INTO THE NIGHT, AS DID THE dancing as we circled Dad and Gina, singing and chanting. Colby really got into the dancing, asking my cousins to teach him some of the more intricate steps. Even Drake and Titus —Grandmother insisted on inviting them—unbent and clasped hands with Dad's friends as they moved around the circle in the firelight.

At last, it was time to go, to leave my father and his bride to begin their life together.

I hugged my dad and kissed his cheek. "Be well." I tried to keep my tears at bay, but they slipped out. His eyes were wet too, and when he hugged me, his wiry strength was comforting.

"Blessings go with you, child." He smoothed a strand of hair from my face. "Mick will take care of you now."

"He already does." I hastily wiped away my tears and pointed a finger at my father's chest. "You'd better give me away at my wedding."

Dad's face creased with his kind smile. "I will. And if your grandmother has her way, it will be an even bigger ceremony than mine."

I groaned and Dad chuckled. We hugged again, then I turned away, happy for him and sad for me, and left him.

Mick and I took Grandmother with us to the Crossroads so she wouldn't have to face an empty house that night, as Dad and Gina were staying in Farmington. They would leave soon for a honeymoon trip to Hawaii, courtesy of Mick. Dad wasn't much for traveling, but he'd gladly taken up Mick's offer, saying he'd always wanted to see the place. Gina vowed she was going to learn to surf. I imagined her, large and calm, standing on a surfboard, wind in her hair, daring the board to dump her over.

At the Crossroads, the extra guests had emptied out. Cassandra was very happy with the money we'd made, though she hadn't charged full price to those staying in the lobby or outside in tents. She stated that the Crossroads was a haven, and she was not out to gouge those in trouble.

Most of the guests had insisted on paying for our hospitality even so, which pleased Elena, because they'd eaten a lot of food.

Mick and I escaped very late and wandered to the railroad bed, where we stood to look up at the stars.

"Our wedding next," Mick said.

"I know."

"Hey." Mick turned me to face him. "I heard that gloom in your voice. You want out of it?"

His question was teasing but I saw the trepidation in his eyes, his fear that I'd tell him, *Yes, let's call it off.*

I let out a heavy breath. "Do you think we can have a wedding without Earth entities, dragon slayers, demons, Nightwalker attacks, dragon binding spells, vortexes opening, or you fighting to the death in an arena?"

Mick pretended to consider this. "We can try."

I laughed, and then I folded my arms, shivering in the sudden coolness. "It's going to be like this all our lives, isn't it? A Stormwalker and a dragon will never be able to stay out of trouble."

"Or cease saving the world." Mick moved behind me and slid his arms around me, his warm lips touching my hair. "But if I'm going to spend my life fighting demons, Night-walkers, dragon slayers, entities, and goddesses from hell, I want to do it with you at my side."

"Why, so you can watch me get my ass kicked?"

"No, so I can watch you *kicking* ass. Like the amazing woman you are."

I turned in his arms and laced my hands behind his back. "Well, if you put it that way ..."

Mick answered me with a kiss. I rose into him, his strong arms holding me safely, while his wickedly sexy kiss stirred up desires I would definitely act upon as soon as we were back inside the hotel.

I ignored the yip of the far-off coyote, which sounded too much like satisfied laughter.

Gabrielle

"Maybe they'll go inside," I said as Colby and I watched Mick and Janet rise into their kiss a little way down the rail-road bed. Mick scooped Janet closer to him, and she slid her leg around his thigh.

"Sweet," Colby said. "You know what *they'll* be doing tonight." He turned to me, his eyes dark in the starlight. "What will we be doing?"

"Sneaking back to Vegas?" I asked hopefully.

Colby took a step closer to me. "That's a long drive. Be morning by the time we get there, and we'll miss breakfast."

"True. But I don't think we'll get much privacy here."

"That is a point." Colby snaked his arm around my waist. "You really like your job at the C, don't you?"

"I do." My heart squeezed. "It's something I can do—something I'm good at. And there's a place for me there. I'm not Janet's appendage, or her insane sister, or *what-trouble-is-she-getting-into-now?* Cornelius is the first person who's seen me as *me*, you know what I mean?"

Colby looked affronted. "Hey, I met you before he did."

I pushed at him but not so hard that I'd dislodge his hold. I liked his arm around me. "Yeah, but you just wanted to boink me."

"Huh. That's what you think. I wanted to know *you*—the beautiful, strong, totally out of the ordinary woman."

I went toasty all over. "Yeah?"

"Yeah." Colby's eyes twinkled like the myriad stars above us. "That is the whole truth and nothing but the truth."

I nestled against him, touching a kiss to his sweatshirted chest. "You should have told me."

"Well, I'm telling you now."

I snuggled in, hearing his heart pound strongly beneath the warm shirt. Colby had not shown any ill effects from being dead for a few minutes. Chandra was right—she was a hell of a good doctor.

Colby and I had been a little shy with each other since then. During the battle, we'd given each other our true names, a large piece of what we were. That sharing was intimate, profound, and we weren't quite sure how to act with each other yet.

"You know," I said, making my voice light. "Vegas is a bit

far, but there's a very nice hotel in Winslow, less than an hour from here."

"Mmm, that's true. And my motorcycle is big enough for two. Of course, the hotel might be locked up for the night by now."

"Nothing we can't get around. We'll pay up in the morning. Their computer won't know we never checked in. Think we should go for a suite?"

Colby's arms tightened around me. "I like the way you think, Gabrielle. This could be the start of a beautiful friendship."

I popped my head up in confusion. "Friendship?"

Colby rumbled a laugh. "It's a line from *Casablanca*. I meant, you and me could have a lot of fun together."

I relaxed. "We can. And we will." I sent him a mischievous smile. "Just because I've realized I'm not totally evil doesn't make me *good*."

He caressed my back, his fingers strong. "Thank all the gods for that." He glanced down the railroad bed. "Wait, I think they're leaving. Libido grew too much for them, I bet."

Mick was leading Janet down the bank, steadying her until they reached the flat land behind the Crossroads. He caught her hand, and they ran for the hotel and the private entrance to her suite, Janet's laughter trailing behind her.

"Aw," I said, my heart warming. "I'm so glad she found someone like Mick. Janet needs to be happy."

Colby kissed the top of my head. He slid his arms from me but clasped both my hands. "Am I hearing you say good-bye to sibling rivalry?"

I watched Mick tow Janet inside the hotel and shut the door, the heat of her need for him reaching me through whatever bond she and I shared.

I turned back to Colby, tilting my head to regard him.

"Oh, I'll keep her on her toes. No need to get maudlin." I glanced back at the hotel, chuckling to myself when the light flicked on in Janet's bedroom and then as quickly off. "But my big sis—she's not so bad."

"No, she's not," Colby agreed. "And I can even put up with Mickey. But I'm happy I'm with little sis." He grinned down at me. "Ready to go?"

"Oh, hell yeah." I started down the railroad bed at a run, Colby giving a startled shout before he ran after me.

I headed for the shed where his bike was, the keys to his Harley flashing in my hand—I'd lifted them from his pocket.

Behind us, the coyote, who hadn't ceased his yipping, raised his head and let his howls rise to the vast sweep of stars.

AUTHOR'S NOTE

Thank you for reading! It's always a joy to return to the Stormwalker world and all its inhabitants.

As you saw, I chose to go into the points-of-view of other characters in this installment, which was both a challenge to write and a lot of fun. Gabrielle kind of took over whenever I wrote her scenes—I never knew what she was going to do! But I learned a lot about her. I adored writing Colby's point of view as well, and also getting inside Mick's head a bit. I hope to explore them further in this way, plus more characters in the future.

Although my writing schedule is so packed I can't always get to every series in a timely fashion, I plan for more books in the Stormwalker series. Janet and Mick have to have their wedding, and there's always something going on in Magellan and surrounding areas. I'll need to check in with Fremont, Cassandra, Drake, and others, and also explore the new dragon in town, Titus.

I was inspired to write Stormwalker a long time ago when driving the roads of northern Arizona, particularly north of Flagstaff and around east toward Monument Valley and Four Corners, and down to Chinle and Canyon de Chelley. I pictured Janet screaming down these roads on her Harley and pulling off to a tiny house in Many Farms, to be greeted by her quietly loving father and her formidable but equally loving grandmother. And then Mick came along, and the first book was born.

I highly recommend a trip to see the Hopi and Navajo lands in Arizona and New Mexico—take several days to wander around Canyon de Chelley and Monument Valley then back to the San Francisco Peaks and Sunset Crater, and plan a trip to Chaco in New Mexico.

The hotel I mention in several of the books, in Winslow, AZ, is real, the La Posada. It's a Harvey Girls railroad hotel, brilliantly restored and absolutely beautiful. It's a good base from which to explore Northern Arizona—it's not far from the painted desert and the meteor crater as well as Chocolate Falls (which run only in spring) and Homolovi, ancient ruins where I set some scenes of *Firewalker*. It's also on the edge of the Hopi and Navajo lands with their spectacular scenery, plus it's an hour from Flagstaff with the Lowell Observatory (where Pluto was discovered), Walnut Canyon, and Sedona. There are a number of lovely hotels in the Navajo reservation as well, and you can even stay in a hogan if you wish!

The La Posada also has a fantastic restaurant, the Turquoise Room—I highly recommend the squash blossom tamales when they have them.

I hope you enjoyed this trip to the Stormwalker world, and I will see you next time!

Best wishes,

Allyson James

(aka Jennifer Ashley)

Wild Wolf

Bear Attraction

Mate Bond

Lion Eyes

Bad Wolf

Wild Things

White Tiger

Guardian's Mate

Red Wolf

Midnight Wolf

Tiger Striped
(novella)

Shifter Made ("Prequel" short story)

Immortals

(Paranormal Romance

multi-author series)

The Calling (by Jennifer Ashley)

The Darkening (by Robin Popp)

The Awakening (by Joy Nash)

The Gathering (by Jennifer Ashley)

The Redeeming (by Jennifer Ashley)

The Crossing (by Joy Nash)

The Haunting (by Robin Popp)

Wolf Hunt (by Jennifer Ashley)

Forbidden Taste (by Jennifer Ashley)

ABOUT THE AUTHOR

Award-winning author Allyson James is a pen name of *New York Times* bestselling author Jennifer Ashley. Allyson has written more than 100 published novels and novellas in romance, urban fantasy, and mystery under the names Jennifer Ashley, Allyson James, and Ashley Gardner. Allyson's books have been nominated for and won Romance Writers of America's RITA (given for the best romance novels and novellas of the year), and several *RT BookReviews* Reviewers Choice awards (including Best Urban Fantasy, Best Shapeshifter Romance, and Career Achievement in Historical Romance), and Prism awards for her paranormal romances and urban fantasy.

More about Allyson's books can be found at the website www.jenniferashley.com or join her newsletter at http://eepurl.com/47kLL.

CPSIA information can be obtained
at www.ICGtesting.com
Printed in the USA
LVHW040259020419
612641LV00002B/95/P